W9-DFC-199

Simon had not gone half a dozen steps before another of the figures from the circle was in his path, confronting him. Then it vanished, but at once he felt its hands clamping his elbows from the rear, pulling his arms behind him, bringing him to a stop. The thing laughed with a high shrieking sound, and Simon saw other figures of the circle close before him, jeering at him. The pressure of the grip on his elbows increased until he screamed with pain. If his arms were pulled a centimeter closer together, the bones around his spine would certainly crack.

Tor books by Fred Saberhagen

A Century of Progress
Coils (with Roger Zelazny)
Dominion
The Dracula Tape
Earth Descended
The Holmes–Dracula File
The Mask of the Sun
A Matter of Taste
An Old Friend of the Family
*Specimens**
Thorn
The Veils of Azlaroc
The Water of Thought

THE BERSERKER SERIES

The Berserker Wars
The Berserker Throne
Berserker Base (with Poul Anderson, Ed Bryant,
    Stephen Donaldson, Larry Niven, Connie Willis,
    and Roger Zelazny)
Berserker: Blue Death

THE BOOKS OF SWORDS

The First Book of Swords
The Second Book of Swords
The Third Book of Swords

THE BOOKS OF LOST SWORDS

The First Book of Lost Swords: Woundhealer's Story
The Second Book of Lost Swords: Sightblinder's Story
The Third Book of Lost Swords: Stonecutter's Story
The Fourth Book of Lost Swords: Farslayer's Story
The Fifth Book of Lost Swords: Coinspinner's Story

*forthcoming

FRED SABERHAGEN
DOMINION

A TOM DOHERTY ASSOCIATES BOOK
NEW YORK

Note: If you purchased this book without a cover you should be aware that this book is stolen property. It was reported as "unsold and destroyed" to the publisher, and neither the author nor the publisher has received any payment for this "stripped book."

This is a work of fiction. All the characters and events portrayed in this book are fictitious, and any resemblance to real people or events is purely coincidental.

DOMINION

Copyright © 1982 by Fred Saberhagen

All rights reserved, including the right to reproduce this book, or portions thereof, in any form.

Cover art by Glenn Hastings

A Tor Book
Published by Tom Doherty Associates, Inc.
175 Fifth Avenue
New York, N.Y. 10010

Tor ® is a registered trademark of Tom Doherty Associates, Inc.

ISBN: 0-812-52386-5

First edition: June 1982

Printed in the United States of America

0 9 8 7 6 5 4 3

PROLOGUE

All yesterday's dead men, and the dead horses too, were slowly becoming visible in the predawn light that came staining slowly across the field. Instead of blackness, the sky was the color of nothingness now. The leader realized that he hadn't slept all, hadn't even taken off his armor. No matter; his next sleep was likely to be long enough.

Out of the mist on his right a figure materialized, and he turned to face it, donning out of habit a leader's confident smile.

"When'll we fight again, sir?" the man asked after a silent pause. A useless question, of course. But something to say.

"As soon as the sun's well up." A useless, unnecessary answer, too, though in his practiced leader's voice it sounded like some decision that he'd just confidently taken.

"There's a many of 'em, sir." Through the opaque grayness that still hid the enemy camp, some hint of their numbers could now be heard in morning stirrings.

"Aye, and few of us." Thank all the gods, he had no need to make a rousing speech now. He and the men who still remained with him were past all that. Any who were not bedrock firm in loyalty had long since gone. He'd say a few words of thanks to them, if he was given the chance. "Go rouse the men. It won't be long now. Stay—see that the wounded are all armed. We can retreat no farther, with the lake behind us, and none will choose to be taken prisoner, I think. Not by Comorr, and Falerin, and . . . and then bring up my horse."

"Aye, sir."

Now, for a little while, the leader stood once more alone. His own wound, he thanked the gods, was in his left arm and not his right. He'd still be able to use his sword to good effect when the time came. Soon now, probably no time for even a speech of thanks. No speeches and no agonizing over plans. Planning, along with hope, had vanished sometime yesterday. No, days ago, when the man who was his true right arm had . . . gone away.

No, he thought again. Months before that, really. There had been no real hope since that same man had been disabled, since—as he'd put it himself—the great stone had come down upon him.

Over there beyond the mist, across the field, men were shouting, taunting, laughing confidently. They knew he hadn't managed to get the remnant of his army away during the night. Their own skilled magicians had seen to that. Now they were already mounting horses over there, ready to begin what would be a slow, confident advance.

That great, damned stone, months past, had crushed all hope. Now the leader had nothing to do but wait . . .

ONE

The dead man centered in the pearly glow of the two portable spotlights sat slumped against an interior angle of the wall behind him, as if he had got his back against those dingy bricks, and had then died fighting. This minor peculiarity of position aside, the scene really held nothing out of the ordinary, Joe Keogh thought. Not for a blind turn in a dark alley off this particular street in this particular neighborhood-of Chicago. So far, Joe was not impressed. In his current assignment, the Pawn Shop Detail, corpses were no part of his day to day routine; still, in a dozen years with the CPD, he had seen violent death more than a few times, and in a variety of forms.

"I don't know 'im," Joe now repeated patiently. He was standing with hands on hips as he contin—ued to gaze at the victim's waxen, gray-stubbled face.

It was the beginning of a warm night in June, and Joe was wearing his suit coat open, shoulder holster barely out of sight. Up and down the alley air conditioners and exhaust fans howled softly or whined shrilly behind grilled windows, gasping a mixture of smells out into the city twilight: incongruous innocent pizza, the fumes of stale beer, and who knew what else besides. In some room behind some section of these ageless bricks some instruments were maintaining a steady, muted pounding that to someone must be music. Another sound just offstage somewhere, this one evidently passing for laughter, kept phasing in and out of audibility. There was, as everywhere and anytime in the city, background traffic noise.

"Is that what you wanted to know?" Joe inquired, when Charley Snider still didn't answer him. "Or am I here for something else?"

Snider, Lieutenant of Homicide, was occupied at the moment with lighting a cigarette. Match flame glinted orange on his dark black face, pale on the pink of his cupped palms. There were a couple of patrolmen in the alley also, one standing just on either side of the bright circle cast by the lamps that had been brought in to help with the photography.

"There's no blood, you see," Snider commented at last, words modulating a long puff of smoke. He threw the match down carelessly; nobody was going to crawl around on the floor of this alley on hands and knees, trying to figure out what brand of match the killers might have dropped. Charley was a big man, now going a little bit to gut and jowls, but having in reserve a lot more speed, mental as well as physical, than showed on the surface.

"No blood," Joe repeated, after a short delay. His own reaction must have sounded slow, but deep inside him something had been very quickly triggered. Memories, no more than a few years old, but with an ancient feeling to them. *Now it begins again* . . .

"His throat's been cut, you see," Charley informed him. "I think it opened the jugular, the carotid artery, the whole shmear. The M.E. just got through commenting on what a neat surgical job."

The expressionless, ageless countenance of the dead man certainly did look paler than most faces Joe had seen, but he had thought that might be only an effect of the lights. Now he bent closer, trying for a better look at the throat. The head of the victim had sagged forward, but now Joe could make out the wide wound compressed under the gray-stubbled chin.

On the shabby shirt collar, just one blood spot was visible, of a size that might have resulted from a nick while shaving.

Standing just behind Joe, Charley Snider cleared his throat. "See, the uniformed people who were first on the scene didn't just call for a meatwagon and load 'im in. They looked him over a little first, and what they saw struck 'em as odd." Charley paused. "I been alerting some of the uniformed people around here on what to look for."

"Oh. So there've been more like this?"

"Three or four. *I* think enough to make a pattern. The people downtown don't agree with me, not yet anyway. They say people are always getting cut up, there're always stiffs in alleys. Well, shit, I know that. They can't see the pattern. I can see it, though."

Joe had only briefly removed his gaze from the body, and now he was again studying it intently. "What sort of pattern? No blood spilled around—what else?"

"Some of 'em, I got to admit, showed a little more blood than this man does. But not the amount there should be. And there's always multiple wounds, including the cut throat, made with something very sharp. All derelicts, like this guy.

When I mention the lack of blood to the M.E.'s people, they scratch their heads and say yeah I guess you're right. Nobody wants to see the pattern, though. Nobody wants to see a bunch of Skid Row stiffs starting to make the news media, especially when they's no suspects in sight.''

Joe shifted his lithe frame forward a little, now squatting close beside the corpse. "Okay if I touch?"

"Okay." Charley's voice was neutral, waiting.

The clothes, Joe thought, were just about what you would expect to find on a stiff lying in this alley—old, mismatched, ragged. Maybe they were a little cleaner than you would have expected—or maybe, again, that appearance was due to the purity of the light. Despite the evident violence of the victim's taking off, he did not appear to have fouled himself from bowels or bladder. The smell of cheap wine came from the body, as seemed only appropriate. But, Joe noted, the smell was of wine only. Absent was the usual inimitable death-on-Skid-Row blend of wine and old sweat and helpless excretions and defeat, as if someone had accidentally left open a nearby door that led down to some anteroom of hell.

Earlier Joe had noted without surprise that there were a number of small holes in the victim's shirt and trousers both. Now he discovered that through a number of these holes he chould see wounds: small sharp cuts, red and raw but almost bloodless.

Joe sat back on his heels, puffing out his breath. That a man should have been killed in this alley was hardly a surprise. Though most winos were harmless, on streets like this there were always a few people about who would kill for a dime, for an argument, for the last mouthful of muscatel. But this was different. Obviously calculated, somehow arranged. And Charley had said that there were others.

Sighing, Joe got to his feet. He ran a muscular hand, not the same hand that he had used to touch the body, slowly through his unruly sandy hair. "He was killed somewhere else," he offered at last. "All the blood spilled somewhere else. And then . . ."

"I figured out that much," said Charley patiently. "Then—?"

"Then he was . . . dressed in these clothes, I guess, and dumped here. Holes made in the clothes, to match the holes in him? I dunno. Dumped here, anyway, with the idea that one more stiff in this neighborhood wasn't going to get a whole lot of attention."

"This lad's been living on the street around here for quite a while," said Charley, anticipating Joe's next question. "I managed to get a make on him from a couple of the other winos. 'Dusty', they called him." Snider made an economical gesture, which was understood by the two patrolmen. They started hoisting the star of the show out of his spotlit corner and onto a rubber-sheeted stretcher on wheels that waited nearby. The body had stiffened. It was going to make the trip in a comic posture, rump sticking up.

"Why'd you bring me here, though?" Joe asked as the spotlights were turned off, one after the other. "Were there pawn tickets on him?" Joe was already sure that he wasn't being brought in on the case by reason of his current official specialty. Charley's summons had come to him over the phone, a personal request very informal and completely outside of channels. And still very much unexplained.

"I just thought I'd let you have a look, man," said Charley now. He and Joe had each started to wrap up one of the portable spotlights on its own cable, while the working uniforms were busy trundling their loaded stretcher on around the corner of wall, into the stagey glare of the streetlight that shone there from the alley's mouth.

There sounded a faint burst of demonic laughter, probably from the beer joint that had to be somewhere behind one of these walls.

"Okay," said Joe. "'Ive had a look. But I still don't know what I'm supposed to do. I've told you I don't know him."

"Never said you might know him, man." Charley's face, dark in dark, was hard to see. His cigarette glowed in his moving fingers as he wound cable: "And I'm not sayin' you have to do nothing. I'm just offering you a look at what my problem is, that's all."

"Oh," said Joe. His suspicions were now confirmed. Charley's motives were about as he'd thought; but he'd had to make sure.

Now, Charley trudging beside him, Joe carried the spotlight on its folded tripod on around the bend of the alley, where he handed it over to one of the patrolmen. Then he got into Charley's unmarked car, which was waiting beside the police van, and shut the door. Now he would get a ride home, and maybe Charley would come in for a beer, and possibly somewhere along the line Charley would be more explicit. Quite possibly not, though. Almost certainly the subject they were almost discussing would not be brought up by Charley in front of Kate.

Joe had just been confirmed in a suspicion that had been growing in him for some time. He himself had acquired a reputation, which by now perhaps ran through the whole department, for having at least one super-exotic informant on the string, for being able now and then to come up with information a thousand miles beyond the reach of anyone else. This reputation, he knew, must rest on only two cases that had touched Joe's professional and personal life during the last few years. Both cases had been weird and spectacular, though on the surface they were unconnected. Neither had been an experience he wanted to repeat. Nor did he want the reputation he seemed to have gained from them. It was quite accurate, as far as it went, but it was hardly even an iceberg-tip of truth.

He wondered now just how much more of the truth Charley Snider might suspect. And then he dismissed the wonder. Charley was street-smart, but he wasn't imaginative to the point of craziness.

After Charley had come in for his beer, and had talked some about the chances of the Cubs, and had then gone on his way, Joe stood at his living room window which was open to the cool breeze, and looked down at the usual evening processions of headlights crowding their way along. The apartment was a fancier one than you would have expected an honest cop to be able to afford, a two-bedroom condo just off Lake Shore Drive on the reasonably far north side. Kate's family had money.

"Charley seemed tired tonight," Kate said. Blond and pretty, she was pacing back and forth in her new housecoat, with the baby over her shoulder, trying to get it to go to sleep. She had regained her slenderness quite nicely after the birth.

"He's got a tough case. Series of cases. He was talking to me about it earlier."

"Oh?"

"Hinting around, that I might be able to dig up some information that would help."

Kate uttered a barely audible *shh*, and turned gracefully away; the kid was nodding off. She left the room, to return in a few moments unburdened and in utter silence, her eyebrows lifted to ask a question.

Her husband, arms folded, was now leaning with his back to the window. He told her: "I know who they want me to talk to.''

It took Kate only a moment to understand. ''I see.''

''*They* don't know who they want me to talk to.'' Joe made a grim sound, like a poor actor trying to get off a laugh. ''Honey, you know what I'm thinking? Maybe I'll just pack it in. The job, the badge.''

Kate sat down on the sofa, whose rich fabric was blanket-covered now in defense against the baby. She patted the spot beside her where she wanted Joe to settle. ''And what,'' she asked, ''will you do then?'' Understanding had left her calm, and made her sympathetic; if she hadn't actually heard this talk of quitting before, perhaps she had been expecting to one day hear it.

''We wouldn't starve. There's your money.''

''Of course we wouldn't starve. But what would you *do*?''

Joe put down his empty beer can and sat down beside his wife. ''What's new with Judy?'' he asked.

Kate accepted her younger sister's relevance to the discussion. ''She's still going with that young man from the University of Chicago. I think things may be getting serious. If you're planning to get in contact with someone, I don't think asking Judy for help would be the way to go.''

''All her involvement with you-know-who is pretty well over, huh? Well, that's good, anyway. That's something. All right, how *would* I go about getting in contact now?''

''There is a certain emergency procedure,'' Kate said doubtfully. ''But I doubt we ought to use that unless we're having a real emergency.''

''If you doubt it, I sure as hell do too.''

Next day, driving through a more or less routine round of pawn shops, helping irate or discouraged robbery victims try to identify their stolen merchandise, Joe had his mind more often

than not on Charley Snider's problem. He heard
no more today from Charley, who, Joe suspected
was working overtime along with a lot of other
people. There was a tip that a mass murderer, a
crazed cultist wanted in New Orleans, might have
come to Chicago. Anyway Charley had already
passed along just about everything that was
known or suspected about the Skid Row killings,
and now he, Joe, was expected to come up with
something helpful if he could. Expected at least to
try. Where and how he got his information would
be considered his own business if he wanted it
that way. All good detectives cultivated informers
whenever they had the chance, and the more valuable the source of information the more likely
they would try to keep it secret. If Joe preferred
to say nothing at all about his source, the whole
department would understand.

So there was no reason at all for him not to try
to help, except he didn't want to.

Joe spent a miserable day. He always gave himself a hard time when he did something other
than what he thought a good cop should.

When he talked to Kate as usual on the phone in
the middle of the afternoon, neither of them mentioned the problem. But when Joe got home that
evening his wife greeted him with a faintly knowing smile.

"We had a phone call," she announced as she
plumped the baby down on the changing table.
"Message for you."

"Oh?" Having read her tone and expression accurately, he sighed. At the same time he felt more
than half relieved. "Let me guess who."

"He says he's fine, thank you for asking." Still
smiling gently, Kate might have been speaking of
an eccentric uncle. "You're to meet him out at
O'Hare Field tonight at eight. That fancy restaurant, you know, the one up on top of the terminal.
Ask for Mr. Talisman."

"Talisman, huh?" Joe looked at his watch and grimaced slightly. He would have to jump right back in his car and drive. "What if I don't want to?"

"He didn't seem to consider that possibility. You know what he's like."

"God, yes." And yet there was an enticing excitement in the evening's prospect. Suddenly Joe wanted to go. He tried to hide it.

"Oh, Joe. It was really a very courteous invitation. Would I ask you if you would be so kind, and so on. Why don't you want to meet him?"

Joe looked at Kate. ·

"Joe. He *saved* our *lives*. To *us* he's never been anything but perfectly—"

"I know. All right, I'll go, all right."

"We can be pleasant to him," Kate reiterated firmly. "Ugh." This last was in reaction to what the opened diaper had disclosed. "You can hardly say that he's made a pest of himself. It's been over a year since we've heard from him. This must be something important."

"Yeah." Now he really did want to go. All it would take now was a little courage.

Courage. He was a tough cop, and carrying a gun, and it still came down to that.

When Joe asked for Mr. Talisman's table, he was conducted to a luxuriously padded booth right beside one of the large, curved windows that looked out over ramp and runways. Tonight clouds had brought darkness before true sunset. Earlier in the day it had rained, and it was misting still, and the outside view was a melange of inky darkness and the glistening reflections of a thousand lights in all colors, flashing, spinning, moving, stationary. The sound of jet engines was muted by thick glass, but still came through. Joe had always liked airports and it had crossed his mind tonight, as it usually did when he approached the place, that he wouldn't mind having duty out here. Airport security was CPD; years ago the city limits had been stretched to take in the square miles of O'Hare along with a narrow corridor of land reaching through the suburbs to connect the airport to the metropolitan center.

The sole occupant of the booth, as usual, a model of courtesy, rose to shake Joe's hand firmly and gesture him to the opposite seat. The voice was just as Joe remembered it, deep and faintly tinged with a central European accent.

"I am told that the Chateaubriand here is quite good. Ah, but you would like a cocktail first, perhaps?" Talisman had a glass of mineral water, still full, in front of him. The waitress, no doubt already somehow charmed, was hovering patiently nearby. It was past Joe's usual dinner time, and he suddenly discovered that he was hungry; these first moments weren't going anywhere nearly as badly as he had somehow feared they would. He ordered a vodka martini, and then expensive food. The waitress disappeared.

"I love aircraft," Talisman commented, turning his head to better observe them through the glass. Joe looked out too, then focused on the faint, vastly distorted reflections of the restaurant's interior on the curved surface of the window. With a little effort he could pick out parts of his own image. That, for example, had to be his own hand, impossibly broadened in a way suggestive of superhuman strength, lying on the white tablecloth. Joe flexed his hand, and watched titanic fingers shift. Of Talisman's image, of the white hands that had no particular look of strength, the elegant dark suit, the angular brooding face, there was not a trace in the reflection. But no one was going to notice that fact who did not look very carefully into the distorting glass. And if anyone should notice, who was going to believe it?

The dark eyes turned back toward Joe. "And how are Kate, and your dear child?"

"Fine." No question had been asked about Judy. That was good. Or was it?

The martini arrived promptly. Joe lifted it in an informal, silent toast. His host, smiling pleasantly, raised his own glass for the first time, barely touching it to his thin lips. The man who called himself Talisman tonight appeared to be about forty years old, a couple of decades younger in looks than when Joe had seen him last. His dark hair, almost straight, almost black, bore at the temples just a trace of distinguished gray. On the third finger of the relaxed right hand was a worn gold ring that Joe remembered seeing there before.

A cup of soup arrived. Joe picked up his spoon and ate. The soup was thinner than he liked, but like the martini very good.

He realized that somehow, with very few words spoken, he had been put at his ease. Or almost. His host, still smiling pleasantly, watched him eat.

"You've been traveling?" Joe asked. He felt no pressure to break the silence, but he was genuinely curious. "I mean, meeting here at the airport . . ."

"Yes," said Talisman vaguely. "Also, as I say, I enjoy watching the aircraft." The dark eyes looked outside, as if yearning, then came back to Joe again. "To business. Tell me, Joe, how are things with the Chicago Police Department these days?"

"Busy, as usual. Varied."

"Ah. I have no doubt that in such a large and complex city the unusual must be usual, if you take my meaning. But what I had in mind was certain specific crimes. I was wondering whether word might have reached you from some of your fellow officers regarding a very unusual series of . . ." Talisman, watching Joe's face carefully, didn't bother to finish.

Joe now told him, quietly and as completely as possible, of the dead man he had seen in an alley, and of the other dead men who went to make up the pattern seen by Charley Snider. "I guess he came to me with it because—well, we're friends. And he must be convinced that I have at least one—somewhat unusual source of information."

"I see."

"Oh, not that he has any idea who my source is. I mean . . ."

Talisman waved two fingers, regally dismissing any ideas that Charley Snider might have regarding him. "Perhaps I shall be able to do something for your friend in Homicide . . . and he, unknowingly, for me . . . yourself, you are still attached to the Pawn Shop Detail?"

"Yeah."

"Therefore you are concerned, sometimes at least, with the location of missing objects?"

"At least I can make a stab at finding out if they've been pawned anywhere in the city. What's missing?"

Talisman appeared to be framing his answer carefully. "Nothing of mine, Joe. And yet something that I believe we must find, or try to find. And somehow I doubt that it is in a pawn shop. Yet we must try every possibility available. I think it is not many miles from where we sit."

"What is it?"

"An edged weapon. Old. I regret that I do not know much about what it looks like."

There was a pause. Joe said: "Unless you can tell me more, I don't see how I can—"

"But you must try. I will tell you what I can."

"Yeah. Sure." Joe took another sample of his martini.

"Joe, there are not many people in the world in whom I can confide freely. So while I enjoy your company allow me to ramble on a little. It may help me to think."

"Sure."

"You see, Joe, I am compelled by circumstances to temporarily take up your profession. In fact, your friend in Homicide and I are interested in the same murder cases; from different viewpoints, naturally, yet I am as anxious as he to see them solved."

"That's good to know," said Joe sincerely. "Then maybe my first private guess was right. When I first noticed the lack of blood. Whoever is killing these winos is . . ."

Talisman was nodding gently. "A member of my community rather than of yours. You may say the word: a vampire. Yes, I have determined that such a one is at least *among* the guilty." Talisman made a sound like a sigh, but without full breath behind it. "I have, in my own community, as you probably know, a certain position of leadership. I have it only by default, perhaps, but there it is. I have discussed this case with other honorable members, who agree with me that some action ought to be taken. I have their moral support if probably no other kind. We will not willingly shelter such a guilty one among us."

Oh? thought Joe. He felt sure that there was more to Talisman's game here than he was yet telling. He also wondered what the couple at the next occupied table would think if they could overhear this chat.

Talisman went on: "Neither your police force nor your courts are equipped to deal effectively with vampires."

"That's for sure."

"Yet you have information, and certain ways of gathering more information, that I lack. Therefore I propose that we informally join forces."

The waitress arrived with Joe's steak. When she had accepted Talisman's insistence that he was not going to order food, and had departed again, Joe said, with a faint smile of his own: "This of course is the point where we always tell people to give us their information and then leave the investigating to the professionals. But naturally in this case—"

"—any such injunction to me would be imbecilic. Naturally. Alas, now that you are ready to help me, I still do not know exactly what aid I may require. There is, as I have said, the weapon to be located. And . . ."

An airliner, taking off, drew faint vibrations through the silverware and dishes.

"There is among the guilty, as I have said, at last one man of my own people."

"How many people in all are there involved?"

Talisman conveyed ignorance.

"This one man who is of your people, as you put it. Do you know his name, what he looks like?"

A headshake, minimal but impatient, dismissed all such commonsensical, methodical questions for the time being. *Now we are coming to the real point.* "Among those somehow involved, Joseph, there is another man who interests me much more." Talisman paused, gazing out the window again. On his face was an expression of quiet excitement, a look different from any that Joe had seen him wear before.

The vampire turned back from the unreflecting glass; he spoke softly, but with emphasis. "Compared to myself, Joe . . . *compared to me*, I say . . . this other man is *something of an oddity*."

"Huh?"

Talisman's manner relaxed a trifle. "But never mind the extremely odd man now. He is not a vampire, nor is he, I think, among the guilty. Sufficient unto the day is the evil thereof. Unfortunately one of my fellow *nosferatu* is killing helpless victims, and I intend to stop him. He is not killing for food; you know that we can obtain all that we really need from the blood of animals. Nor are his crimes of sexual passion. He is engaged in wicked ritual. I get the impression that he is offering blood sacrifice."

Joe was too much the professional to be put off for very long from the professional attitude. "You mean one of these cults? Devil-worshippers and so on?" And immediately there crossed his mind the thought of the man from New Orleans, that Charley Snider and many others were presently trying to ambush. "I don't know how frequently people in your, uh, community engage in that kind of thing."

"Not as frequently," said Talisman, "as people in your community might suppose. Of course, Joe, there are many ways of worshipping the Devil. Just as many, I suppose, as there are of praying to his great Adversary."

The first taste of steak had been delicious, but already Joe had forgotten it. "Let's stick to the facts, if we're going to help each other. Give me all the details you can. Leaving the magic aside, you're looking for two men, and one old knife."

"Two men in particular, yes. One object. A weapon. It might be bigger than a knife. But we must be careful what we leave aside. Ah, Joseph, what is magic?"

TWO

The applause swept up enthusiastically, quite loud for the few dozen people in the audience. As plainly as if he could see her, Simon Hill knew what the woman in the tenth pew back, the most recent volunteer, looked like now: half pleased, half nervous, entirely mystified. It was all in the sound of her voice as she had to agree that it was indeed a diamond wedding ring that she had been holding in her fingers. Like most subjects she was glad that the trick had worked successfully, and at the same time she felt a core of resentment, perhaps unconscious, at not being able to figure out how it had been done. If Simon had explained the banal truth to her, about the elaborate voice-code established between magician and assistant, she would have felt quite disappointed.

It was the end of the performance. They'd done enough, though not quite everything planned, and he had to end it on a burst of applause like that, even though there was some chance of a certain

kind of trouble whenever a mentalist failed to
finish on an illusion-breaking note of farce.
Signalling Margie by his gesture that they were
cutting it off right here, Simon turned back to
face the audience, meanwhile pulling off his
white, thick blindfold, blending the two actions
expertly into a sweeping bow. Margie, tripping
lightly back from her place at the side of the last
volunteer, took Simon's outstretched left hand
and joined him just in time for the second bow.
The organ, in its loft far in the rear, sounded a
long chord of finale.

Simon Hill was standing in the chancel of the
great chapel of St. Thomas More University, on
the lakefront on the north side of Chicago. A few
spotlights, mounted under an immensity of gray
pseudo-Gothic vaulting almost a hundred feet
above his head, picked accurately down at him
and Margie where they stood, rather like Our
Lady's juggler in the old fable, before the flat,
plain, modern altar table. Some of the more lib-
eral faculty members had been arguing for some
time that if it was all right to perform *The Play of
Daniel* here in the chapel, then why not also some
other entertainment of the medieval tradition? Simon had heard the president quoted as objecting
that if a conjuror were to be allowed this year,
then next year someone would be milking a goat
in the nave as well, in authentic medieval style;
but eventually the liberals had prevailed, and
here was Simon the Great working and getting
paid. All the performances here were after all
supposed to have something to do with the Summer Medieval Festival, and, short of goats, what
more fitting than a *jongleur* of some kind in the
cathedral? A mind-reader in the chapel came
close, anyway.

Still hand-in-hand with Margie, Simon was taking the fourth or fifth bow, to gradually dimin-
ishing applause, when a pale, masculine face to-

ward the rear of the occupied section of pews caught at his eye and then tried to catch at his memory. The face and the short figure that went with it were undoubtedly familiar. But they were so out of context here that it was hard to assign them a name or a relationship.

The applause, following the one law that inexorably governed it, died out, and with that the bowing had to cease also. Five or six people, mostly from the front pews, hesitantly moved forward to offer what promised to be more personal praise and congratulations. The pale-faced man in the rear edged forward too, but tentatively, as if he were modestly willing to wait until the others should be done, and only at this point did recognition of that face come. It brought something of an inward chill. Almost fifteen years, Simon counted up mentally, since he had seen that face. It hadn't changed noticeably in fifteen years.

From the corner of his eye he noticed Margie's face turn toward him, and he realized that his grip must have just tightened on her hand. Simon squeezed her fingers once more, this time lightly and reassuringly, and then he let her fingers drop. Together he and Margie nodded and smiled and murmured thanks to the people who had come forward to speak to them individually. Just as the last member of this group was moving up with timid determination to confront Simon, Father Gibson, the evening's MC, approached also. With his microphone on its long cord looped round his sport-shirted neck, he was obviously eager to get in a few remarks before introducing the evening's main event.

The last member of the group who had come up from the audience was a middle-aged woman, well dressed. Simon at once recognized not her but the look in her eye, and his heart sank a trifle.

"I'm sure you have some remarkable powers," the woman began, with a quiet earnestness that he found frightening.

Simon shook his head, and smiled deprecatingly. "It's all trickery, ma'm, I assure you." And he broke eye contact with the woman at once and started down the center aisle toward the rear of the chapel, away from her and the altar and Father Gibson.

The woman kept pace. "My own wedding ring is lost, you see. And my husband has just recently passed away, and . . ."

It was too late now for anything farcical to be an effective mood-breaker. An attempt at lightness, humor, now would be a personal insult. Simon said as gently as he could: "What I do are only tricks. You could do them yourself with just a little practice."

Margie came to his rescue, taking the woman by the hand and sympathetically leading her aside. For which act, Simon told himself, he certainly owed her one. In deference to the setting, Marge's costume this evening was much more demure than usual: long, bloomer-like pantaloons and closed midriff, while Simon himself was in the evening dress that he usually wore on stage. He kept going now, pacing toward the rear of the chapel. The nave was almost long enough for a cathedral, and with tonight's lighting concentrated toward the front, the rear was quite dim. There was to be an intermission now, probably just long enough for Father Gibson to get in a few announcements, and followed by the main event, the *Play of Daniel* itself. Simon and Margie had been planning to hang around in a rear pew and watch Nebuchadnezzar's downfall.

"Mr. Hill?" The pale face, remembered voice to match, was waiting for him. But, Simon realized with surprise, it was as if the man speaking had never seen Simon before; had no idea that they had ever met. In a moment surprise vanished; of course it would have been more astonishing if Gregory Wedderburn *had* recognized him quickly. He hadn't been Simon the Great as a boy in Frenchman's Bend, or even Simon Hill. At five-nine he was now several inches taller than he had been then, and he was heavier by thirty or forty solid pounds. His brown hair was no longer short, but almost shoulder length, and he had grown a mustache.

And Simon certainly felt no necessity of recognizing Gregory Wedderburn as an old acquaintance. "Yes, what can I do for you?"

"My name is Gregory Wedderburn, sir. First of all, I would like to compliment you on the performance." No, Gregory certainly didn't look as if fifteen years had passed; he was almost exactly as Simon remembered him. Of short stature, age indeterminately somewhere between forty and sixty, a face that any casting director would immediately type as belonging to a tycoon and not a servant.

"Thank you," Simon replied, neutrally.

"You're very kind," contributed Margie, just coming up. She must have managed to get away from the widow before the subject of seances could even be broached. Simon hoped so, anyway. There was a trace of a frown on Margie's face as she regarded him; she knew him well enough now to be able to judge his sometimes sudden moods with considerable success.

Meanwhile Simon was being shown a side of Gregory that he had never seen before, the face of the obsequious servant. "Secondly, sir, I'm here tonight as an agent." A gentle imitation of a laugh. "No, I'm not volunteering to be your booking agent, or whatever the right term is. I'm representing my own employer. He would like to hire you for a private performance."

Simon thought he knew who that employer was, and curt refusal was on the tip of his tongue. Yet he couldn't quite come out with it. The germ of a daring idea, very intriguing even if still very hazy, had been born. He had to find out more. It was completely obvious by now that Gregory had not the faintest idea of who Simon really was.

"You come quite highly recommended, Mr. Hill." Gregory managed to sound smug, servile, and snobbish at the same time. "Miss Vivian Littlewood, ah, my employer's sister, saw one of your performances not long ago."

So, now he works for Saul. That was a minor surprise. "And who is Miss Vivian Littlewood?" Simon enjoyed the chance to make his own tone condescending.

Gregory almost flushed. He drew his short frame perceptibly more erect, and looked up at Simon frostily. "My employer is Saul Littlewood. You'll recognize the family name if you're at all familiar with Chicago."

"Oh, you mean the old meatpacking family." It was fun to be knowledgeable but not impressed.

The little man had regained his smoothness. "Mr. Littlewood is planning a rather lavish weekend in his suburban home, starting one week from tonight. I realize that this is quite short notice and that you may well have some previous engagement. But I am authorized to say that Mr. Littlewood will make it quite worth your while." Gregory smiled rather vacantly and nodded in Margie's direction, as if assuring her that the guarantee applied to her as well. "The theme of the party will have to do with the medieval, you see."

"Evidently a popular theme these days."

"And in this case, as you'll see, very appropriate indeed for a house-warming." Gregory displayed the faint smile of superior knowledge. "Mr. Littlewood has authorized me to offer you one thousand dollars for one evening's performance, on Friday. Then you and your assistant will be welcome to remain as guests for the remainder of the weekend if you wish. That would of course be an all-inclusive fee for both of you, meant to cover expenses—"

"A thousand dollars?" Simon couldn't help showing surprise. "I'm hardly one of the big names of show business. What do I have to do? I mean, I don't have any big production numbers, or . . ."

"The only requirements are, first, that you provide yourself with some medieval costume, authentic in appearance. Secondly of course you are to give the best performance of which you both are capable, a point I am sure I need not emphasize. You are of course free to choose your own tricks, effects." Gregory paused meaningfully. "You will of course cooperate in so far as you feel able, with any special requests that members of your small audience may have."

Simon shrugged. "Insofar as we feel able."

"Yes. And there is a fringe benefit that you may consider of some importance."

"Oh?"

"Yes. Among the guests will be a few who are quite influential, I understand, in the world of entertainment. You say you are not now one of the big names of show business, but . . . I of course know nothing of magic myself. Would there be any special equipment, or prearrangements that you require?"

Margie was about to speak, probably with questions to ask, but Simon had taken her hand and now squeezed it gently, signalling for silence. He said: "We can provide all the special equipment we'll need. Where's this house?"

"In the far suburbs—rather far out even to be called suburbs, I'm afraid; about two hours' drive. You'll need rather detailed instructions on how to get there." Again, the small superior smile. "When you see the house, you'll understand what I mean about the medieval theme being fitting."

THREE

Mrs. Hildegard Littlewood, nee Hildy Nordberg, was dressed for tennis, having just recently ascended from practice on her court. She was standing on the roof of her castle, leaning her forearms and elbows on what her bridegroom had recently told her ought to be called a merlon. It was the portion of a battlement that stuck up like a giant squared tooth. With fingers hooked over the rising edge of stone, Hildy could feel how her thick new golden wedding ring caught and grated on the edge. With her eyes closed in summer sunshine, she was trying to fight back a threatened bout of near-hysterical giggles. She had the feeling that if she once let the laughter get started it was going to get out of hand at once. Sometimes lately it had seemed to Hildy that if she could allow herself one good bout of hysteria she would get it out of her system and would then be able to settle down. But she wasn't familiar enough with hysteria to know if it might be managed that way.

In fact she had never had trouble with it before. And she wasn't sure, either, how long she was going to be alone on the roof before someone came up looking for her.

She told herself now for the thousandth time that she had no realistic cause for unhappiness. Quite the contrary. Absolutely the contrary. And in fact she wasn't really unhappy. It was just that two months ago she had been a part-time student and part-time waitress, supporting herself after a fashion by dishing out pizza in a roadside place just outside Los Angeles. And today here she was just finished with a workout on her own tennis court in Illinois, with more money in more bank accounts than she knew what to do with, and standing on top of her own imported, reconstructed . . . no, it was just too ridiculous.

Hildy pulled hard on the mortared stones. A sound between a laugh and a faint shriek escaped her lips. But then nothing more came. A genuinely relieving outburst was evidently not as near the surface as she had thought.

She released her grip on the edge of the parapet and turned, opening her eyes to summer sunshine that warmed the stone-paved castle roof and the nearby treetops that screened away most of the outside world. *If you could see me now* . . . but what made her overload of success all the more traumatic was that there was practically no one to whom she could say that, even on the phone or in a letter.

Hildy had moved around a lot in her young life. What little had been left of her family when she was growing up had been second and third generation Californians, with Okie restlessness intact. Continual moving continually made the latest crop of new friends drop away, and old friends were non-existent. And then her mother, the remaining family remnant, died. And there Hildy had been, waiting on tables, that day two months ago when Saul Littlewood had just happened to come in looking for some lunch.

One of the less visible changes in her life since that day was that now her trains of thought tended to become easily derailed. Another recurrent thought came interrupting now: some of these treetops really ought to be trimmed, at least a little. And then, every night, one light ought to be left on in one window of the upper castle, probably right in that narrow window of the single tower that rose above the roof and battlements. That way they could have the place photographed for a paperback book cover . . . Hildy had tried this joke a couple of times on Saul, who each time had looked at her indulgently, smiled a little helplessly in his serious way, and hadn't appeared to really get the joke at all . . .

Whenever Hildy tried to tell someone, calmly and factually, what had happened between the two of them on that first day in the pizza parlor, she wound up having to say that she had simply let him pick her up. Which was undeniably true as far as it went. But putting it that way didn't begin to tell the truth of what had happened between the two of them at first sight.

All right, she advised herself now, run through it once more in your mind, and then stop dwelling on it, and then let's concentrate on where life ought to go from here.

Once more, now, she told herself that at the time she first met Saul, she hadn't really been Cinderella. Neither dirt-poor nor uneducated. Anyway, poverty, Hildy had decided, was far more a state of mind, or perhaps a statement of social position, than it was a measure of actual money available. It was just that when she first met Saul she had been only nineteen years old and her own sole support, and the degree in computer science that was going to make her independent and successful was a number of years that seemed like a good part of a lifetime in the future. And Saul was still far from being used to the possession of wealth himself, though wealth had been in his family for generations. He was still walking on air with the reality of the whole vast inheritance, that day when he just strolled into the pizza place, and looked at Hildy and said—

Hildy's rather feverish reverie was broken at this point by the sound of a door opening. In contrast to the stones surrounding it, it was an ordinary-looking twentieth century door, only a few decades old. Sturdy, weatherproofed wood with a no-nonsense modern lock, it was set in the side of the round watchtower that extended up ten feet or so above the roof. Old Grandfather Littlewood, as Saul and Vivian kept saying, might have been eccentric to import and rebuild himself a French castle, but he had not been daft enough to want to live in an unmodernized one.

As the door swung outward across stone flags, a young woman's face wreathed in black curls came into view around its edge. The face lit with a friendly smile at the sight of Hildy.

"There you are." This was Vivian, Saul's sister. At the twenty-eight she claimed, she was a couple of years younger than Saul, and looked considerably younger still. Her basically pale skin, like her brother's, seemed to resist tan and sunburn alike; but recent weeks in Hawaii and California had managed to impart a light bronze tint to both of them. Vivian was not as tall as her brother, but even more innately elegant. Hildy, in contrast, had white-blond hair and Scandinavian blue eyes. Her short frame was shapely enough, and not at all fat, but she was definitely on the sturdy side. With slightly improved reflexes she might have made a tennis champion; she could never have become a fashion model.

Vivian, wearing jeans and a trim shirt that displayed her own thin figure to good advantage, came forward smiling. "If you're in the midst of some serious meditation I don't have to interrupt it."

Hildy, who had found herself getting on much better than she had expected with Vivian, was determined to be cheerful. "Oh, I can meditate any time. What's up?"

Her sister-in-law put on a look of mild concern. "It's just that the great housewarming weekend starts in a very few days now, and we were insisting that all the guests and all the help have medieval dress of some sort. And I'm afraid that so far *I* have done zilch about what I'm going to wear, and—"

"Oh, the weekend. Oh my God yes, a costume. There's been so much else to do I've just completely—"

"I know, dear. Me too. Anyway, Saul and I have just decided to dash into the city. He with more business to be done, as usual. Me to track down this place I've heard about where they make you costumes that are really clothes, if you know what I mean."

"Oh. Oh yes. I'd better come along. How are you going?"

"Your husband wants to fly, he's really happy with his new license. We can land at Meigs, that's right on the lakefront you know, and be in and out of the city in no time, comparatively speaking."

"Great idea." Hildy looked at her new wristwatch. "Give me ten minutes to get changed?"

"Sure. I doubt we're going to leave inside of half an hour anyway. The great tycoon's still on the phone."

"Good," said Hildy, wondering not for the first time if it was this casual put-down attitude of Vivian's that kept her from getting married. And Hildy started for the door in the tower and the stair inside it. But then she found herself delaying involuntarily for one more look around.

"There are moments," said Vivian, watching her now with quiet amusement, "when I envy you."

"Why?" Hildy asked in wonder.

"Because. To you all this is so very new. This was more or less our family home, Saul and I spent a fair amount of time here, visiting Grandfather, when we were kids. There was wealth around, even if we didn't have much." Vivian waved her hand. No need to go into all that again now; Hildy had heard often enough already the tangled tale of family politics, quarrels, disinheritance, legal maneuverings. But now the older generation were all gone and the courts' final ruling had come down. The castle and its grounds were only a small part of Saul's and Vivian's inheritance.

"*I* envy *you* most of the time, I think." Hildy murmured now. "That you can take to all this naturally." She looked around again. "I think I'm falling in love with the place."

The roof where they stood was perhaps two hundred feet above the broad, brown surface of the Sauk, which flowed at the foot of the high bluffs on which the castle perched. The river, slow now with summer, was visible only in dots and patches hazed by the green of the nearby crowns. In fact, when you looked out in any direction from the roof, what you could see was mainly the tops of nearby trees. The grounds of the castle, small airstrip included, covered about ten or twelve acres, most of it right atop the riverside bluffs and down their slope. The bluffs, heavily wooded, were much too steep ever to have been cultivated, or even put to pasture. The river and its shorelines along here, Hidly had thought, probably looked much the same now as they had during Indian times.

The rich countryside that surrounded the river on both sides could be seen from the castle roof only in leaf-clouded patches, through and over the uppermost branches of trees that must have been little more than saplings, if indeed they had existed at all, when Grandfather Littlewood bought the land. If Hildy let her imagination try, it could build on the hints of things seen tantalizingly through the summer trees, working to convince her that she was now in fact the mistress of some huge feudal domain. If the land in feudal times had not really looked like this round the castle's original site, it should have.

There were vast fields of summer corn out there, along with square miles of other crops that she could not so easily identify. There were sprawling, sloping creekbed pasturelands, supporting tidy herds of dairy cows, with here and there some sheep. Most of the fields were bordered by thick hedgerows that Saul said sheltered small game in plenty. Orchards and pastures provided patches of woods, besides the wooded land of the river bluffs and islands. Saul had told her that there had been wild deer here in the valley when he was growing up, and he thought there probably still were, at least a few. He could remember Grandfather Littlewood telling stories of wild wolves, running right here along the Sauk . . . the more Hildy heard of Grandfather Littlewood, the more she wished that she could have met him.

The trees around the castle prevented a rooftop observer from being able to see any of the prosperous modern farmhouses and barns very plainly; with very little effort a feudal illusion could be sustained. What buildings were visible through clear gaps in greenery were miles away, too distant for detail to be seen. In winter, Hildy supposed, with the leaves gone, the view of the countryside around must be considerably

plainer—and of course it must then be easier for
the outside world to see the castle, too. To see it,
for example, from the narrow highway that
threaded along the river's farther shore, and
maybe even from Frenchman's Bend, the little
town on the far shore half a mile upstream. She
could see nothing of the town now, and very little
of the highway even when the breeze stirred
branches. The breeze was picking up a little now,
she noticed, and there were gray clouds in the
southwest.

"I suppose we'd better get moving," Vivian
commented, looking in that direction, shading her
eyes against the sun. "We can spend the night in
town if we decide to, but the ace will want to get
there before the thundershowers do."

The two women entered the tower; Hildy closed
the door firmly behind them, and they started
down the winding stone stair. The narrow stair
curved counterclockwise as you descended, Saul
said to give a defending right-handed swordsman
the advantage as he retreated upward. As she
passed one of the narrow decorative windows
Hildy looked down into the courtyard some sixty
feet below, and saw that the workmen were giving
the swimming pool a trial filling. It certainly
ought to be ready for use by Friday afternoon.
Now, in a matter of minutes, she was going to get
into a machine with her lover Saul at the controls,
and fly. She felt dreamy, drifty, ready to let go
and enjoy the ride.

She asked Vivian: "What were medieval
swimsuits like, I wonder?"

Vivian's laugh was quietly musical. "They
looked very much like medieval pajamas, I'm
afraid."

"Not a stitch in sight?"

"Exactly. Saul and I got away with skinny-
dipping in the river a few times when we were
little. One of our cousins from across the river

put us up to it . . . he was quite a nasty little boy. But we'd better not encourage the weekend guests to carry this medieval thing too far."

The stairway brought them into a hallway that had not existed in the original structure, on the third level of the castle above the ground. Again the walls were stone, and ancient sconces held unlighted torches against the walls. But there were electric lights as well, recessed and inconspicuous; there were bedrooms, bathrooms, closets, designed in at the time of reconstruction in the early twentieth century. The old place was really in remarkably good shape, thought Hildy, considering how many decades it had been standing almost empty and almost unoccupied since it was rebuilt. She had to admit that old Gregory, though she didn't like him, had certainly done a good job as caretaker.

Saul, still in tennis clothes as was his bride, was standing halfway down the long hall, telling some more workmen in which room to put an antique bed. The process of refurnishing was coming along faster than Hildy had thought it would.

Hildy hurried to embrace her tall husband, bury her face for a moment against his chest, smelling of sweat and exercise and sunlight. Saul, murmuring something, returned the hug; he seemed half-distracted, as he usually was these days, thinking about business.

The three of them walked on down the hall, one young woman on each side of Saul.

"It's been fun, kids," said Vivian. "But soon I'm going to be moving out."

"Oh?" Hildy, feeling vague alarm, looked across at her. "Where to?"

"Sometimes I wonder, how are you guys ever going to *heat* this place in the winter? This isn't southern California, you know. It gets cold in these parts."

Saul put in: "The old hot water system is still

working. And there are a lot of fireplaces." He turned to Hildy with a vague expression of concern. "We could think about having some baseboard electric put in, I suppose."

"Don't start that before the weekend," his sister cautioned him. "By the way, Gregory tells me that the magician he wanted to get is coming."

Saul said: "Fine. It looks like everyone we invited is going to be here."

FOUR

At dawn he had been sitting crouched on the curb. His feet, in their broken, mismatched shoes, were braced in the littered gutter, as ready as they could be made for their part in a quick spasmodic effort at getting his body erect. When the morning sun started to get warm, the sense of desperation and impending peril faded, and he moved into a building's shade and got his aged shoulder-blades against a solid storefront. It was not the shade he sought; such warmth as this northern sun could generate could never really bother him. It was the support he wanted. He was very tired. If he dared let himself lean back against anything during the night, he tended to go to sleep; if he slept he could not remain on guard, and it was imperative to remain on guard during the hours of darkness. Whenever he nodded off by night lately he came jolting awake, crying out through his old throat in nightmare's helpless terror.

He found himself wondering, sometimes, why

the prospect of his own murder could shake him so. His life had long been robbed of everything that would make it worth worrying about. But this wondering was no defense against night's terror.

Now morning daylight lent his surroundings gritty reality enough for him to be able to rest in metaphysical security. As he allowed himself to sit leaning back against the building, his hands, stubby-fingered, the basically pale skin polished beyond grime, could be let down to rest one on each side of him on the Chicago sidewalk. During the warm June night just past his hands had stayed most of the time clutched round himself as if he might be cold, as if his own embrace could possibly protect him from the terror that walked—and flew, and crawled, for all he knew—by night. Now, in daylight brightness and warmth, and with people nearby—even such people as the Street afforded—maybe now he would be able to get some sleep.

Even if dreams came before wine.

News of the killings, of the evil, blood-draining torture-slaughters of helpless old men, had in the past days traveled up and down the Street like wind. Borne somehow in alcoholic breath, in muttered half-words, in faces frightened into speechlessness. Even though you might think that none of the people here ought to be afraid of death . . .

His eyes closed, already drifting near sleep as he leaned back against the building, he heard a pair of feet in unmatched shoes approaching, slowing to a stop. Without bothering to open his eyes he could identify their shuffle.

"Hey, Feathers?" called the expected voice.

Despite himself the man called Feathers sometimes remembered that in some dim lifetime before he'd hit the Street his name had been something else. But that didn't matter, hadn't mattered for a long time now. He smiled now with what teeth he had left, knowing what this approach meant. Already it seemed to him that he could taste the wine, and he opened his tired eyes with quiet joy, ready to listen.

As he had expected, his visitor now launched into a long, detailed and almost completely unnecessary explanation of a simple scheme of pooling coins from several contributors in order to obtain a bottle. To the organizer of the scheme its prospects appeared bright. The man called Feathers grew impatient well before the end of the explanation, but some people deserved to be treated with courtesy, and anyway he understood what the organizer himself perhaps did not, that listening patiently and sociably was really part of the payment for being allowed to participate without being cheated. And so Feathers listened, nodding with assumed patience whenever agreement seemed to be called for, and in the end he contributed half a dollar. It was his only money in the world, and he gave it in trust, having done business with the firm before. The agreement promised that sometime today he would share wine, and he could at least hope for enough that bad dreams would be again postponed.

Alone again, still sitting on the sidewalk with his back against the storefront, he watched a pair of drunken women reeling along the far side of the street. There was a sight offensive to morality. The two suddenly broke into a quarrel, letting out horrible sodden gasps and cackles . . . that women should be here at all was a terrible thing, and he could see that one of these had been lovely and young not long ago . . . never again . . . in pain, Feathers closed his eyes again, willing his thoughts elsewhere.

Today, as sometimes happened, the sleep that he had expected and yearned for refused to come. The day continued to pass anyway, as all days did. He waited for his investment in wine futures to

bear fruit. Meanwhile he did his best to avoid
thought. Just for variety he moved back to the
curb and sat there for a while again. And then
once more he shifted into shade, getting his back
against a different building.

He dozed at last . . .

"Hey, Feathers? All I need now's a quarter. One
more fuggin' quarter, man."

"Got no more money." Under the circumstances
he considered that a courteous reply.

"You got a dime?"

He closed his eyes again. His bladder pained
him lightly. Soon he would have to decide if it was
worth the trouble of going into an alley before he
voided. Yeah, he had lasted a long time on the
Street. A long, long time. Still there had been a
time in his life before the Street, when things
were not like this. Not like this . . .

Had he perhaps been here for a million bottles?
How many bottles a year would that be? Numbers had never been his strong point. But he was
sure that his Street had run through many other
towns beside this one, and many other years.

He opened eyes—awoke, perhaps?—to find himself still sitting alone, in shadows that had to be
those of afternoon, shadows slowly lengthening.
No wine in sight as yet. Well, he could be philo-
sophical. In time another bottle would be his, one
way or another. Bottles and people, he'd seen
them come, he'd seen them go. Usually pretty
thoroughly drained. Even if some men had
amounted to something in previous lives, now on
the Street they were all pretty much the same . . .
pretty well drained . . .

He was ambushed unawares by delayed sleep,
and dozed again, only to wake with a sharp start
from some bright unbearable dream of youth and
greenery, and hideous, monumental loss. For a
moment there he'd been a long way from the
goddam Street, but he didn't think he could sur-

vive many more moments like that one.

Oh, God, it had been years since he'd last remembered . . . in memory he heard the last note of a woman's laugh, biting now like a knife point.

It didn't matter, it was all over, over, over, and none of mattered now a goddam bit. But somewhere deep inside he was shaking.

Propelled into movement by a different feeling, an impulse that it took a little time to recognize as hunger, he tottered to his feet. There would be a bowl of soup or stew available somewhere, a sandwich maybe. He knew a couple of likely places to get a handout. Neither place was very far away, though getting there by shuffle would take some time. Time was one thing he had plenty of, baby. There had been a song about that. A year ago? Feathers knew he tended to lose track of years.

The heat of the day, such as it was, had already passed its peak and was abating. Sun's heat felt good on bones as old as his.

Sing a hymn—no, you didn't really have to do that any more—and get a meal. Eventually, he could still hope that it would be today, a wine bottle would appear.

Leaning against a lamppost, he fumbled to open his trousers' frayed fly, discovered it already open, and drained discomfort from his bladder. If the cops saw him now they'd certainly take him in. There were a lot worse places than a Chicago cell in which to spend the night.

But no such luck today. He was going to have to go to the hymn-singers and get a meal, and then prowl after wine. Somehow, sometime, a bottle would appear.

A pawnshop window half-mirrowed the sidewalk's heat, and his own ragbag figure's shambling progress. His gray whiskers looked like fur glued on in handfuls decades past and unattended since. Behind the window's armored grillwork were old musical instruments, radios, a tiny television with a dead dusty face. At the bottom of a short literary stack there was one thick, serious-looking volume, and something about that bottom book stirred vibrations deep in memory, roiled more sorely things already stirred by that last dream.

There had been books, yes, once there had been many books. Books revealing marvels ancient beyond guessing, and ancient marvels in themselves. And summer greenery as in the dream, and a young woman's laughter . . .

. . . NO . . .

It didn't matter. He had to cling to that. If he let himself panic now, over nothing, over what was dead and buried, it could finish him off. Really it didn't matter now. Whatever his life had once contained of beauty, and of power, was all forgotten now. More than forgotten, buried and dead. He no longer wanted change, improvement, success. He no longer remembered what those things were. Now he wanted nothing at all beyond another bottle, or at least a share in one, and then to be left alone. The wine, the power, the sacrament. The Word of the Lord urged softly, in eternal pigheaded hope. The Lighthouse, the Salvation Army kitchen. And by now he was near enough to smell the soup.

At one time—it was so easy to lose track of the years, no, so difficult actually, but he'd managed it—at one time it really had been necessary to sing a hymn for them before they'd give you a handout. It was all handled differently now, more scientific and more merciful at the same time. Institutionalized love. The Work and the Word of the Lord going hand in hand . . . oh Lord, oh God, why is it still needful that I still be cursed with a functioning mind, or anyway one that sometimes functions? How many million bottles of wine are needed to work the miracle of deep forgetting?

For a moment he stood swaying on the streetcorner, arms raised, fingers spread as if to grasp and tear the sun.

. . . world without end, amen. The Street was a world truly without end within the world, going on infinitely echoing itself. As an empire it had outlasted many others. And he had seen a lot of the Street. A goddamned lot.

When he came out of the soup kitchen, having eaten, and having skillfully put off the clever overtures of the social worker, it was dark again. The sun was certainly down, the shadows cast by streetlights had grown out in their fixed places on pavements and the fronts of buildings. The sky was a starless blur above all lights. He was leaving a fresh young woman behind him disappointed, not the first time he'd done that, ha hahh.

The soup had evidently given him some kind of strength.

. . . now was that real laughter, somewhere?

Hardly. Only some of the usual noise made by the usual two-legged pigs of the Street. Though at the end there had sounded one true, wild note . . .

Get a meal, sing a hymn, get a bottle sometimes. Get busted, sleep in a cell, get out. Oh yeah, and fear the eventual return of winter. In winter life grew hard.

Get a bottle, then try for a safe place to sleep it off. The pitiful shelter of some flophouse with its chickenwire barricades at best. At worst—

Great God but death was coming, prowling the street in the next block. Feathers, seeing the dark-suited figure under a streetlight from a block away, recognized it instantly and knew an instant convulsion of terror. His ancient heart leaped up to pound savagely under his ribs. He instantly ceased his shuffling progress to nowhere, and stood leaning like an abandoned store dummy against the nearest building front. For all his immobility he was suddenly more awake, more alive, than he had been for years. With all the energy that he could muster, he willed himself unnoticeable, invisible. Meanwhile death in a dark elegant suit came pacing on in his direction. The seeking butcher, pale angular face brooding above a neat collar and red tie, stalked past Feathers not a body-length away, without a sign of being aware of him. Feathers did not breathe. He saw a worn gold ring on a white finger. The dark eyes in death's wan countenance did not turn toward him. The moment passed with Feathers still invisible, and then the embodiment of death was gone.

He breathed again. He gasped, and sweated too. God, why did he cling so frantically to life, erect his flimsy chickenwire barricades of the mind, just to give the throatslitters a little more trouble in getting their hands on him? But cling to life he must, there seemed to be no choice.

Now he really had to get a bottle. He'd seen death on the streets before in recent days, but never so close. He needed a bottle, and then some place where he could rest.

Against a half-familiar storefront he let his legs give up their burden. His shaky knees folded, and he slid down to sit on the sidewalk. His once-strong hands caressed the solid, physical concrete, still warm from the sunlight of the day just past.

"Feathers?"

This was a new voice, one that did not sound as if it ought to be on the street at all. Its owner had somehow contrived to approach without being heard. The old man roused in surprise from his near-trance, noting with shaky relief that the newcomer was not in a black suit, even before he could get a good look at the man's face.

The man standing over Feathers was no one he had ever seen before. Maybe one of the Street missionaries, except few of them were blacks. This man had skin the color of coffee heavy on the cream, features half African. Coatless, his dark shirt open at the collar, but well-enough dressed in the dirty dusk; in fact, dressed too well by far to be a genuine member of the Street himself.

The man was smiling at Feathers softly. He was of average build, and somewhere under forty. "I heard your friend over there call you by that name not long ago: 'Feathers'. We could use another name if you don't like that one." His accent was not American Black, but not quite Standard American either. Maybe Caribbean?

"No friggin' friend of mine. Who're you? You're no friggin' friend either." And all the while Feathers felt a weak relief that this was not dark death returned. Speech and thought, as they so often did, seemed to be springing from different founts inside his head, each going its own way almost unrelated to the other. He was being discourteous. Well, sometimes that was actually the best way to cadge a drink, and anyway most people deserved it.

"I could be your friend." The stranger's dark eyes were vaguely luminous. "I'll buy you a drink. Where's the best place?"

"Drink. All right. I'm your man." Still sitting on the pavement, Feathers suspiciously eyed the street to right and left. The choice of a place did matter, because—"Not right here." There was a tavern within spitting distance on his right. "If we go in here, all my goddam friends will see and come in after us. Bumming drinks. Leeches."

"Okay," agreed the stranger good-humoredly. "Where, then?"

"Place just around the corner. Down the side street." Feathers' feet had by now somehow become positioned under his center of gravity. Standing up was now possible, with a little help from the stranger's hand, which felt stronger than it looked. Shuffling, leaning on a building now and then for balance and support, Feathers led the way around the corner.

When you turned this way the world changed quite a bit in just one block of gritty sidewalk. Proceeding a second block in this direction would have brought them to an alien country, whose horrified inhabitants would boot a Skid Row bum right out of their taverns. But Feathers had no intention of going that far. One block was just right. The corner tavern on the borderland would let him in, if he had a companion who looked as if he could put down some money on the bar. And here the leeches were not likely to dare to follow.

In the doorway of the borderland tavern they were met by cooled air, the smells of stale beer and staler pizza. This atmosphere had a certain degree of class. It bore no noticeable traces of bad wine or old vomit. The people already in the bar, none of them with their clothes torn or their flies gaping, looked up coldly at Feathers when he entered. But he had judged correctly, they weren't quite ready to throw him out on sight when he came in with someone better dressed.

"How about some food?" His soft-voiced benefactor, helping him get settled in a booth, was becoming solicitous. Maybe he was queer. It was a long, long time now since Feathers had felt the need to worry that anyone would approach him in that way. He doubted that was it.

The two of them sat facing each other in a dim plastic booth, and drinks, drinks, were on the way at last. The bar in this tavern had arranged on it the trimmings for serving food: paper napkins, mustard, salt and pepper, sharp pointed little plastic picks. A sign on the wall said SAND-WICHES.

"I'm a reporter."

"Like shit you are."

"Oh?" Fierce insult appeared to have provoked

no more than gentle amusement. "What am I, then?"

"How come you picked me to talk to? Buy drinks for?"

"There's something about you. Something interesting."

Wine was set before Feathers, a small portion of a wine-dark sea bounded in a glass. Plunging in shielded one from all else.

The coffee-colored hands on the other side of the narrow table cupped a clear glass, holding what could be gin and ice cubes. Or maybe it was vodka. "We could go somewhere else if you'd rather. I have a car not too far away. I know a party where you'd be welcome. They have a lot of drinks just sitting there waiting. You know what good wine is like?"

"Ah."

A second glass of wine replaced the first, which had been drained. And now sandwiches were being carried to the table too.

"Won't you eat something?"

On close inspection the plastic points turned out not to be honest simple toothpicks at all, but pink miniature swords. One of them had been skewering an olive in the black man's drink. Good God. Feathers stared helpless, hypnotized. His host had eaten the olive and was holding the pink sword right against the clear liquid in the glass, sparking an explosion in Feathers' brain of ancient memories . . .

. . . and present knock-out drops . . .

Oh God no. His reaching fingers could no longer find the wine.

FIVE

It was about three on a hot Friday afternoon when Simon Hill and Margie Hilbert arrived in Frenchman's Bend in Simon's five-year-old car. For Simon, the drive out from Chicago had also been a trip back into memory, back into time. It had been enjoyable in spots, but mainly—he wasn't sure why—it had been disturbing.

"Frenchman's Bend," he said now, slowing in anticipation on the two-lane concrete highway, almost roofed by the arches of overhanging trees. "I bet they still don't even have a population figure on the sign."

Margie in the right front seat was looking past Simon and across the broad expanse of the Sauk, which was high for summer. She had been quietly admiring the scenery since they had crossed the river at Blackhawk, now almost twenty miles upstream behind them. "Si, you say you know these people who own this place we're going to?"

"Yeah. Sort of. Actually we're distant cousins.

We've been out of touch."

"Not only that, you don't like them, do you?"

He grunted.

"I get the impression that you're even out to get back at them for something."

Simon didn't answer.

"It's just that if I'm going to wind up in the middle of something, I'd like to know what's going on. We're supposed to spend a whole weekend there."

"I guess I wouldn't count on doing that." He kept expecting to see the recognizably final bend in the highway, and it kept being just a little farther on than he had thought. Now he glanced at Margie, who was still waiting for a real answer, and had to admit that she had a point. The trouble was, he didn't know what answer would be the truth. "Well," he said, "it's a long story. Would you believe, I won't know how I feel about these people until I see them again? Right now the feelings are not too good. But . . ."

"You were just a kid when you saw them last, huh? What kind of a fight did you have? Was it one of these family things about money?"

"No. My branch of the family was never in line for any of that anyway." He drove for a little while in silence. "I was fifteen years old. Saul was maybe twelve. Vivian was about a year older than me, I guess. I had my first affair with her. She's the Miss Littlewood that old Gregory mentioned. Actually . . ."

"Yeah?"

"Actually I'm not sure what role old Gregory played. I have some confused memories about him." He glanced at Marge; she wasn't understanding this; well, that was the point, he had never been able to sort it out himself.

Margie, practical as usual, was thinking ahead to other matters. "You think the old guy was just conning us about there being entertainment people in the group for the weekend?"

"I don't know. I just don't know."

The last bend before Frenchman's was here at last. The highway curved sharply, under graceful arches of tree limbs. On the right a hill rose up, too steep for farming or even grazing, heavily wooded; on the left, a gently sloping bank only a few yards wide fell to the broad surface of the Sauk. This part of the highway was threatened with flooding fairly often 'in the spring. Just ahead, the bank going down to the river widened somewhat, and a few old buildings came into view, still half concealed by the summer growth that lined both sides of the highway.

"This is it," said Simon. "I was wrong about the population sign. They don't even have one any more." There was, at the moment, no other traffic in sight to worry about. He pulled left across the single oncoming lane and onto a clay-and-gravel shoulder that blended into a broad stub of road or driveway serving the three or four buildings that made up this side of the hamlet. A couple of other cars, unfamiliar to Simon, were parked here; no people were in sight. He braked to a gentle halt in the shade of a huge old elm, familiar once he saw it again, but till this moment forgotten. The elm was the biggest healthy specimen he could remember seeing anywhere, having somehow survived the Dutch disease that had all but exterminated its species in these parts a few decades back.

Like all the towns along this part of the river, Frenchman's Bend straddled the highway. Four buildings, including sheds, on the side toward the river, maybe twice that many on the other. In his first look around at the place, Simon could not see that anything at all had changed in fifteen years.

He got out of the car, listening to cicadas drone, looking around some more. The stub of road that he had parked on continued to the edge of the low bluff on which the houses stood, then plunged down through a broad cut in the bluff to the shoreline just a few feet below. The bluffs along this side of the river were considerably lower than those lining the opposite bank, several hundred yards away. Over there the land rose abruptly from the shoreline well over a hundred feet, a height exaggerated by the tallness of the trees atop the bluffs; all that could be seen of the far shore was a continuous soft leafy mass.

In Frenchman's Bend the old frame houses stood as Simon remembered them. Whether it was the same paint covering them now or not, it looked no older than the paint of fifteen years ago. The two parked cars were unfamiliar, though; even here some things had to change.

With Margie following him silently, Simon turned his back on the houses for a moment and walked to the place where the road cut through the bluff. He stood there looking down. On the gravel shingle just below was an abandoned pile of clamshells, left over from the decades before plastic buttons, when the freshwater shells had had some commercial value. Simon remembered the shell pile as soon as he saw it again, as with the giant elm.

No one around here built a permanent boat-dock; the spring ice-jams and floods tended to be too fierce, tearing away anything weaker than a bridge abutment. But there was an old rowboat, too lacking in distinction for Simon's memory to feel sure about it, tied by padlocked chain to the trunk of a stubby, familiar willow. And, on the narrow strip of sand that at the water's very edge blended into rich mud, an aluminum canoe, unlocked, had been inverted, with a wooden paddle partially visible underneath it. If this was the same canoe that he remembered—

Motion and whiteness, along the wooded shore of an island a hundred yards out in the stream, caught Simon's eye. He looked up sharply.

Margie, who had been gazing out across the water in a different direction, turned toward him. "What is it?"

"I thought I saw . . . someone out on the island." The impression, momentary but convincing, had been of pale flesh, completely unclothed, and dark curly hair. Of course what was much more likely was that he had seen someone wearing some light-colored summer garment.

At the distance, he reflected as he watched the island, it would be hard for even the steadiest gaze to perceive curliness.

An insect droned from across the water. "Looks like a real jungle over there," said Margie without much interest.

Was his imagination continuing to add details, or had he really seen the figure, in that one doubtful moment, as beckoning to him with one arm. He closed his eyes. An inner voice said that, even if he couldn't remember it, there was good reason why he hadn't come back here for fifteen years.

Simon opened his eyes again before Margie could take notice. Now on a sudden impulse he climbed a few steps, from the road to the lip of the bluff. From here he stared downstream, between islands, along the longest visible reach of the river. He knew where the castle stood, half a mile downstream, atop the high bluff opposite. Simon knew the exact direction in which to look, or thought he did, because he had seen it often enough from this very spot in winter, its gray stone angles standing out starkly amid a tracery of black branches, against gray winter sky . . .

A crow, cawing sharply as if disturbed by someone nearby, came up from amid the trees of the nearest island, the one where Simon thought that he had seen the figure. Well then, there was someone on the island, and what of it? But he felt relieved.

"I've never been in a canoe," said Margie, looking down toward the shingle. "Is that how we're going to get across?"

"We'll see," Simon told her. "Look, we'll just check it out as far as we can go, the secret passage and the rest. When we hit a snag that could stop us we'll give up the idea and come back here and drive back to Blackhawk and around and drive up to the castle by the front door like they're expecting us to do, and put on our alternate act. But the secret passage just makes too beautiful an opportunity to resist, if it's still there and we can use it. Right?"

Margie had been doubtful all along. "The people who own the place now don't know this passageway is there?"

"I tell you I don't *think* they do. And it can't hurt anything to try." Simon resolutely turned his back on the water.

There were two houses on this side of the highway, along with a couple of outbuildings. In front of the bigger house a wooden sign said BOATS. The ANTIQUES sign Simon also remembered had disappeared sometime in the last decade and a half; he thought he could make out from here the slightly discolored spot on a tree trunk where it had been nailed.

"Canoes are all right," he said to Margie now. "You can tip them if you try, or if you jump around wildly in one, but you're all right if you just sit still. I can do the paddling." As he spoke he had started walking toward the larger house, with Margie keeping at his side. Now he could see that the name on the rural mailbox a few yards from the house still said *Colline*. And when he squinted through the heat-shimmer of the concrete to the far side of the highway, it seemed to Simon that he could still make out faded letters on one of the mailboxes over there: *Wedderburn*. That house on the far side stood next to a building that had once been a farm equipment store, though even in Simon's earliest childhood memories it had been generations out of date and closed. If Gregory should appear in one of those doorways or windows now, would Simon, seen once more in a familiar context, be recognized?

But no one at all appeared. Simon led Margie on, toward the house-antique shop. Their feet made a sound that evoked memories for him, crunching lightly on an ancient detritus of broken clamshells, waste from the clam-fishing decades, pulverized by time and by now almost turned to soil.

A few steps from the closed front door of the house, he halted Margie for a moment. "My aunt and uncle used to run this place as an antique shop. For all I know they still do. I don't know whether they'll recognize me or not. If they don't, I'd just as soon leave it at that."

Margie frowned at him—she liked to think sometimes that she was softhearted on family relationships—then shrugged, pretty shoulders moving in the light, longsleeved shirt. "Whatever you say. It's your town and your family, and you're the boss on the job."

Simon felt like kissing her, and knew she would resent it at this moment. Without giving himself time to think about it any more, he turned to the old familar door and pulled it open. A moment later they were both stepping into the half-familiar semigloom of what had been—no, apparently still was—the antique shop's main room. The place was crowded with dusty shapes that on a second glance turned out to be not junk for sale but only cases and mountings for displays. There was less actual merchandise on view than he remembered, but there was still some. Business appeared to be languishing even more now than it had been then, which he supposed was hardly surprising given the current absence of a sign out front.

The antique bell that he remembered had tinkled when they came in. Now Simon watched the curtained doorway that led to the living quarters in back. He was bracing himself for the sight of his aunt or uncle. The curtain stirred as he watched it, and in the fraction of a second before it was whipped aside he knew that if his relatives didn't recognize him he wasn't going to tell them who he was, either before or after the performance.

Except, of course, just possibly—Vivian. Had Miss Littlewood recognized Simon the Great when she saw him in performance, and had she sent Gregory with an invitation for that reason? Since the night in the chapel at TMU, Simon had tried a thousand times to picture what Vivian must be like now, at thirty. He had tried to analyze what he thought about her now, what his feelings were at the prospect of shortly seeing her again. The analysis had proved impossible. The thoughts and feelings would not fall into any ordinary category, except the inadequate one of curiosity.

And now the curtain was moved aside, and the world, as it often did, surprised Simon. The teen-aged girl who emerged into the shop was a stranger to Simon's memory, looking like no one in particular that he remembered from Frenchman's Bend, looking as commonplace as any kid he'd seen on the way out from Chicago. The girl had dark hair, but there ended the resemblance to Vivian or to any half-glimpsed water nymphs. Here instead we had a moderately dumpy, banally adolescent figure in denim shorts and loosely swaddling halter top.

"Can I help you?" the girl asked, in a voice as reassuringly ordinary as the rest of her. She had put her hands on the counter near the kerosene lamp. Whether that particular lamp had been in stock fifteen years ago Simon had no way of telling. There was fluid in its glass reservoir, and the wick was charred. The house had electricity, of course, but that lamp had been used recently.

Simon smiled confidently. "I see you have a canoe down there. I'd like to rent it for a couple of hours."

"No," said the girl, shaking her head. It was a surprisingly quick, definite answer, as if such requests came frequently and she had been trained how to respond to them. But then she added unexpectedly: "If you want to go over to the castle, my brother can paddle you over."

Simon blinked deliberately. "I didn't say anything about a castle. You mean the huge house on the other side of the river?"

The girl surveyed them calmly. "You don't look like you're going fishing, or on a picnic." Simon exchanged glances with Marge; they were both dressed casually, in practical jeans and long-sleeved shirts against expected mosquitoes. Marge had on light white gym shoes, Simon brown suede loafers. But they weren't dressed for fishing, and apart from Margie's large shoulder bag they were carrying nothing.

Tuning up his smile to about its second most charming level, Simon told the girl: "We're not waterskiing, either. All right, then, we'll hire the canoe and your brother too for a couple of hours. Does he have a regular rate?"

"Talk to him," the girl advised. "I'll go get him." She came out from behind the counter and scuffed on bare feet toward a side door.

In the dim light Simon looked around at tawdry, scanty merchandise, at junk, at dust. Marge's eyes were alert and expectant but he had nothing to communicate to her at the moment. Listening carefully he could hear the girl's quiet voice drifting in faintly from beyond the side door where she had gone out. He couldn't hear what she was saying. There was a private yard out there, on the side of the house away from the highway, or at least there had been one when Simon lived here.

Shortly the girl came back into the shop, followed a moment later by a boy who in apparent age, about fifteen, might have been her twin, but who otherwise resembled her only vaguely. He was tightening the fancy belt buckle on his jeans; his lean chest showed under an unbuttoned gray shirt, and his feet were shoeless like his sister's.

Simon asked him: "Five bucks an hour okay?"

"Yeah. Fine." The youth sounded moderately eager.

"Our car's not going to be in your way out here, is it?"

The girl assured them: "Nobody'll bother it."

Then Simon and Margie followed her untalkative brother out through the side door, past a couple of lawn chairs in the yard, and down a narrow path toward the water. The river, Simon thought to himself again, was quite high for midsummer; the lands to the north and east, along the upper Sauk and its tributaries in far northern Illinois and Wisconsin, must have been getting heavy rains lately. And he could see rainclouds now, in the southwest sky, beyond the wooded bluff where the hidden castle waited. When you lived in the city steadily, he thought, you lost touch with the weather, caring only how cold it was at the moment, whether you might be going to get wet. Anyway he estimated that the next rain here was still hours away; it shouldn't interfere with what he and Marge were going to try to do.

Simon helped the boy turn over the canoe and get it into the water. Marge, following directions and making no fuss about possible tipping, got in without incident. Simon loaded his own considerably greater weight in near the middle of the craft; and then their barefoot guide shoved off and hopped in skillfully behind him.

Their guide's presence restricted conversation somewhat. Simon had planned to use this portion of the trip for briefing Margie further on history and local conditions, but he would be able to do that later when they were alone. He sat in the canoe and looked around and thought.

So far, the view from the water only reinforced his general impression that nothing much had changed, except for people. He wondered without concern where his aunt and uncle were. Surely, if they had sold out or otherwise departed permanently, the name on the mailbox would have been changed by the new occupants. Of course the boy and girl might easily belong to some branch of the family. They would hardly have been born fifteen years ago, and Simon hadn't kept up with any family events. He wondered idly if perhaps they were really twins; that would be consistent with their being relatives. It seemed that multiple births were more common in the complex of locally interrelated families than they were in the general population.

"It's really pretty here," said Margie, almost dreamily. She was sitting relaxed in the prow, as if she had in fact come here only for the scenery.

"Actually is," Simon agreed. In his own mind the view upriver from Frenchman's Bend was quite ordinary. In the far distance, a couple of miles above the town, the girders of the aging bridge had been repainted at some time and it was evidently still functional. Between the bridge and the town a scattering of tied-up boats and floating docks were visible along both shores. People from Blackhawk or elsewhere maintained riparian summer cottages along here, and farmers sometimes kept small craft tied up during ice-free weather, going fishing when they could. In the middle of a broad stretch half a mile upstream, an outboard towing a water-skier was droning in determined circles, like some huge insect magically confined.

Change in the scenery came swiftly as soon as the Sauk curved west and south from Frenchman's Bend. Simon, looking back now, realized that he had always understood somehow that in the downstream direction ordinariness no longer applied. Looking ahead now as the canoe moved with the current, he saw what might almost be one of Mark Twain's rivers. It would scarcely be a surprise to hear a steamboat hooting from a couple of bends downstream, feeling for the channel. In his childhood the old people of the neighborhood had talked about how in Twain's day a few boats had actually ventured this far up from the Mississippi, seeking cargo.

Here, just below the bend, the Sauk ran for a time even broader than above. And here the width of the river appeared to be stretched by a flotilla of islands, all but the tiniest of them heavily wooded. Naturally being broader meant that the river here was shallower as well. With the exception of the elusive and sometimes shifting channel, vast stretches were no more than knee-deep even when the water, as now, was relatively high. This made power boating here below the Bend a very tricky proposition, and usually all the recreational boaters stayed above the town. Canoes, rowboats, and rafts, could certainly ply here without any particular trouble, and yet with the exception of the few craft owned by Frenchman's Bend people they rarely did. No other boats were to be seen now, anywhere ahead. Nor were there any cabins along the shore. Of course you wouldn't want your cabin on a flood plain ten feet from the highway; and on the far shore the bluffs were too abrupt for cabins.

"It's wild, too," Simon said, belatedly continuing his response to Margie's comment.

The boy, still silent behind Simon, just kept on paddling. He evidently knew the best routes among the islands as well as Simon had known them at his age. To reach the castle landing by the quickest way from the Frenchman's Bend landing, you angled downstream between a certain large island and the small one next to it, which gave you the benefit of a slightly accelerated current; coming back upstream, if you hugged either shore you'd find yourself in slack water much of the way and have to work against the current.

Already the great gentle bend of river behind the canoe had taken the railroad bridge and most of the distant cottages out of sight, as well as the buildings of Frenchman's Bend itself. They were now passing between the two islands, both thickly overgrown. All of the islands here were small chunks of permanent wilderness, preserved from cottage-building by the high water that drowned them at least once a year, the spring ice jams that gouged bark from their trees and sometimes sprinkled them with kindling that had once been a boat dock or a shanty somewhere upstream. In summer the islands tended to be well populated with flies and mosquitoes, but they were visited sometimes by picnickers and fisherfolk nonetheless.

The island now passing on the right of the canoe was large, a couple of hundred yards long. It was the one where Simon earlier had thought he'd seen a figure moving. No reason, he repeated to himself now, why someone couldn't be there. It was just that the figure he'd seen had seemed designed to evoke things in his memory.

No boats had been visible on either side of the island, which was the shape and he supposed about the size of a large ship, prow and stern carved narrow by the endless flow of water, maybe fifty yards across the beam amidships. In a couple of places along its shoreline, willows hung far out with their leaves trailing in the water, making under the curve of branches green dim caves in which a small boat might possibly lie tied up in concealment. Simon, gliding past, stared intently into the shadows under the willow branches, until he was sure that there could be no boat. A narrow shoreline rim of mudflat running virtually the whole length of the island was unmarked, as far as he could see, by any kind of recent human activity. At a faint splash of the canoe's paddle the mud gave up a droning wasp, and then the blue-green drifting stiletto of a dragonfly. Simon could feel sweat trickling on his face. The middle of the island would be a green Brazilian wilderness today, with a thousand insects whining in the heat. Not a place where anyone would want to spend much time.

Now, for a minute or two, all the works of humanity save for the canoe and what was in it, had completely vanished.

Trickle of water from the paddle, and a drab hum of insects. And then there on the shoreline was some broken glass, and this was after all not the Amazon. A moment later the canoe had emerged from between islands, and now it was again possible to see a stretch of highway running close along what was now the farther bank. A car was passing a grumbling semitrailer, only a quarter of a mile away.

To Simon's left, on the small island he had not been studying, something now moved slightly but suddenly in the bushes, and once more a crow flapped up with raucous noise. Simon turned his head sharply. Under the crow's racket he'd heard a half-note of something that was almost music—from insect, bird, or human throat? It had reminded him of laughter . . . but now there was nothing to be seen by the near-jungle quiet in the heat.

The canoe was now aimed more directly toward

the southeastern shore. Ahead Simon thought he could make out the place where the castle's floating boat-dock had once been moored. He was not surprised to see that it was gone. All the better for his plans if there were no regular landings here. But the girl had asked him at once if they were going to the castle; that certainly suggested that others had recently come this route.

He turned his head to speak to the boy. "Do you carry many passengers this way?"

"Nope." The youth didn't seem to think anything of the question one way or another.

"Have you taken anyone before us?"

"Unh-unh." Inflected to mean no.

"Your sister just seemed to assume this was where we were going. I wondered. By the way, are you twins?"

"Yep."

As they drew near the landing place, now simply a narrow spot of sandy beach, Simon could detect no sign that other boats had recently come to shore. When the canoe grated on bottom, he edged past Marge, hopped ashore, than reached back to give her a hand. Then he turned to the boy, who was watching them uncertainly. "Just wait for us, okay? It could be as long as a couple of hours, but it could be just a few minutes. I'll pay for your time. I'll throw in a five dollar bonus. Will you wait?"

"Yeah," said the boy. He got out of the canoe and with Simon's help pulled it far enough out of the water to keep it from drifting. Then he pulled a paperback book out of the hip pocket of his jeans and sat down crosslegged on the sand, as if prepared for a lengthy wait.

Margie had her bag slung on one shoulder and looked ready for whatever came next. Simon smiled at her and led the way. In the narrow strip of riparian grass the path was less defined than he remembered it, in fact it was almost completely overgrown. All to the good. The new heirs were evidently no longer river people. They certainly must have more expensive toys now than canoes, and they could seek out more inviting waterways than this. They'd probably forgotten this part of their domain.

As there was almost no flat land at all along the shore, the path had no choice but to immediately angle up the bluff. The first tall trees closed in around it, and as soon as he entered shade the first mosquito whined in Simon's ear. Good thing he'd remembered to have them both use repellent. He led the way on up, with Marge following in the narrow path.

Here what was left of the trail became somewhat more visible. Along most of its course the path was not as steep as the slope it climbed; it looped its way upward in sharp switchbacks with long legs of gentle ascent in between. At the second switchback Simon paused briefly to look down. Through a fragmentary screen of branches he could see that their guide had changed his position slightly, to sit now with his feet in the cooling water, his dark head bowed over the white pages of the book.

"He's going to talk to people, isn't he?" murmured Margie, who had come to a halt at Simon's side. "About ferrying us over here."

"I suppose he will. But not until the show's over, I hope. I can promise him another five, and five for his sister, if they'll keep quiet about it until tomorrow at least."

"Last of the big spenders," Margie murmured.

Simon winked at her, and, turning, climbed on. The path now ran through the full thickness of the woods. The tall tree trunks were not quite vertical, compromising with gravity and the steep angle of the land. After twenty yards or so, at the next switchback, Simon paused again, this time looking up. He took Marge by the arm and pointed. Now, indistinctly through a haze of summer growth, they had their first partial glimpse of the castle itself. Its gray stone walls, magnified ominously by their position, towered almost directly above them.

"It's *huge!*"

"Well, yeah. Actually small for a castle, I suppose. It was a real castle once, in France. Somewhere in Brittany. Part of it dated from the tenth century or so, I seem to remember being told. Old Man Littlewood, Vivian's and Saul's grandfather, bought it and had it shipped over here, on barges I guess. He was caught—" Simon paused. He had been distracted by a snuffling noise; it was faint and distant and something about it struck him as very odd. Somehow his mind couldn't simply dismiss it as a noise made by a dog. He thought of bears, which of course were not a reasonable possibility in Illinois.

"What is it, Si?"

"Did you hear anything?"

Margie turned her head, seemingly sniffing the air. "No."

"It was nothing, I guess." And now a dog, a real dog, was barking frantically; but very far away, no doubt on one of the nearby farms. Simon stared upward at the gray walls again.

"What were you going to say about their grandfather?"

"There was some kind of fire or explosion here one night and he was killed. That was before I was born, I think."

And he led the way on up. Now the path, working its way across a hillside grown stony, almost a cliff, grew steep enough to require very careful footwork in a couple of places. Anyone not reasonably agile and confident might feel better clambering on all fours at these spots, and even an athlete might reach for a nearby branch or treetrunk as an aid to steadiness. At the trickiest climbing turn, a wooden handrail that Simon remembered had now disappeared. Only the wooden roots of it were barely visible, like decayed tooth-stumps in the rich mossy soil.

And here in places the limestone bones of the earth stuck out, their naturally squarish shapes serving the climber briefly as stairs. He'd once hurt a toe on one of them, Simon remembered . . . but right now he didn't want to dwell on that previous ascent; that whole mysterious day. Right now he and Marge were here as workers with a job to do. It was probably the only way he could ever have brought himself to come back here at all; and he had long wanted to come back, to face certain things again, to try to rediscover them . . . Simon was in good physical shape, he took pains to stay that way, but still his breath had quickened with the climb . . . as he'd felt it quicken on that other, mysterious day . . .

When the path bent in its fourth switchback Simon looked down again toward the landing. He wanted to make sure that the canoe was still there. The screen of intervening greenery was now much thicker, but he could still see glints of aluminum. And the kid . . .

For just a moment, when the breeze stirred intervening branches in the proper way, Simon caught a glimpse of dark human hair, tanned human skin. For just a moment he saw clearly, though only partially, the figure he had glimpsed on the island, beckoning. It was Vivian, naked, waiting for him.

Marge was looking down too, doubtless trying to see what had so interested Simon. He moved back a step to stand for a moment with closed eyes. He swore to himself with silent savagery that he was not going to let his eyes or his mind or whatever it was play tricks on him. Never again. Could there be something about this place, this physical location, something chemical or atmospheric that brought on hallucinations, at least in certain susceptible people? How was he ever going to be able to sort out the truth, the fantasy, the dream, about his last days here if even now he was still subject to—

Simon opened his eyes. Marge was watching him with curiosity, but all she said was: "Looks like our guide's still waiting for us."

"I couldn't see too well through all the branches. What did you—?"

Still her eyes probed at Simon. "He's still sitting there reading. That's about all I could make out."

"Ah." Simon nodded, and faced uphill again, and climbed. Toward a real meeting with Vivian. Just as on that unforgettable day when he'd climbed alone. All he could really think about, then or now, was her. He wondered now if anything about that damned crazy experience had been real. Damn her, damn her anyway. He was suddenly angry at Vivian, angrier than he had ever suspected he might become at this late date. Whatever had really happened to him on that day fifteen years ago, it was a wonder that it hadn't done him permanent psychological damage.

And maybe it had. Simon knew a sudden chilled feeling deep in his gut. Maybe it had. Could it have anything to do with his being still unmarried?

Of course there were a lot of people, no more damaged than anyone else, who for one reason or another just didn't want to get married. Marge was one. Simon deliberately fell back a step to watch her climb ahead of him, her trim body moving smoothly in jeans and long-sleeved shirt. Her evening's costume, along with a few other items that might be useful, was in her shoulder bag.

They had reached the fifth, penultimate switchback of the path. Here just as it approached the turn the path sloped briefly downward. Looking up from here you could see the tall hedge, almost as impenetrable as a wall, that marked off the rear of the castle grounds proper from the surrounding woods. From this angle the hedge was tall enough to block sight of the forbidding stone walls beyond it. At the tip of the switchback loop Simon halted momentarily. From this point a branching path, even fainter than the one they followed, went off on a level course to the right. After going a few yards in that direction it curved around a protruding limestone shoulder of the bluff and vanished completely. Not, Simon realized, that the branching path was still really visible at all; it was just that he knew that it was there.

He glanced round quickly. As far as he could tell, Margie and he were still utterly alone. Then he quickly led her along the unseen trail to the right. Not only had grass and weeds completely overgrown the way during the last fifteen years, but now the new branches of small trees had to be put aside. And here in the deeper shade were more mosquitoes.

Simon moved around a second limestone shoulder, perhaps thirty yards from the place where the pathways had branched. And came to a stop. At least he knew now that he hadn't dreamed or imagined this part. Before them was the grotto, and the cave.

Within and against the natural limestone face of the cliff, the two concentric arches of the grotto had been constructed so that a natural small cave was at their center. It had all been done in the time of Grandfather Littlewood, of course, along with the rest of the construction. A knee-high rustic wall of stone surrounded the small area paved with flagstones before the grotto, an area centered on a stone construction that Simon in his earlier childhood had taken for a simple picnic table. He couldn't remember the first time that he had seen it; but he couldn't forget the last. He approached this central tabular structure now and stood staring down at it, for the moment oblivious to all else. It was a little less than waist high, built solidly of stones that on second glance were not quite the same in color and texture as the flags below, or the castle walls of which one corner was now partially visible through greenery above. The top of the table was flat, circular, and perhaps eight feet across. In its center, as if to provide the only reason for its existence, was mounted an ancient-looking sundial, a spherical cage of green-patinaed metal; probably copper, thought Simon now. An all but completely illegible inscription ran round the sundial's metal base.

Simon didn't look long at the dial or its inscription, though. On the flat stones of the tabletop faint brownish stains were visible. There was no telling how old the stains were or what had made them.

"What weird statues, Si."

He looked up; he had actually managed to forget the statues, along with piled clamshells and much else. There were six or eight pieces, mostly life size, cast concrete or carved marble, disposed on pedestals made for them around the little paved court before the grotto. Staring at a crude, fig-leafed imitation of Michaelangelo's *David*, he said: "The story goes that there was an artists' colony of some kind in the woods near here, when Old Man Littlewood was putting up his house. He just about bought out their stock of things they'd done for practice, stuff that was heavy and hard to move and that no one else wanted to buy. He didn't want it in the house, evidently, but it was good enough for decoration out here in this . . . whatever this is . . . out here in the woods."

"They're weird."

"Yeah. Let's get to work." The grotto at the cliff

face was about ten feet deep, if you were to have measured it from the outer of its two concentric arches to the heavy iron grillwork, like a jail door, that closed off the twisted mouth of the natural cave. The cave mouth was almost too small for an adult to enter anyway, and when looked at from the outside gave no indication of being any bigger farther in. The grillwork door was guarded on each side by a piece of fantastic statuary. When Simon moved up to the door for a close look it was obvious that no one had opened it for some time, and he muttered his satisfaction. The chain and small padlock holding it shut were both rusted, probably enough so that he could have broken them with relative ease. He pulled on the door, tentatively, swinging it through the few inches of play given it by the chain, creating a small aperture through which his adult body could never be made to pass. Then he decided on a more subtle way than breakage.

"Pass me the tool kit, Marge." Escape work, opening locks, was not his strongest act. But he had dabbled.

Margie dug into her shoulder bag and pulled out the packet of folded cloth, the size of a billfold. It opened to show pockets filled with a jeweler's, or an escape artist's, selection of instruments. Simon selected a small pick and went to work. The lock didn't look terribly expensive or difficult.

Meanwhile Margie retreated to stand just inside the mouth of the grotto, on watch, looking out and listening. Once she turned to ask him in a whisper: "Did you hear something?"

He paused, ready to be irritated at the interruption, but still believing that she would not have interrupted him for any commonplace sound. He listened, but could hear nothing out of the ordinary. "Maybe a bird?" he suggested. "Some animal in the woods?"

Margie shrugged. Simon went back to work. The cheap lock gave up after only a couple of minutes, unrusted parts of its shackle sliding into view. With a mutter of triumph he undid the chain and set it down; and now, with a minimum of skreeking, the jail door could be swung open. A few spider webs tore soundlessly. Inside lay blown dust and dead leaves, untrodden.

When Margie had got herself wedged into the cave mouth with him, he closed the door again behind them both, and re-wrapped the chain as convincingly as possible. He secured its links with the lock, which he almost closed. "Now," he said.

Margie had already repacked the tool kit, and now had a tiny flashlight ready. With this in hand Simon led the way into the cave. It was a way along which progress at first looked hopeless; it seemed that you must run into a wall before you had gone more than the length of your body. But around the first corner the light already shone into deep blackness, showing where a small natural crevice had been carved wider. Simon went down on all fours and inched and scraped his way ahead, with Marge groping at his heels. He slid down, deeper into the hillside. A moment later they could both stand up.

"Wow," whispered Margie. "I'm starting to believe your story."

The passage was too narrow for more than one person at a time, but adequately high. From here it snaked slowly upward through the hill, presumably following some path of least resistance through the rock. It darkened briefly to almost pitch blackness, then brightened again somewhat as they approached the outlet of an air-and-light shaft that pierced the solid stone roof ahead. The outlet of the vent at or above ground level was obviously very well concealed in some way; Simon had never had an opportunity to try to learn where or how. The last time he'd come this way,

he hadn't had a flashlight with him; he could recall groping and stumbling; and he told himself
now that those memories at least had to be real
enough.

The secret way did not continue underground
for very long. After fifteen yards or so, and one
more small vent for light and air, they reached a
steep, short flight of stairs, cut out of the native
limestone just like the rest of the passage. Then,
when they had climbed about ten steps, walls and
stair alike became construction instead of carv-
ing. The passage had brought them up within the
main castle walls themselves, twelve feet in thickness at the base.

Here the way was as narrow as before, and still
quite dim. The air was fresh-smelling, but considerably cooler than outdoors. Unexpectedly, a
branching passage appeared, twisting away to
one side and again downward; Simon remembered the branch but hadn't explored it before,
and wasn't going to check it out just now; maybe
a little later, if everything else went well.

Another stair. At its top, natural light, dim but
adequate for movement, was coming in through
one side of the passage. Simon flicked off the
penlight and gestured Margie to silence. At the
top of the stair they stood together, looking out.
On this side of the passage a deep niche built into
its stone wall terminated in an actual window,
covered with a thick wood screen through which
only a few small holes remained open. Heads side
by side in the recess, they each put eye to hole and
found themselves looking out into what Simon remembered as the great hall of the castle. It was
certainly a vast chamber, whose size was difficult
to estimate in this constricted view; but from this
strategically placed spyhole almost all of it was
visible. In the enormous fireplace a huge spit
turned, and the smell of roasting meat confirmed
that some sizable animal was indeed being

roasted whole. A long, crude trestle table, the chief article of furniture, was dwarfed by the size of the room around it. At the moment no people were in sight; the spit was being turned electrically, a cord from a small motor running to an outlet in the gray stone wall, as incongruous as it was inconspicuous.

Simon turned his head, putting lips to Margie's ear. "This panel should open from in here if you push it. This is where you'll come out. Think you can squeeze through?"

She pulled back, looked at the dimensions of the window in the stone. "A little tight. I can manage, though, if it doesn't tear the damn gauzy costume off. How far down is the floor out there?"

Simon looked again, estimated. "I think just about the same as the surface we're standing on in here. I'll look it over from the other side, tonight, before I give you the final signal at dinner. Okay?"

"Okay. I'll give it my best shot."

"Good guy," said Simon, and kissed her gently on one ear. Marge had fits of women's lib of varying intensity, and being called *girl* sometimes caused an argument.

"If this works, you'll be a good guy yourself. If it doesn't . . ."

"We've got an upper level to check out," Simon whispered. Flicking on the penlight again, he led her to and up another flight of stairs. This was steep and went up a long way. At the top of this the passage, now so narrow that even Marge scraped both side as she passed, ran level for a considerable distance. At intervals of a few yards more niches were built into the wall, on the same side, again with spots of indirect light filtering through them. These spy windows were quite low down in the wall, and each of them gave into a separate bedroom, four or five in all. Peering into one of these rooms after another, Simon and

Marge found them empty of people but all furnished and apparently ready for use. The passage they were in still followed the outer wall of the castle, and the windows in the bedrooms were under their feet. In a couple of the rooms luggage had already been deposited.

At the spyhole to the last bedroom, Simon indicated a division in the section of paneling that showed through the stone window. "Give a push here and it should swing open, if for any reason you have to get out this way." It was always good to have some kind of fall-back plan.

"Like looking for the ladies' room, maybe. It's only about two o'clock now—I could be in here another six hours or so, and then have to go right into the act."

"I guess I didn't think . . ."

"I'll cope. I'm resourceful."

"Sure you will." Simon kissed her, quickly but with real affection. They had been working together and occasionally sleeping together for a year now, and sometimes he thought that something permanent had grown between them and then again he didn't know. He turned away, then back. "Here, you'll need the flashlight. Almost forgot."

"Can you grope your way out?"

"No problem." And he was on his way; in moments at the top of the uppermost stair, down which he felt his way on his soft-soled shoes.

The first part of the trip out was uneventful. It was as if every foot of the way had already been engraved upon his memory. But when he had got as far as the branching tunnel in the base of the wall he was surprised to see that light was filtering upward very faintly from the branch. Probably just the penlight in his hand had been enough to mask it when they were on the way up. Simon paused, watching. The light was possessed by a tiny flicker, as if its source were flame. Before he left Margie alone in the tunnel system, he ought to check this out.

Down a short turning stair in the branch tunnel, and he came to what surprised him, a real door. It was made of crude wood that seemed to fit with the rest of the decor, and was swung partly ajar, out into a sizable stone room with stone-flagged floor. In the room a torch in a wrought-iron wall scone burned dimly, making the illumination that had drawn Simon here. Against the wall not far from the torch there stood on two legs a metal object that Simon at first took for a suit of armor. It took him a few moments' staring in the dim light to realize that it was some kind of iron maiden, a complex instrument of torture.

At best the old man had had a bizarre sense of humor. Whatever this sub-basement was being used for now, the open door, the torch, meant that it was certainly being used for something, and that what Simon had thought were the secret passageways were known. He would have to go back and get Margie and get out. But first he was going to try to find out exactly what . . .

When he peered cautiously round the edge of the door, the whole room, or almost all of it, was visible. Besides the iron maiden, other peculiar instruments stood about in it. Most notably a bed-like rack, with great spoked wheels made to give leverage for disjointing the victim's limbs. And the rack was occupied . . .

Simon stepped back, closed eyes and rubbed them, mumbled something halfway between a prayer and a curse, then stepped forward and looked again. The rack was occupied by the naked body of an old man, gray-whiskered, paunchy, whose wrists and ankles were bound to the machine by the provided heavy straps, and who looked as if he were not dead but certainly unconscious.

Moving without conscious volition, Simon pushed the door open farther and stepped out into the room. Eyes fixed on the rack and its' occupant, he moved forward slowly. He'd been working up to an hallucination like this one all afternoon, and now it was here, and he was almost glad, knowing that it couldn't possibly be real.

The old man was quite motionless except for gentle, faintly snoring breathing. A small rope of saliva trailed from one corner of his mouth. The leather strap holding one of his arms felt like a taut strap when Simon touched it, and the old man's forearm, puffed slightly by the tight bond, certainly felt like flesh. But this couldn't be—

Simon started to take a step backward, and without warning a strangling grip clamped on him from behind. His neck was caught, one arm pinioned. He could no longer breathe and his head was going to burst and he knew that in a moment more he would be dead.

SIX

In Chicago pawnshops they had looked at enough samurai swords, at least imitation ones, to have conquered China; enough Nazi bayonets, most of which Joe Keogh thought had never been farther east than Gary or anyway New England, to have repelled the Russians. With Charley Snider he had seen bolos, Bowie knives, trench knives, stilettos, sabers, machetes, and cutlasses. They had confiscated illegal switchblades, that no claim of being a bona fide collector could save. They had looked at razors and cleavers and spearheads and God knew what, had handled today every variety of pigsticker that either Joe or Charley had ever heard of, in the process coming upon a few types that were new to both of them. And they had failed to find, or at least failed to identify, what they were looking for. Of course two men, or ten men, could not have covered all the pawnshops in a single day, and there was tomorrow to look forward to. Right now the men were deep in the basement of central headquarters, rummaging with fading hope through the last few days' take of confiscated goodies. Along with enough blades to furnish a field of grass, there were blackjacks here, zip guns, and, once more, God knew what.

Charley was squinting doubtfully at an odd kind of homemade brass knuckle outfit. A small length of chain had been rivited onto it. Charley had been detailed to work full time with Joe today because of a report that a black man exactly fitting the description of Carados, the west coast murderer, had been seen in conversation with a bum known as Feathers in a tavern just a block off Skid Row; and Feathers was now nowhere to be found; and Joe had allowed it to be known informally that his informant might just possibly be able to provide some lead.

"I guess," said Charley, trying the quaint artifact on his right fist, "if you don't get 'im with the punch you maybe take an eye out with the swinging end."

"I guess," agreed Joe. With a faint groan he straightened up from the table full of treasures he had been turning over; when he got home to Kate he was going to request a backrub.

"So now," Charley sighed, "looks like you can tell your boy when he calls again that we came up empty trying to find this special blade he talkin' 'bout. What exactly was this cutter supposed to tell us when we did find it?"

During the day's labors Joe had already managed to put off this question a couple of times. Of course it would have to be answered sooner or later, and he had been giving some thought to how. He tried now the best answer he had so far been able to come up with: "If we found it, and could describe it exactly to him—add details beyond what he already knows about it—then he thought it would help him, maybe, to put his fin-

ger on the guys we want." Joe had to admit to
himself that his best answer sounded purely
terrible.

Charley took his time considering. "Well," he
said at last, "I guess this cat has really come
through for you a time or two in the past."

"Yeah. He has."

"For Carados," said Charley, "I'll go to a lot of
trouble. I'll even take a chance on making an utter
damn fool of myself and wasting a lot of time.
When's your guy supposed to call you again?"

"Tonight, I hope. He wasn't sure." Last night,
when Talisman had called Joe at home, to give
him the first detailed information about the
sword, Joe had been able to hear the subway
trains roaring in the background. And it had been
midnight. Joe wouldn't have cared to hang around
a subway station at that hour, not without Charley Snider and maybe a small squad of marines.

His caller of course had not been distracted by
any personal concerns. After describing the
sword he was trying to find, Talisman had told
Joe of the existence of an imported castle, a European building reconstructed out on the Sauk
River, that really ought to be investigated. "The
man I began by looking for is there, you see, as
well as the truly remarkable man of whom I
spoke.

"The oddity."

"Yes. And I can sense now that there is a
woman to match." For a moment Talisman's
voice seemed to hold nothing but deep masculine
appreciation.

Joe protested. "The Sauk River's really way out
of my territory, as you know. If I call the sheriff
out there, or the state police, I can't just tell them
to look for a vampire."

"Obviously, Joe. It is possible that a man named
Carados, from New Orleans, is there also. His existence they believe in, his possible presence will

greatly interest them. But say nothing yet. The
time is not yet ripe. More important matters than
I had dreamed are involved here."

"Why are you telling me now, then?"

"Someone besides myself should know, Joseph.
If I should disappear, if I should die. I am going to
visit that castle presently. The duty I have assumed compels me to. But the powers of evil
there are greater than I knew, and it may be that
they will slay me."

SEVEN

When you had just been strangled to death it seemed not surprising that your next experience should be a peculiar dream. But even under the circumstances this was starting out to be a very peculiar dream indeed. One moment Simon was nonexistent in nothingness, and the next he was adrift on the Sauk in an old rowboat, very like a boat he had sometimes played in during the summers of his childhood, when his grandmother with whom he usually lived in Chicago brought him out to visit his aunt and uncle who ran the antique shop, and the assorted cousins living in Frenchman's Bend and on some of the farms around.

In this dream—he was almost sure it was a dream—Simon was a child again, or not much more than a child. He was wearing green swimming trunks, like a pair he had once worn. It was summer, and the rowboat that bore him was adrift, oarless, among the islands of the Sauk. The lack of oars was nothing to worry about. Whenever he wanted to get back to shore he could stick his feet out over the stern and splash hard enough to propel the boat, even straight against the sluggish current.

For a short while Simon was convinced that he was indeed a child again. Then he looked down at his body, and thought about himself, and came to understand that he was fifteen now. He was waiting for Vivian. That realization frightened him, but the fear was swallowed up in the idea's overwhelming fascination.

He was expecting her to appear somewhere in the distance first, but instead she burst up with a violent, surprising splash from the brown water right beside his boat, something she had never done in real life, and Simon understood that she must have come swimming underwater for a long distance just to startle him. The effort succeeded; he jumped. Vivian, with green weeds as from the ocean tangled in her dark curly hair, clung to the gunwale looking at him wickedly.

"I am the lady—" she began, and then pantomimed biting her tongue, acting broadly the part of one who has started to say something that must not be revealed. She was unchanged, no older than when Simon had seen her last, except that her eyes now danced more openly with evil. With a single lithe splashing movement she now pulled herself completely up into the boat. There was a sound as of a faint creaking of bedsprings. At once Simon was compelled to stare at her body, which was clothed in nothing but a very small green bikini. Wetness gleamed on her tanned skin, and he gazed at her helplessly, and Vivian smiled knowingly to see the effect that she was having on him.

"I have to do this," Vivian told him in a whisper, and her voice was altered, diffident, almost apologetic. She lay down in the bottom of the boat, which was now conveniently furnished with a mattress and white sheets. Then, "Take off your trunks," in the same odd pleading whisper, at the same time whisking off her own bikini top. The breasts revealed were all wrong, were large and pale and soft, but Simon obeyed, and thrust his body toward her. He had no choice now, if he had ever had.

The frightened face below his was not Vivian's, but that of the girl from the antique shop, and they were in a bedroom, on a bed. Simon saw this but nothing he saw affected what he had to do. He crouched atop the female and entered her, just as the bed that was once more a boat began to sink in a vast pool of blood, red rivulets running in from every side across the stark white sheets.

Now they were struggling on the flat stone altar in the court before the grotto. Seed pumped from him in dull mechanical spasms. When he was empty he rolled from the female onto the altar's flat, cold stone, sticky where small pools and maculations of blood were drying. The stone squeaked like bedsprings. Simon knew that now the blood was on him too, and for the first time he grew aware of a ring of watchers, of evil beings who now had him firmly in their power . . .

. . . and the door to the grotto was a prison door in truth, with a host of victims caged behind it. One by one, they were being led forth by strange beings, led to the stone altar and a death of horror. They were young and old, male and female, some in rags, some richly dressed, some in the clothing of centuries long past. Some were innocent, some deep in blood as were the sacrificers themselves.

A young man with a face of perfect beauty and evil watched from a central throne nearby, and Vivian stood by his side. She was arrayed now in the costume of a queen, and her face wore a queen's haughtiness. Saul, at the age of twelve, in jester's cap and bells, sat cross-legged at Vivian's feet, a wooden sword in his hand, staring solemnly at Simon. Old Gregory, in medieval costume, led a young girl victim forth and bit her in the neck. Another old man, horrible of countenance, stood beside the smoking altar which was empty now, and waited for the next victim to be brought. All round the altar blood-drained corpses lay.

The sword in the executioner's hand was smoking, dripping, reeking . . .

The sword . . .

Swords, for there were more than one . . .

Came interruption. A resonance of light, a calling back and forth between the blades of light and darkness, like trumpets of opposing armies. The calling altered everything, unseated evil that had held the world in undisputed bondage. The evil young king rose up roaring, and Vivian had to shield her eyes. The watchers broke their circle, scattering. The victims who could still move fled, some hobbling on mutilated limbs. Only Simon, who drifted disembodied now, was able to see perfectly, not dazzled by the sword of light or blinded by the blade of evil darkness. *I can always see*, he thought, *better than anyone else*. It seemed a profound truth.

And then, for a time, he was nonexistent in pure nothingness again.

He was lying flat on his back, in what felt like a bed. He could tell from the feeling of air passing gently over his body that he was completely naked; but thank God, thank God, there was no stickiness of blood. Or of sex either, for that matter.

A dream. Of course. Only a dream.

I can always see better than anyone else. He had to hang on to that much of it at least.

There came faintly, from somewhere in the distance, the notes of some stringed instrument, one by one, as if being plucked out by a beginning player. The halting melody had a medieval sound to Simon.

Where the hell was he?

Simon opened his eyes. Then he lay for a moment without moving, staring at his surroundings in blank puzzlement. He was alone in the bedroom he had dreamed about, or a room that much resembled it. Stone walls were only partially concealed by paintings and rich tapestries. The single tall, narrow window pierced an outer wall at least four feet thick, the high ceiling was of vaulted stone. Simon recognized at once that he was in one of the many bedrooms of the castle; he was not sure if he had ever been in this particular room before, nor had he the faintest memory of how he had got here now.

Or why . . . but no, of course, he and Marge had come here to give a performance. Hadn't they?

And then he'd found an old man, bound naked and unconscious on a medieval torture-rack . . .

Simon sat bolt upright in the antique-looking bed, the motion making the bedsprings squeak. Where had reality stopped, where had dreams begun? He was awake now. If he couldn't feel sure of that, he might as well give up on everything. Yes, he was awake.

He *thought* that the last episode of reality before this had been himself struggling in the grip of some skillful, powerful attacker, an arm at his throat choking off his wind. The fantastic sight of the old man bound, then the attack, and then . . .

Simon looked about him. He was sitting on a bed, with covers turned neatly down, in a well-appointed bedroom. All the furniture he thought was modern, though in an expensive style suggesting the antique. Faintly, from somewhere in the distance, the notes of the stringed instrument still sounded.

On a chair beside the bed his clothing was disposed, half-carelessly, just as he would have left it before stretching out for a nap—except he would ordinarily have retained his undershorts. On the cool stone floor beside the chair sat his overnight bag, the one he remembered leaving in his car parked on the other side of the river.

Simon raised exploring fingers to his neck. He could swallow and breathe without pain or difficulty. He could feel a slight soreness in his neck muscles when he pressed them. It seemed a very inadequate proof of having been choked into unconsciousness.

There was a mirror on the dresser and Simon got off the bed and went to it and examined the image of his muscular body. There were no bruises or scratches evident, no sign that he had ever been attacked.

Simon didn't usually take his wristwatch off if he was just stretching out for a rest, but now it was lying on the dresser. It said six forty-seven. The last time he could remember looking at it, it had read a little after three, three twenty, maybe. That had been just before he'd left Margie in the secret passage.

"My God, Marge," Simon breathed aloud. He quickly looked about him, at the walls. This was not one of the rooms into which the secret passage opened. He really *had* left Margie in the tunnel, hadn't he? He could remember doing so—just as clearly as he remembered, for example, an old man strapped on a rack.

He turned back to the chair where his clothes were and began mechanically to dress. Think, try to think. He'd left Margie in the passage, according to plan. Then he'd passed through the dark tunnel again, turned aside at the descending branch limned with faint torchlight. And then that crazy scene in the—the dungeon, including the attack. Then the dream. Then this. Leaving the dream aside, no part of it seemed any more or less real than any other part.

Six forty-eight. Outside the window it was still broad, warm daylight on a long June afternoon, or evening.

Somehow, someone must have admitted him to this house, conducted him in some manner to this room.

Still, in his memory, only the strange dream, more than half forgotten now, intervened between the attack on him in the dungeon, and this room. He had dreamed of embracing Vivian, and she had turned into the young girl from the antique shop.

Simon was zipping up his pants when someone tapped at his room's door. Feeling half alarmed and half relieved, he went to open the door a cautious crack, having to unlatch it first from the inside.

Gregory was standing outside, in the stone-vaulted hallway that Simon's memory told him he had last seen fifteen years ago. The dignified-looking man was dressed, or costumed, in a loose brown tunic, long hose to match, and vaguely pointed shoes or slippers that looked as if they might be made of felt.

"Did you have a good rest, sir? Most of the other guests are here now. Miss Littlewood sent me to tell you that you'll just about have time for a swim before cocktails, if you wish."

"Er—thank you." As far as Simon could judge, who was no expert, Gregory's costume looked authentic. He'd brought his own, of course, packed in his bag. "Gregory, did you happen to notice what time it was when I arrived?"

Gregory blinked. "Why, no sir, I really didn't. I suppose it must have been about two hours ago."

"I suppose . . . oh, and Gregory?"

The man had been in the act of turning away. "Sir?"

"Any word from my assistant?" Simon congratulated himself on having phrased that rather cleverly.

"Not to my knowledge, sir." And for just a moment Simon had the impression that Gregory might be offering himself the same kind of congratulation.

"Thank you. Tell Miss Littlewood I'll be right down for a swim."

Simon closed the door, and turned round once more to face the enigmatic room. There was his bag, there were the clothes he had been wearing. He crossed the room, and looked out and down from the window as well as he was able; the view was restricted by the narrowness of the window embrasure and the thickness of the wall it pierced. The remodeling installation had provided the window with a wooden sash and glass panes, the wood painted gray to almost match the stonework of the wall. The window was open about a foot to the warm weather, and Simon lifted it higher, putting out his head and shoulders; there was no screen.

Probably screens against insects hadn't been considered necessary this high above the ground. He was at about the ordinary fifth-floor level, he guessed now, looking down. His restricted view was of the paved area just in front of the garage; the garage of course had been built of the same stone as the rest of the castle, but still looked awkwardly anachronistic.

Among the three or four automobiles that were parked in his field of view, he recognized his own.

His car keys were in the pocket of his pants.

He shrugged, took off the pants again, and left them on the chair. Then he stripped completely and got the swim trunks out of his bag and put them on, noting in passing, as if the fact were of some significance, that they were not green. From the private bath attached to his guest room Simon grabbed one of the huge, plentifully supplied towels. At the door to the hallway he paused; he didn't have a key to this room, and he hesitated just briefly at the idea of leaving his things in it unlocked. Then he smiled at what, in the circumstances, struck him as a ridiculous concern.

He had to make contact, as soon as possible, with Margie. If she was still in the secret passage, and all was well, then he was going to have to make a medical appointment for himself next week, and talk to someone about hallucinations. If, on the other hand, she wasn't . . .

The hallway outside Simon's room was medieval in most of its materials, but not at all in its plan, if Simon's hazy ideas about real castles were at all accurate. On one side of the hall, a row of doors led probably to rooms much like the one in which he had awakened. On the other side, a balcony railing of wood and stone guarded a drop of forty feet or so to the stone paving of the main entry room on the ground floor; this was not the room that Simon thought of as the great hall, but one almost as large. It was dim down there, from lack of windows, and flames glowed on candle and on torch. He still had not the faintest memory of coming up this way today.

Now he had to locate one of the connections to the secret passage, and try to signal Marge. Here was a door that puzzled him at first, until he realized it must be that of an elevator, discreetly almost hidden. He thought that some of the other rooms that he was passing on his way to the descending stair must connect to the secret passage. But most of their doors were closed, and the one that was ajar showed someone's luggage on a bed. He wasn't going to chance entering any of them right now.

A young man Simon didn't recognize, dressed just about as Gregory had been, in what was evidently servant's garb, passed Simon in the hallway. Simon nodded and smiled, getting only the faintest of responses. It struck him that if everyone were really dressed in the style of six hundred years ago there might be problems in distinguishing fellow guest from worker. And he wasn't really accustomed to dealing with servants anyway, he hadn't had that many invitations to the homes of the really rich.

Anyway, outfit of towel and swimsuit would presumably signal guest. Arrayed in his own leisure-class uniform, Simon reached the broad curving stairs, and padded down them. The feel of their stones under his bare feet evoked memories again. But he'd had all he wanted of memories for now. But in a moment he was probably going to see Vivian . . .

The stair passed an intermediate floor, whose rooms Simon recalled only hazily, and of which he could see almost nothing now. The ground floor rose to him round the next curve of stair, the natural persistent coolness of its great rooms grateful today. Here were the candles he had seen from above, set about on tables and sideboards, in rooms so vast that almost any furniture would have left them feeling empty. Flame flickered also in the fireplace of the great hall, which he now entered. The roasting that he and Margie had observed from inside the secret passage had evidently been completed, though the rich odor of it still hung in the air, assuring him that he had not imagined everything. The motor-driven spit had been dismantled and except for a few tiny flames the logs had burned down to a bed of glowing charcoal.

The sound of the stringed instrument that he had heard upstairs was plainer now, coming from some room not far away. The effect was somehow distractingly beautiful.

Modernity intruded again, this time in the form of splashing sounds, from outside but not far away; the pool was in use as announced. Simon had just turned toward the wooden screenwork covering one end of the great hall, behind which the secret passage burrowed, and Margie presumably waited silently, when he was stopped by the sight of a painted portrait. The picture was mounted on the screen itself, and so of course had been invisible earlier when he had looked out from behind the screen. It showed a middle-aged, powerfully glaring man; and Simon was sure it hadn't been there fifteen years ago, the last time he remembered entering this room.

It stopped him for a moment, but the need to contact Margie dominated. Still facing the screen, as if he were studying the portrait, he raised one hand, brushing momentarily at the hair behind his right ear—and saw at once the answering wink of Margie's penlight through the screen.

Relief was intense. Being still alone in the room, Simon could allow himself a great unburdening sigh of it. Amnesia and hallucinations were bad, but not as bad as the fear that reality had turned treacherous on him. He allowed himself also a smile and wink toward Margie.

As he turned away, his eye was caught once more by the portrait. Its glaring subject was dressed stylishly in the fashion of the late nineteenth century. Simon had last seen him holding a dark sword in his hand, as he stood beside a bloody altar.

EIGHT

As soon as Simon had left her alone in the secret passage, a little after three o'clock, Margie put her shoulder bag down on the dusty floor, with the silent hope that nothing was going to crawl into it. Actually the risk didn't seem great. The passage was basically free of vermin, as far as she had been able to see, except for those few spider webs near the entrance. It wasn't really dirty except for the inevitable layer of floor dust. This dust was thin in most places, and had been untrodden everywhere until she and Simon had left their tracks in it.

A faint, unidentifiable sound was coming from somewhere now, doubtless from deep in the house. Marge reacted by looking through a spyhole again, into the nearest bedroom. The room was well furnished in a sort of pseudo-antique style, and there was no sign that anyone was currently using it. She guessed that a door in one wall, standing ajar, led to a private bath. It would be great to be able to nip in through the secret panel and use the can, but there was no evidence that the bedroom was going to remain unoccupied for the next two minutes. Things weren't desperate yet.

Marge sighed, and removed her eye from the peephole, and looked up and down the dark passage as well as she could without using the flash. She wished for a chair. Somehow she felt reluctant to sit, even in her utilitarian jeans, on the old dust of this floor. She supposed that in a few hours she'd change her mind and stop being so finicky.

She wished she knew how she was going to spend the next four or five hours or more, until perfomance time. She wished there were a ladies' room available.

Well, she might be able to do something about that difficulty, if she were to scout around a little. When people designed elaborate secret passages, it seemed possible that they might design some kind of secret comfort facilities in. If not she could always come back here and risk the secret panel. Marge really didn't want to do that, though. She could imagine herself pushing the panel open, while unseeable against its inner surface there stood a little table holding a priceless something-or-other. Probably a vase. Crash, and then an interesting social situation. No, she would explore some other possibilities first.

In a moment Marge had shouldered her bag again, and was creeping as silently as possible back along the passage in the direction from which she and Simon had ascended. Simon had said there were panels opening into two of these bedrooms, and the others were open to hidden observation. She wondered if she and Si were going to be put up in any of these rooms. Yep, the old guy who had imported and rebuilt this place had been a little kinky, all right. At best, he'd nourished a fondness for a kind of humor Margie didn't appreciate. She wondered how the heirs, when they learned about the secret passage, would take the revelation of the sort of guy Grandpa had been. Or, could she and Simon do the act so well that the existence of the passage still wouldn't be suspected? That would be a real achievement. Possibly they could. They were good, as good as anyone, Marge thought, when things were going right.

Again there drifted muffled sound from somewhere. These were faint, but Margie got the impression that there was something spasmodic and desperate about them. Probably someone just horsing around. Or wrestling with some heavy furniture. Of course it could be people really fighting, dead serious about it. Even as Marge paused to listen, the noise ceased. She waited a little, but could hear nothing more, and moved along again. She wanted to get down to the lower passage, which she recalled was a little wider and ought to offer a more comfortable place to wait in.

It still didn't really make sense, she thought, that Si knew about all these secret ways and peepholes, and the people who lived here didn't. She wondered why he had seemed so shaken today, at a couple of places while they were climbing the hill through the woods. He'd said that someday he'd tell Margie the whole story, about his growing up in these parts; which meant, if Marge understood Simon as well as she thought she was beginning to understand him, that he would never tell her any more. Simon wasn't a bad guy, and Marge liked working with him. He was all professionalism, as a rule, when it came to the act. As for the love life, well, he wouldn't be her first choice for that. There was always the feeling that he was really thinking about something or someone else.

Marge was passing another peephole, and without much of a struggle she yielded to the temptation to pause and take a look. Another bedroom, with a suitcase on the floor. The spyhole gave a perfect view of the bed, which had two people sitting on it. A grossly heavy, swarthy man, just sitting there, turned so Marge couldn't see his face, half dressed. Another half-dressed figure, facing the other way, a body so thin that Marge wasn't sure for a moment that it was female, staring into space. Almost immediately Marge turned away. Ugh. There had been a *wrongness* in that room. She felt as if she had just spied on people laboriously inventing some new perversion. They looked as if they might have just finished such a task.

Now, if and when the secret passageway became general knowledge during the weekend, that couple, all the guests, would wonder who might have watched them doing what. Ugh. Complications.

Marge moved on, for the sake of silence scraping the walls as little as possible. She traversed what was left of the upper passage and then went down the long, steep stairs, using her light. When at last she reached the peephole giving a view of the great hall, nothing had changed. The great logs still crackled in the enormous fireplace, the pig or whatever it was continued roasting. The aroma made Marge hungry. In her shoulder bag were a couple of candy bars that she meant to eat later. Anyway she certainly wasn't just going to camp in this spot waiting for Simon to appear. He'd need an hour, at the very least, to get back across the river and then drive round, by way of the bridge at Blackhawk, to approach the castle by road in the manner of an ordinary guest.

Using her flashlight sparingly, keeping its beam aimed low, Marge went on down, following the tunnel underground. A minute more, and she had

passed the branching way—without giving it
much thought—and was back in the cave, peering
out into the now-gloomy daylight of the deserted
grotto and its paved forecourt with the statues
and the curious stone table. The fact that a cloud
had come over the sun made the whole place now
look somehow ominous. But, reassuringly, it was
as quiet and uninhabited as ever. The jail-door
was closed and bound with the chain and
lock—Simon on going out must have been careful
to leave it exactly as before, which was only what
you would expect from someone as meticulously
professional about details as he was. Now Marge
ought to be able to do the same thing with the
gate, and just slip out for a minute into these deserted woods . . .

It took a little more than a minute, maybe two
or three. Then she was back inside the cave again,
physically relieved and ready to concentrate properly on the job at hand. She carefully bound up
the chain and lock just as before, and retreated
into the underground portion of the passage. The
next step, she had decided, would be to get a little
rest. She would find a relatively dustfree place
and stretch out, maybe catch a little nap. Marge
knew her own habits; the danger that she was
going to oversleep was just about zero.

Within a few minutes Marge was dozing on the
tunnel floor, shoulder bag serving as a pillow.
When she awoke it was with a start, and the feeling of having been asleep for some time. At first
she had no faintest idea of where she was or how
she'd got here.

Memory returned, bringing with it reassurance
of a sort. The gloom in the tunnel was much
thicker than it had been when Marge dozed off;
darkness had obviously fallen outside. She had a
bad moment, wondering if after all she could have
overslept. But no, her watch showed it to be only
a little before seven. Some shadow must have

come over the inlets for air and light. Perfect timing, she thought, or close to perfect. They had decided dinner probably woudn't start till eight, and the show would go on after dinner.

Marge rose without haste and stretched. Then she picked up her bag and hurried along to the agreed-upon primary rendezvous, the peephole giving into the great hall. She braced herself in a standing position at the lookout, watching and waiting for Simon to appear.

Her wait was short, so short that she again sent up a silent cheer for perfect timing. Here came Simon from another room, alone, wearing his swim trunks now and carrying still-dry towel. The expression on his face told Margie of controlled worry, concern deeper than the usual pre-preformance tenseness. Maybe, she thought guiltily, Si had been here at the rendezvous before, trying to signal her about some problem.

He gave the primary signal now, brushing at his hair, and Marge felt another twinge of guilt to see his relief when she answered at once with the flashlight, signalling that she was in place and everything was fine. And then Marge could feel relieved, for Si signalled to her nothing about difficulty or cancellation; he only paused for a moment, looking up at something above Marge's head and out of her range of vision, and then he walked on out of the great hall, doubtless to have his swim. She thought it must be something other than the performance itself that was worrying him. Maybe he'd been told that the fee wasn't going to be a full thousand after all.

Anyway she could now relax again for a little while. Things were rolling, the act could go smoothly, just the was they wanted it. They might even pull off a really spectacular effect. Marge could imagine how it would be for the audience, a roomful of people absolutely certain that they were facing solid stone walls, when a voice spoke to them out of nowhere, and then in response to a magician's gesture the figure of a young woman took shape out of thin air . . .

It wasn't too early now for her to get her costume on. She slipped it out of the handbag and inspected it as well as she could in the poor light. Diaphanous was the word. She had debated with herself about how much to wear underneath it, and was glad now that she'd decided a full leotard wasn't too much. She had the leotard on now under her shirt and jeans, and a good thing too, if that fat man she'd just been spying on upstairs was going to be in the audience, as he undoubtedly was. Something about him made Marge shudder inwardly, and she hadn't even seen his face.

She exchanged her white gym shoes for black ballet slippers for the performance; not that it was unlikely that anyone would be studying her feet very closely.

She had just finished changing, except for her shoes, and had got the street clothing crammed into the handbag, when new distraction came, in the form of what sounded like a groan. It was a faint sound, yet gave the impression of coming from somewhere uncomfortably close. There couldn't, thought Marge, there absolutely couldn't be anyone else in this unknown passage with her. And yet it certainly sounded like it.

Another faint groan wavered in the air, again too close for comfort, too close to be ignored. Was Margie herself now to be the target for some kind of trick?

That was one of the first thoughts that leapt into her mind. She had to know. Penlight in hand, Marge prowled the tunnel. Not that way, this way. The moaning sound obligingly repeated at irregular short intervals. She was led to the branch passage going down, but paused at its top step. She had assumed, when Simon ignored the branch, that he knew where it led and that it could be disregarded.

Now that she looked carefully, she could see one set of footprints in the dust of the stairs before her. It was hard to tell if the faint prints were going up or down.

She sat her shoulder bag down carefully on the floor, leaving herself freer for quick action, and tiptoed down the stairs, stepping in the tracks. She came to a thick wooden door, standing slightly open. The groans emanating from its other side. When she snapped off her tiny flashlight she could see faint torchlight flickering through the opening around the door.

Marge stood still, thinking. She didn't need to think for very long. Groans and an open door, whatever else they might mean, indicated that other people besides herself and Simon had to be aware of the supposedly secret passage. They meant, at the very least, that the whole elaborately planned trick had to be considered blown. They meant—

She had to find out what they meant. It was impossible to do anything else until she knew.

The door swung back easily, with only the faintest squeaking of its antique-looking hinges. What lay beyond it resolved no questions for Marge, but only raised them to a new level.

In her short life she had seen a lot of acts, good ones and bad ones, from inside and out. She could tell at first glance that the semiconscious old man bound to the torture rack was no willing participant of any act. His arms and legs were almost plump, his ribs scrawny. His head, shaggy with gray hair and beard, rolled slowly from side to side. His eyes were closed. His mouth, open to reveal bad teeth, drooled a little from one corner.

Marge approached. She prodded the old man gently with a finger in the ribs. The only response was another groan. Then she reached to loosen the leather strap binding the old man's left wrist; it looked so tight that she was sure it must be hurting him. The buckle, of an odd design, and very stiff, resisted her first efforts. Margie's fingernails were of a practical short length, but she was afraid for a moment that she'd broken one, maybe because all of a sudden her hands had started to shake. The strap came loose at last. The old man's pinched wrist was relieved, but his arm stayed where it was; he wasn't going to wake up.

"That's it, then," said Marge to herself, aloud and decisively. At that moment she completely abandoned all thoughts of being able to go on with the performance as planned. This old man was real, and really hurting. She had to reveal her presence and get help.

As Marge turned away from the rack, the idea had just begun to form in her mind that Simon might be in some kind of serious trouble too, and for that matter herself as well. If the people in charge of this castle were people who did things like this—

The thought had no time to develop. A muscular young black man wearing a dark shirt was standing in a second doorway to the room, looking at Marge. It was a recessed doorway that she had not noticed until this moment. The man's skin was the color of creamed coffee, and his face was handsome in a way that struck Marge at first glance as somehow, indefinably, flawed. And he was looking every bit as surprised as Margie felt. It wasn't the old man tied on the rack that had surprised him, though. It was Marge.

"How in hell many of you are there?" he murmured in a soft voice. The question seemed not to need an answer; in the next moment he took a step toward her.

Marge, who had just begun a protest speech, cut it off and instinctively stepped back. Whatever it was about the man facing her, posture, movement, look, she was warned. On nimble feet she got the only large obstacle in the room, the rack with its still-groaning occupant, between herself and the advancing man.

With the rack between them, she gazed at the black man, and he at her. The dim light in the room flickered, the torch guttering on the wall.

"I'm asking you, who else is in here, woman?" The man had paused in his advance. He swung a quick look around him now, at the door to the once-secret tunnel standing wide open, then at once back to Marge.

Marge couldn't answer. She wouldn't have been able to speak, even if she'd had words ready; there seemed to be something wrong with her throat. She was pretty well boxed-in behind the rack, with little room to maneuver. The stone wall touched her back.

"Come here." The man moved toward her slowly. His eyes were unblinking, and in them grew a frightening happiness. Then he smiled lightly, as if at the foolishness of simply telling her to come to him.

His strong-looking arms were half extended, fingers curved for a quick grab.

"No."

"Oh yeah. Oh yeah, lady. Here to me."

If the man lunged straight across the rack he would be able to grab her. And now he did lunge, with unexpected, cobraish speed. He had Marge by the wrist, trying to pull her toward him.

Marge had wiry strength, and desperation. They struggled together for a moment like obscene actors, across the old man's naked torso. Then something happened, Marge couldn't tell what, but the crushing grip on her arm was suddenly broken. Her assailant made a strange sound, slumping back, sliding down to one knee.

Gasping as if she had been knifed, Marge scraped herself out from behind the constricting rack and ran for the tunnel door. Wherever the other door might lead, her attacker had come from there, it was his turf, there might be more of him that way. Her one thought was to reach the open air and daylight. Once out in the tunnel she climbed the stairs in a mad all-fours scramble that brought her back to the main passage. Then she turned to her right and ran, gambling that she could run in this thick gloom without disaster, rather than delay the fraction of a second needed to get the flashlight from her costume's pocket.

Daylight had all but disappeared when Marge reached the cave mouth. In her terror she saw this fact as another phase of an attack aimed at her. Sobbing, she threw herself down at the base of the barred gate that held her in the cave, fumbling in a mad panic to loosen again the padlock and the chain. With every second stretched in terror she heard imagined footfalls of pursuit. And yet no horror arrived to seize her from behind. Somehow the lock did open in her fingers; the chain rattled through them, tearing at her skin.

Marge burst the freed door clanging open and ran out. A few heavy, preliminary drops of rain were striking on the paved court, on the stone table with its obscure sundial. A statue gaped in her path, glaring at her with dead gray eyes; she ran around it. The heat of the day had dissipated now in the damp hush before the storm; the shadow of the castle lay enormous on the woods around her now. She scraped her shin, uncaring, on the low stone fence that rimmed the courtyard from the woods. Tree branches hanging motionless in gloom scraped at her as she fled. The path was not really visible now, but here there was only one level route a path could take. Marge sped along it gasping, the branches that clawed at her threatening to turn into apparitions.

Even with the forest altered by dusk the intersection of paths was unmistakable. She turned downhill, running without pause. In what seemed nightmare slowness the switchback curves of the descending path flowed past her. It was now so dark that she was sure the sun was down. A single raindrop struck her cheek. Through gaps in the trees, by the light of an odd sky, she saw clouds coursing thick and low, like airborne giants hunting across the valley of the Sauk.

The ugly realization overtook Margie as she ran: there would be no boat waiting at the landing below. Simon would already have taken it back across the river.

Then she would plunge into the water, swim, wade, do whatever she had to do to get away. At least, thank God, no one was chasing her.

And then she heard, from up the hill behind her, that someone was. Or something. Not even human feet. In a moment the sound identified itself to her fear as a pounding, four-legged run, as of some monstrous dog.

Terror compounded, escalating into something approaching madness. Just as Marge rounded the last steep descending turn of path, exhausted muscles failed and her foot slipped, the ankle starting to twist. She came down heavily, in rough grass and weeds. With superhuman speed her pursuer was catching up. The sound of onrushing feet was mixed now with a hideous growling and snuffling, the noises of a menacing dog amplified to the proportions of a bear.

Marge screamed, her mind gone in blind panic. Just as she lunged to regain her feet, a shaggy, stinking shape loomed over her. What felt like a furred muzzle struck her on the cheek, hard enough to knock her down again. She had a moment's glimpse of literally glowing eyes, and monstrous fangs.

Marge screamed again, a hopeless quavering. The pressure of a paw at her throat kept her down on her back. At last with pure relief she heard the running arrival of a pair of human feet, she cared not whose.

The black man's soft voice, panting, was hot with anger now. "You got her. Good." It sounded as if he were speaking to another person, not a beast. Then his tone shifted, purring at Marge: "One more yell, and he'll take a chunk out of you where you won't like it. Believe me?"

"Yes," said Marge. And the animal, as if her answer had satisfied it, at once removed its pinning weight.

"Get up," the man said.

Marge got up, very slowly, surprised to find herself practically unhurt. What had been a gauzy costume was little more than trailing rags. She and the man were both still gasping from the downhill run. Meanwhile the impossible beast— Marge couldn't convince herself it was only a dog—sat on its haunches staring at her. Its black fur was long and so was its lolling pink tongue. There was something thickly, horribly human about that tongue. In its sitting position the beast was almost tall enough to look Margie in the eye.

"Now don't run," the man advised her, getting his breathing under control. "Don't do anything now but what I say. Just walk back up the path. That way you stay alive."

Surely, thought Marge, before she had climbed as far as the castle again, she could somehow manage to wake up. No nightmare went on indefinitely. And at the same time she knew better. Across the river, its sound carrying freely over the broad water, a diesel semi was taking the narrow highway at high speed. Its headlights might as well have been shining somewhere on Mars.

"Get moving."

Slowly, wordlessly, Marge turned and started up the path. At least her ankle wasn't really twisted. But she kept to a slow limp.

The man, climbing only a pace behind her, spoke in a low voice almost in her ear. "Tell me, how many of you were in that tunnel altogether? Who else is there?" And another few steps behind them both, the breast paced slowly. From its throat now came a straining growl, as if only with the greatest effort could it keep itself from seizing Margie in its jaws.

Marge would have been quite willing to answer the man's question, if she could have understood it. To ask how many were in the tunnel seemed to mean—

This time the four-footed run approaching down the path was almost silent; for all its size the pale bulk that hurtled leaping in the night was almost on top of Marge, before she was aware of it. She made a small sound and tried to throw herself aside. A furred shape as heavy as that of the first beast brushed her in its passage, knocking her aside. This time Marge fell softly. On the slope below there sounded impact, as if a rolling boulder had collided with a tree. Marge slid into tangling bushes on the steep slope. Nearby was thrashing confusion, savage noise as of great beasts in combat. When Marge freed herself from the bushes she slipped and again rolled over on the slope. Her mind spun dizzily.

Half stunned, she raised her head. The black man was nowhere to be seen. The beast that had threatened her, the dark-furred one, was down on the ground while the pale newcomer crouched over it, attacking, driving for the throat. The position held for only a moment. Then the dark beast with a great yowl of agony fought to its feet. Another cry, and it had torn free of its attacker and burst into flight. It hurtled past Marge, ignoring her, its eyes glaring redly. Its next howl, receding, seemed to reach her ears from a long distance away.

The merciless clarity of a lightning flash showed Marge the second beast turning her way. Its own glowing eyes were now fixed on her, and dark stains were already matting dry on its pale fur.

Marge rolled away. With horrible ineffective slowness she got herself up on all fours. She knew even as she moved that before she could even begin to run again the great pale beast was going to land on her back . . .

Lightning flashed again.

"Wait," said a man's voice, close behind Margie, just as she crouched to run. It was a deep, compelling voice, one that she had not heard before.

Poised for hopeless flight, she turned her head. The pale-furred animal had vanished. Where it had been, a tall, lean man now stood, dressed in black trousers and a black turtleneck shirt. His eyes did not glow, but they were fixed on Marge just as the eyes of the pale wolf had been. The man appeared to be bleeding heavily from his left shoulder, up near his throat, but still he stood erect.

Marge whimpered.

"Softly," the deep voice commanded. "Calm yourself; for the moment you are safe. Tell me who you are. My name is Talisman."

NINE

Thunder was grumbling in the distance as Simon walked out through the french doors into the courtyard that held the pool. This was a stone-paved expanse, containing an island or two of tended grass and nascent flowerbeds, and surrounded on three sides by the sprawling bulk of the castle. On the fourth side there was more lawn, then a tennis court, and beyond that a tall, thick hedge. Through the hedge a driveway came curving into the grounds, from a public road that could not be seen from here. And through it, also, an even more private and unmarked path led down to riverbank and grotto.

With the flow of clouds above, sunlight came and went across the water of the pool, which was near the doors through which Simon had emerged into the courtyard. From its irregular shape it was clear that the original plan had been to suggest a moat. The last time that Simon could remember standing on this spot, fifteen years ago,

the pool had been drained and dry, the bottom littered with dust and dead leaves, the dry sides
marked with broken and discolored tiles. The
stone gargoyles round the rim, that now pumped
circulating water into the blue depths from their
stone throats had then been gaping, dry-throated
monsters, eerily discolored too. But recently the
pool, like almost everything else about the castle,
had been almost perfectly refurbished. A dozen
deck chairs had been arranged round it in the
shade of modern patio umbrellas. At a white
painted table of wrought iron on the far side of
the pool there sat a gray, elderly couple wearing
conservative swim suits and dark glasses. They
looked rather, Simon thought, like uncertain
guests at some posh hotel.

The dark glasses made it impossible to tell
whether the couple had taken notice of him or
not. He decided to delay approaching them until
after his first good plunge; on a day like this cold
water might be a tonic to clear the mind. The div-
ing board was new and resilient. Simon's first
dive took him deep, and he prolonged it into an
underwater swim across almost the full diagonal
of the pool.

As he came up, shaking water from his long
hair, his eye fell on a small group of young workers, dressed in antique garb like Gregory's, who
were unloading something from a van parked at
the edge of the drive. Among them Simon could
recognize the teenaged girl from the antique shop.
His dream came back to him, but distantly, without impact. She and her brother were probably
distant relatives of some kind, his own as well as
his hosts', Collines or Littlewoods or Picards; people living in or near Frenchman's Bend were more
likely than not to be some kind of kin to each
other. The two kids might well be talking about
their boating customers of the day. Well, it was
too late to worry about that now. And Simon had

bigger things to worry about, like being unable to remember the return boat trip at all.

Right now he had to think about being a guest, which was evidently one of the things for which he was being paid. He pulled himself up out of the water, retrieved his towel, and approached the gray-haired couple in their poolside chair, meanwhile determinedly sticking out his hand. "Hello, I'm Simon Hill."

The man jumped up at once, obviously glad to have the ice broken. "My name's Jim Wallis—spelled with an eye-ess on the end. And this's Emily."

Emily, somehow conveying an impression of bright friendly eyes without removing her glasses, lifted herself halfway out of her chair to shake Simon's hand. "Pleased to meet another guest. I bet you're the fella who's going to do the tricks tonight."

"That's me."

And, having said that, Simon forgot that he was supposed to be having a conversation. Even Marge in her hidden passageway was for the moment forgotten, as was the act.

A female figure in a bikini had just appeared, framed in the French doors on the far side of the pool. It was Vivian, and she was still only fifteen years old.

For half a breath the illusion was utterly convincing. Vivian was no imaginative vision, but solid reality, and looked not a bit older than she had fifteen years ago. And then she moved, stepping to one side of the doors to speak quietly for a moment with one of the servants. When she moved, changes in her were immediately apparent, in her expression and manner if nothing else, and Simon could see that she was after all a very youthful thirty. In the same moment it passed through his mind, on some level devoted to irrelevancies, that her bikini today was yellow, not green as it had been on that day when he saw her last.

Now, finished with her instructions to the worker, and ready to enjoy her own party, Vivian moved to the edge of the pool prepared to dive.

At that moment a shrill scream sounded. It came from somewhere in the distance, down the bluff perhaps, in what sounded like a young girl's voice. Kids horsing around somewhere, thought Simon absently. He couldn't take his eyes or his thoughts from Vivian.

As if she too had been momentarily distracted by the sound, Vivian hesitated briefly on the brink of her dive. A faint smile crossed her face, and her eyes looked to one side. Then she plunged in smoothly, swimming straight across to him.

Simon, as if by prearrangement, bent to give her a hand out. There was electricity in the touch of her hand. Pulling her from the water was surprisingly easy, as if she hadn't gained a pound in fifteen years.

"Thank you," Vivian said brightly, bounding up lightly to her feet. Her voice was different, more mature. Her fingers retained a grip on Simon's. "And you're Simon the Great, of course. Sorry I wasn't on hand to greet you when you arrived. I'm Vivian Littlewood." And then, before Simon could find the words he was groping for, she added: "I've watched you perform, you know." There was no faintest hint in Vivian's eyes or in her voice that she knw who Simon really was, who he had been. No trace of acknowledgement of the fact that a hundred and eighty months ago, or thereabouts, she had once held his straining body clamped between those finely muscled thighs . . .

"And where was that?" asked Simon, with what he felt was a good imitation of cool detachment. He had wondered how strongly the old magic would work on him again. He needn't have wondered. It was all he could do to pull his eyes away from the small breasts inside the little strip of yellow fabric. For a moment the dream he had just had, a very strange dream indeed, echoed in his mind.

Vivian named a dinner theater in one of the more fashionable northern suburbs. No reason why she couldn't have seen him there, he'd worked the place a couple of times. He could remember quite well his last time there, in the preceding fall; it had been something of a disappointment, like most of the rest of his career to date. Every time he seemed to be on his way, some setback came. Now magic was gaining popularity again, and he still couldn't make a breakthrough. He found himself yearning to tell Vivian his troubles.

But before he could speak again, she said "Excuse me," and turned and plunged back into the pool. On the far side, Gregory, brown-garbed seneschal, knelt at the edge with a worried expression, waiting. For some reason he had put on a wide-brimmed hat for this brief outdoor appearance. Something Saul had once said about Gregory, years ago, came and went in Simon's memory before he could quite be sure of what it was. Maybe the man was allergic to the sun, Simon thought vaguely. He'd heard of cases. Though right now there was hardly any sunlight left.

The subject under discussion over there on the other side of the pool must have been serious, for Gregory's distinguished face was grim, and on hearing the first words of whatever it was Vivian pulled herself rapidly out of the water and skipped straight into the house. Her servant followed with quick strides.

Another couple were coming out through the French doors just as Gregory hurried in. These two were wearing beach clogs on their feet, and expensive T-shirts damp and rumpled over swimsuits. After studying the man for a few moments Simon felt reasonably sure that it was Saul; if so, he now looked older than his sister. The young woman on Saul's arm was a very pale blond, short and rather stocky, though not fat. She was somewhat given to freckles, and pretty in her own fashion, which was a long way from Vivian's.

Saul shot a distracted glance after Vivian and Gregory as they hurried into the house, then exchanged a few words with his blond companion. Then the two of them started walking around the pool, obviously coming to mingle with the guests.

"Don't worry about it now," Simon heard the fair one reply to Saul. "Whatever it is, Vivian will want to handle it anyway."

They joined the small group standing at poolside, and introductions went round. Saul's wife was named Hildy, Simon learned, and they'd only been married a few months. From the way they talked and joked about it, their honeymoon so far had been a complete rat race, marriage and the final victory in the complex legal struggle over the inheritance coming almost simultaneously, followed by taking possession of the castle and getting it refurbished. This weekend was in celebration of it all. Saul showed no more signs of recognizing Simon than Vivian had.

Now, in conversation, it came out that the Wallises were both former members of the artists' colony that half a century ago had flourished in some cottages nearby on the bluff, and had incidentally provided some of the odd statuary now decorating the grotto.

"I look forward to seeing it," said Simon, making no particular effort to put conviction into his voice.

"And we were really friends with the old man," mused Wallis now, looking back in time as he spoke. "Even if we were just kids then, he took an interest. We were what you'd call hippies now, that's what we were."

"The old man?" asked Simon, as if he did not know.

Wallis nodded toward Saul. "This fella's grandfather. That's his portrait on the wall inside, in the huge room where the fireplace is. Augustus Littlewood. One of the great Chicago tycoons. He built this place. Bought the whole shootin'-match when he was on one of his excursions to France, and had it shipped. Believe it or not. Barges full of stones were coming up the river here, all the way from New Orleans up the Mississippi. It's nice that the younger generation remembers us now. We were really surprised to be invited." Wallis sounded as if he were determined to hang onto the pleasure of the invitation, even if he didn't expect to enjoy the party much.

It was full evening; underwater lights had come on in the pool. Now Emily Wallis put in: "Here come the other people we met earlier." The dislike in her voice was not well concealed.

Emerging from a door in a side wing of the castle were a grossly fat, swarthy man of early middle age, and a very thin young woman with discolored hair and huge breasts, who wore a European style bikini. The man wore a robe over vast swim trunks, and Simon thought he could see where his neck was bandaged, under a scarf. He moved slowly and tiredly. Engrossed in some private discussion, the pair settled in chairs on the far side of the pool. Saul began awkwardly to urge the people with him into a mass migration, wanting to get everyone introduced.

The fat man was introduced as Pierre Arnaud. His accent might not have been French, but Simon judged that it was not American. There was something familiar about him, as if Simon might have seen his picture somewhere. The post office suggested itself. Arnaud's thin companion with the silicone implants was introduced only as Sylvia; she looked nervous, and remained almost silent. Simon hadn't thought that a swimsuit substantially smaller than Vivian's could be made to stay on without tacks, but here was proof.

No one was much interested in swimming, and conversation soon tended to lag. Simon was not surprised. He could rarely recall seeing at one party a collection of guests as apparently mismatched as these. The Wallises, despite protests of youthful hippiness, looked firmly elder middle class, whereas these others . . . maybe more guests were scheduled to show up, enough to form two convivial groups. *Someone active in the entertainment field.* So far Simon had seen no one he thought might qualify.

A spattering of rain came as an actually welcome interruption. At the same time Gregory appeared in the French doors again, in his almost-monk's garb that somehow was not as ridiculous as it should have been, now that he'd got rid of the foolish sun hat somewhere. At Gregory's announcement about cocktails, people wrapped in towels began to drift back into the house, where they helped themselves to freshly provided snacks and drinks.

Standing towel-wrapped between Saul and Hildy at the outer end of the great hall, Simon gestured with his glass toward the wall at the far end. "It's an impressive portrait." The dream and its several characters refused to fade completely. Besides, he realized, he was actually stalling, hoping to catch one more good look at Vivian before she changed out of her bikini.

Saul smiled vaguely. "Our grandfather, of course, as Willis was saying. The old gentlemen was largely responsible for the position in which I find myself today." He looked round him with an odd, doubtful expression, as if he might still be reserving judgment on the desirability of all that he had inherited.

"Your dominion." Two servant girls hurried by, one of them the antique-shop twin. She looked at Simon and quickly away again, and there was something private and frightened in the look. The dream throbbed in his mind.

"Oh yes," said Saul. His eyes flicked as if with surprise. "And Vivian's."

Vivian and Gregory were nowhere to be seen. Simon caught just a glimpse of the retreating backs of Arnaud and thin Sylvia, heading off into the castle's other wing.

Saul was gazing at the portrait again. "It's been in storage for a long time, of course, along with a lot of other stuff that survived the fire. He died twenty years ago. What with other deaths in the family, and various complications, it's taken the courts and lawyers that much time to straighten everything out. Unbelievable, isn't it?" And Hildy at her husband's side nodded solemnly.

"Yes," agreed Simon slowly. He must have seen the portrait long before it showed up in his dream. He must have seen it, somehow, on one of his childhood visits here—when it had been in storage.

From his point of view, everything wasn't straightened out even yet.

TEN

"My name is Talisman," the wounded man repeated calmly. He stood on the trail in the thickening dusk, gazing steadily at Marge, ignoring the blood staining his shirt, and the other blood, some of which must have been his also, that was spattered over the leaves and branches round him. "What is your name?" he asked again. "Who are you?"

"Margie Hilbert." There was something soothing in the man's steadfast gaze, so soothing that Marge could almost begin to relax. As she spoke, she straightened up slowly out of her strained crouch. Her breathing and her pulse were easing back toward an approximation of their normal rates. In the surrounding darkness the ordinary noises of insects were returning, filling in the hush that had followed the mad clamor of the fight. "I'm here with the magician," Marge added. Then she blinked, shook her head, and tried to become practical. "You're badly hurt."

If so, the dark-clothed man seemed quite successfully to be ignoring the fact. "*Who* do you say that you are with?" The question came with sharp emphasis on the first word.

"The magician."

"The . . . you are with him?" The man's voice held urgency and disbelief.

"Yes. Simon—Simon the Great. We're supposed to be putting on a show here this evening. But then I saw . . ." It was hopeless, thought Marge. Where could she start?

"Ah. A show." Her questioner relaxed somewhat. Now he moved closer, until he loomed tall at her side. His eyes were dark, yet she could see them very plainly in the gathering night. She felt unable to do more than wait, in mental and physical exhaustion, for whatever might happen next.

"Yes," the tall man said at last. "I believe you. Stage magic." His wound did not seem to be bothering him at all. In the darkness Marge couldn't see whether it was still bleeding or not. "Stage magic," he repeated. "And yet I sense great power near you, connected with you. It dwells in, flows from, one you have touched recently . . . this stage conjurer that you speak of. Is he up there now?" Talisman motioned with his unwounded arm toward the top of the bluff.

The thought of Simon still up there in the castle, in danger from God knew what, was enough to restore some of Margie's energy. "Yes, at least he was there a few minutes ago. I don't know what's going on, but—" She paused for a deep breath. "You see, there's a kind of a tunnel up there. A secret passage. And I was in it, looking around, and I found this old man trapped, tied up—"

"An old man? Very old?"

"I don't know. Yes. He's in a—well, it's a dungeon. He was strapped down on this device. Then another man—" Marge paused, looking around her. "There was another man here, a black man.

He chased me down here from the castle, along with the—the animal."

"We shall perhaps hear from the black man and the animal again. Or from their associates. But meanwhile I think we have a few minutes to ourselves; let us use them wisely. It is important that I see this old man you speak of. Is he truly in a dungeon?" It seemed that Talisman would be only mildly surprised if it were so.

"He is. I saw him. But we have to go somewhere and get help."

Talisman looked around at the dark woods, the leaden, rolling sky, as if he were keenly interested in the weather, or listening carefully for some particular sound. "Getting help, Marge, at this stage, would be even more difficult than you imagine."

"At this stage? Stage of what?"

"I shall explain when there is time. First lead me to the dungeon." The words were delivered with a commanding gesture.

Long ago Marge had learned, or decided, that there were some people who could be argued with and others who couldn't. She realized already that this man was definitely in the second category. She could run away from him (or could she?) and spend the rest of the night probably stumbling exhaustedly around the countryside; she didn't think she had the strength left to get herself across the river. And she didn't want to waste what little she had left in argument.

"Trust me, Margie Hilbert."

Somewhat to her own surprise, Marge found that she was inclined to do so. With a weary nod she turned and once more started slowly up the tral, this time not bothering to pretend a limp. The silence behind her remained absolute, and she had to turn her head to make sure that Talisman was following her. To her surprise he was only two steps back. Another lightning flash revealed a great bloodstain drying on his dark shirt, which was torn near neck and shoulder; otherwise there was no indication that he had been hurt at all. His steady, eerily silent movement gave an impression of great strength.

"Go on." Talisman's eyes prodded her impatiently along.

Marge turned and climbed. Gradually she moved faster, feeling a compulsion to get this—whatever "this" was, exactly—over with. The remainder of the ascent was silence, and mosquitoes, and an occasional spatter of rain.

Not until they had reached the deserted grotto did she pause again. The barred door of rusted iron hung open as she, or perhaps her pursuers, had left it. She pointed to indicate the way.

"I see," said her companion. Then he stood back for a moment, looking over the situation, peering straight up the bluff and then to right and left as if he could see perfectly well in darkness. "Then it is not a true dwelling," he said. "Not here, at least. Let me try whether I can enter here uninvited."

At least those were the words Marge thought she heard. By now she had about given up hope of anything this evening making sense.

Talisman stood in front of the iron door and bent his head. And there, to Margie's troubled vision, he seemed to disappear. A moment later she was aware of his figure standing just inside the cave. "Come," he urged her softly.

Fatalistically she followed orders. Otherwise she'd have to turn away to run and stumble through woods and mosquitoes again, listening for pursuing feet; she still wasn't ready to try that again. So she moved forward, groping after Talisman, one hand on his back for guidance. He moved through the tunnel at a good pace, as if he now knew just where he was going. The only sounds that Marge could hear were those of her own soft-soled shoes, and her own faint breathing.

Before Marge had quite realized how quickly they were progressing, they were at the branching passage and turning down it. From here on guidance was provided by faint, flickering torchlight and continued groans. Now Marge could see that the door to the dungeon room stood wide open.

The room was as she had first seen it, occupied only by the old man still on the rack. His left arm, the one that she had freed, now moved with little brushing motions across his chest, as if conscious, he were trying to reach his other bonds.

Talisman took two paces into the dungeon and stopped momentarily. Muttered speech, full of outrage, burst from him in some foreign tongue. Marge paused, watching warily, as Talisman stepped quickly forward again. The three remaining straps opened their stubborn buckles to three quick flicks of his fingers. The old victim's limbs, freed, contracted.

And now the eyes of the victim opened at last. Hooded still by age-carved lids, their cloudy gray-blue was the color of sky between storms. Still half dazed and on the brink of terror, the old man uttered guttural sounds. He raised himself on his elbows and looked around him in bewilderment.

Talisman moved a long pace back from the rack, to stand beside Marge. Then, even as the freed man on the rack edged himself on his elbows farther from his deliverers, half-snarling at them in fear, Marge was astounded to see her tall companion go down on one knee, facing the old one.

"Maistre," murmured Talisman softly. At least it sounded like that to Marge: one foreign word, of French or Latin probably.

The old man wheezed in chest and throat. He hawked up phlegm, and spat it toward a corner, all without taking his eyes from Talisman. He said at last: "Don't gimme any of that crap." The words came out in a weak gargle, and yet the dominant impression that they conveyed was of force.

Each breath in the old man's throat was a wheezing rasp, evidently accelerated by fear. His eyes remained fixed on Talisman—they had identified importance. The old man's arms and legs, now that they were freed, looked as much muscular as they were fat. And now that he had turned on his side, his belly bulged paunchily, matted like his chest with gray-brown hair. Ample maleness, half hidden in the heaviest fur, had something about it that struck Marge as somehow peculiar—the old man was uncircumcised, she realized. And she almost blushed, to have taken notice of such a thing at a time of death and danger. She felt as if some mischievous power had forced her to do so.

Talisman had risen to his feet and was waiting silently. At last the old man spoke to him again. "Who the hell *are* you? I thought you was some butcher, when you come after me on the street."

In the guttering torchlight, the dried blood on Talisman's shirt might have been no more than shadows. His voice now sounded proud, offended, and yet constrained to remain respectful. "You must realize now that when I sought you on the street I meant no harm. I sensed that a worthy master, a man of great stature, was nearby and needed help. In honor I could do no less than try to find you. I would have offered service, but I was prevented from recognizing you there. Your own powers prevented—"

"Service, shit!" The words came in a double snort, of what sounded like contempt and wonder mingled.

Talisman's voice rose briefly louder, to override an objection that was in itself too contemptible to deserve a more direct reply. "I would not offer unsought help to many now alive. Understand that. I have been prince, in my own land. And I am now—what I am. If your powers could hide you from me on the city streets, then of the strength of your powers I am sure. As I am sure that once you had nobility. And that you are now the prisoner of the scum who hold this house above us."

"Sonovabitch," the old one said. He spoke in a milder voice, as if he were impressed despite himself by Talisman's ringing speech. "Look," he bega in a reasonable tone. Then he paused to consider his own nakedness, to look at Margie, and at the room around him. He seemed to come fully awake now for the first time. "'Scuse my foul mouth, little one. What've they done with me? But I'm still alive. Still alive."

Talisman answered him. "What has been done to you, *maistre*, I can only conjecture. But truly the powers that did it must have been formidable."

"Whatinell you mean?"

"I mean that I cannot accept your rejection of my service. Not until I know that you make it knowingly, and free of all enchantment."

That last word seemed to Marge to hang echoing in the dim dungeon air. *Antment antment antment.* She no longer felt able to pass any judgement on what made sense and what did not. She waited for what might happen next.

The old man was looking at first one of them and then the other, meanwhile muttering as if in calculation. Then he shook his head, as a man might who was indeed trying to clear it of some spell.

"Dunno what you mean." His voice rose. "Where's my friggin' clothes?" And now his eyes were fixed on Marge, as if perhaps she ought to be in charge of wardrobe. The old man's whiskers were pure vaudeville decoration, sticking out in all directions. His whiskers and his hairy paunch

almost succeeded in making him a complete joke,
a comic satyr strayed from some ancient Roman
stage. Almost, not quite, because there were his
eyes. Blue-gray eyes, hard-looking inside their
baggy lids. They had not blinked often, those eyes,
even when the aged body had cringed in fear, and
they contained something frightening.

For a moment Marge could only stare back
in fascination. Talisman meanwhile spread his
hands, a weary, exasperated gesture, and turned
to look into the corners of the room, where almost
perfect darkness reigned. And where there
seemed to be no clothes to be discovered.

Marge felt a sudden urge to do something, anything, to solve the problem. "Wait," she said, and
turned and hurried out of the chamber and into
the narrow ascending tunnel. As she ran she
pulled out her little flashlight from her ruined
costume's pocket. In a moment its beam had
found her shoulder bag, waiting on the floor just
where she'd left it. Looping the strap over her
shoulder she hurried back to the dungeon, meanwhile rummaging in the bag. As she rejoined the
men, she was pulling from the bag a garment of
thin but closely woven brown cloth. Marge had
got this from her costumer, whose idea it was of
what a medieval jongleur ought to wear. She had
brought it along as an alternate costume for
herself, in case the gauzy materialization
outfit—what a total loss that was now—should at
the last moment prove unworkable or inappropri-
ate.

When she extended the robe to the old man, he
at once hopped down from his awkward wooden
couch, demonstrating in the process that he was
very little taller than she. He grabbed the offered
garment from Marge's hands and pulled it on over
his head. Somehow she had assumed that the effect was going to be bizarre, a hairy old man in a
dress, and somehow it was not. The bright, mean-

ingless symbols that decorated the cloth suddenly seemed to acquire a potential significance. The ancient knotted the robe's simple tie at his waist, and stood before them in new dignity.

To Marge he absently muttered something foreign, that she supposed might have been a thank you. When he spoke to Talisman it was no longer as a cowering derelict, though fear was still audible in his voice. "Whadda you think they want with me? The ones who brought me here?"

"To the best of my belief," Talisman told him calmly, "they intend to use you as the next in a series of human sacrifices."

Unconsciously Marge had retreated from both men. Her back was now against the stones of the dungeon wall. And a part of her mind, having now recovered somewhat from the terror of the beast, was trying to tell her that she ought to believe none of this. That this talk of powers and enchantment and sacrifice had to be part of the biggest show, the biggest act, the biggest scam . . . She knew that nothing she had seen or heard here had been part of any act.

Talisman was speaking to the old man, as if in explanation, again speaking what might have been French or Latin. Whatever it was, the old man understood it, and nodded slowly; his suspicions, or some of them, were being confirmed.

"And I have fought the *loup garou*," Talisman added. He was still inexorably calm. "Within the hour. And only a few paces from these walls."

The old man nodded again, in fear.

Talisman went on "Some dark dominion has its center in this house above our heads. Among its evil powers there may be—nay, must be—some greater even than the werewolf. But you know this. You must."

The ancient one regarded Talisman hopelessly, then closed his eyes, as if he could bear to hear no more. "We must be a hundred friggin' miles from the city," he muttered hopelessly.

"At least that far." Talisman paused. "That *you*
should have been plucked from the streets at ran-
dom seems impossible. They chose you deliberately. Or they were led to choose you. Who, what,
might have led them?"

The old man had no answer.

"There are powers at work here, honored one,
that are beyond my experience and comprehension. Tell me, what is it that you so greatly fear?"

The ancient was rubbing at his forehead. "I
wonder what the bastard put in that wine . . . you
figure it out, why they picked me. I don't give a
damn, I'm leaving, whatever I have to do. If I can
remember how."

Talisman was quietly upset by this announcement. "The place for one of your stature to
be is here, in confrontation with your enemies
who kidnapped you and brought you here. Honor
and wisdom alike forbid that you should simply
leave."

"Screw honor and wisdom. Whadda you know
about wisdom?"

"Do you not see . . . ?"

But plainly the old man was not listening. Having glared once more at both his listeners, as if
they were the ones guilty of kidnapping, he had
closed his eyes again and was now muttering sys-
tematically. His toneless voice fell into the
rhythm of a chant.

"Master," said Talisman. To judge from his
tone he was now closer to offering violence than
service. "I do not insist on courtesy from you; it is
not my place to do that. But more than courtesy is
at stake. I ask you to behave with common sense.
For your own good, as well as for the sake of the
innocent folk of this time and place."

"Shuddup, will ya? How in hell's a man supposed to think? To remember?" The blue-gray
eyes closed yet again, the mumbled words came

louder, faster than before.

Talisman uttered a sound that was not quite a sigh, and took one step forward. His right arm flicked out like a lash. Marge winced at the sound his hand made, hitting the old one on the temple. The old man's eyes stayed closed, and his jaw sagged open in mind-chant, displaying snaggled teeth. Talisman caught the body gently, just as it began to fall. He lifted it easily, to put it back unbound upon the handy rack.

And at that point a soundless explosion overcame the world.

For a moment Marge actually thought that a bomb might have been detonated, so powerful was the sense of almost instantaneous change. But what happened was silent, and did not blast or burn, and was just a beat too slow to have been the effect of chemical explosives.

Marge saw herself surrounded by gray, glowing haze. Talisman had disappeared, but she caught just a glimpse of the great pale wolf-beast bounding away in flight. Raging men and women who she had never seen before surrounded her, their hands outstretched to clutch. Angry creatures she had never imagined bared fangs larger than the dark wolf's had been.

A hideous paw that was not quite a hand slid past her face and down. A woman's face, all malign beauty under dark curly hair, snarled in surprise and fury, then was shocked into pale marble when the woman's eyes fell on the supine figure of the old man.

Still dressed in Marge's surplus robe the old man lay on the rack, unconscious but unbound. She had the impression that reality was swirling like fog round his unmoving head.

Marge could take no more. She went down, huddling with hands over eyes, until the madness should end somehow.

She landed, sitting, on something at once

springy and soft, finely divided, and softly irregular. It wasn't a stone floor.

No touch came from the clutching hands, no pain from snapping jaws. Everything was quiet.

Inside the protective cage of her hands she unclenched her eyelids just a trifle, until she saw bright light nudging through. It turned the flesh of her caging fingers incandescent pink.

Not until a breeze caressed her face did Marge realize that she was sitting on long green grass in bright sunshine.

ELEVEN

When the world blew up around Feathers with a great shock, it left him drifting like a shed plume amid the smoky wreckage of what had been the local atmosphere. The shock didn't stun him, though. In fact it partially cleared his mind, at least enough for him to understand that it wasn't really the atmosphere that had been wrecked and stirred and scrambled, but something more fundamental. And also that now he wasn't Feathers any more.

Shit, he never had been, really, not with any sense of identification with the name. And with one false name out of the way, he was able to understand, willing to remember, more.

A great deal more.

And stop saying *shit*, he admonished himself. Stop speaking foulness when you are with gentle folk. How have you fallen into such a habit?

It serves, he answered himself, to help keep the

gentle folk, or some of them anyway, away from me.

And why do you want to do that?

You know why.

But, if he did know, he didn't want to think about it. Actually he couldn't think about it, not just yet.

But change had come again, and he was going to have to adapt to change once more.

Here was another item that he hadn't wanted to think about: he'd really known for a long time that something in the nature of that blowup was coming. It had to be coming sooner or later, no special powers were needed to see that, only a minimal intelligence and a knowledge of the situation. When you dammed up something long enough, when you repressed it, as that new young social worker at the soup kitchen would doubtless say, then sooner or later it would come bursting or leaking through in one form or another.

A good blowup, like this one, reduced tension. But it also created problems. For example, when he opened his eyes, where was he going to be? The answer when he discovered it might not be pleasant. But he was soon going to have to open his eyes, whatever—

His thought was stopped, totally, by the sound of a woman's voice. It was a soft voice, not ten feet away from him, and it wasn't laughing this time, as he had heard it in those ghostly warning pre-echoes that his powers had provided for him on the street. No, it was only talking, but its tones of subtle venom were unmistakable. Never in this world or any other was he going to forget the tones of that voice. The shock of them now was such that at first he had no idea what the voice was saying. It took him a little while to get his thought going again.

Then he who had once been known as Feathers opened his eyes. His surroundings hadn't changed as much as he had feared. His body, strictly speaking, was no longer lying on the rack; rather he now floated horizontally in the air six inches above it. Around him, the tight swirl of his protective powers made what his eyes could perceive as a knotted blanket of blue smoke. Things had very recently been trying to reach him through that blanket, he perceived also, and had been defeated by it. With a little effort he could see some of those things now. They were squatting much like giant toads, in the four upper corners and two of the lower corners of the stone-walled chamber.

But he hardly noticed those things now. All his attention was fixed on the woman who was their mistress. She stood in the approximate middle of the stone-paved floor, almost within arm's length of the strange torture-bed above which his body was suspended. She was facing him, hands on hips, poised like a sentry who had just heard a suspicious noise—or, he thought, almost like a housewife discovering a mouse. Her attitude was made no less serious by the fact that she was wearing nothing but two tiny strips of yellow cloth. In physical appearance she'd changed very little since he had seen her last.

If she had been anywhere near as surprised as he was by this meeting, she'd had time to get over the first shock of it before he looked at her.

The man who had been Feathers saw no point now in being chary of his use of magic, and therefore no need to struggle with joints stiffened by hours of immobility. Instead of straining to sit up now, he simply willed himself standing. The knots of smoke that held his body tugged and tightened; their network lifted him gently from his suspension above the rack and turned him vertical and set him gently on his feet, a little closer to the woman than he had been before. He noted with secret joy the effort that it cost her not to step back.

He was about half a head taller than the top of her dark curls; familiar measurement.

"Hello, Nimue," he said softly.

She didn't have an answer for him right away. There was a lot going on behind her mask of calm control; he could feel it, but he wasn't able to identify it all, and in fact he did not try. Long seconds passed and still Nimue did not speak. She might have tried words on him while he was still unconscious. If so he felt sure that none of them had been well-meant, and as far as he could tell none had been effective. He and this woman had long ago reached an equilibrium of sorts. The smoky blanket of his powers protected against more than claws.

While waiting for her to speak now, he thought about the creatures, the activity, he could perceive in the room around him. He calmed the local atmosphere somewhat toward normal, while taking good care that the effectiveness of his defensive powers should not be hindered. Their full mobilization was one good effect that the blowup had produced.

Meanwhile his memory was privately examining a recent image: that of a dark man dressed in darkness. A rather tall man, not met before, except in passing on the street, claiming with sly tongue to be well-meaning, prating about honor. And effective. Oh yes. He who had been Feathers could still feel the bruise on his temple, throbbing just a little. The dark-clothed man had been wise enough to know the moment in mid-incantation when it would be possible to strike, and he had had nerve enough to take the risks involved. And speed, and controlled strength. And the old tongue. It all added up to vampire. One of the old, honorable . . . oh, piss on it, what did it matter now?

And—oh yeah. Some little girl had been here too, dressed up like a stage fairy. In fact this robe bemerded with idiot symbols that he was wearing now had come from her. There was probably some damnfool masquerade planned here, that doubtless had behind it some evil game of Nimue's, and the girl was just an innocent caught up in the mess. Pretty thing, too. Well, too bad. The world was full of innocents in trouble through no fault of their own.

Only at this point did it occur to him, provoking in him first amusement and then faint concern, exactly what had been the probable fate of the vampire and the girl when the blowup happened. Serve the old blood-drinking bastard right, he told himself, feeling his sore head. And then the innocent girl . . . he sighed.

Nimue had at last tired of her game of silent waiting. "By what name shall I call you now?" she asked. It was certainly a banal way for one adept to begin a conversation with another. And a pointed reminder of his own discourteous bluntness in using her own true name at the start. Well, some people deserved courtesy, and some . . .

Nimue had addressed him in one of the language from old Brittany; he couldn't recall the name of the damned tongue now, if it even had a name, but as soon as he heard it again the sound and meaning of it flowed smoothly once more in his antique brain cells.

He spoke the tongue of Brittany, for the first time in a thousand years "I'm leaving. You need not worry about what you ought to call me."

"I should prefer to be able to use some name." Nimue's voice was smoothly unrevealing. "For reasons of courtesy."

"All right. Hawk is a good name." Then, switching to modern English: "Mr. Hawk, to you." And then, after a pause: "I don't get it, what you're trying to do here. I mean, why me? And tied down on a rack. I mean, what the bloody hell, woman? Did you just want to see the expression on my face when I woke up?"

Nimue only smiled faintly, and shook her head. They both knew that she didn't have to explain anything at all to him. Because . . . because . . . the reason escaped Hawk just now, but he knew it was a damned good one.

"Just fate, I suppose," he meditated aloud. "That's why I'm here. Or somebody's plan?"

Still the enigmatic smile. Nimue raised an open hand, and made a small gesture with two fingers, and two of the things—in the old days he would probably have called them familiars—from two of the top corners of the room went flickering away upon some errand. They were pre-instructed, evidently, or maybe pre-programmed was the modern word.

Nimue said: "No plan of mine, Mr. Hawk. You can leave here any time you want to, for all of me. All we wanted was some human who would not be missed, so it will be easy enough to obtain a replacement. The rack was just a handy place to keep you, nothing more. By the way, would you like a good bottle of wine to take along? I understand that wine had been your chief interest ever since we last spoke."

She couldn't resist a chance for petty cruelty. Hawk shuddered. The emotion that made him do so was not quite recognizable. "Just 'some human', hey? And you got me. How about that man who picked me up on the street? Some private plan of his, maybe?"

Nimue looked as if she would like to remind Mr. Hawk of his expressed wish to leave, but was at the same time afraid that any word from her might have an opposite effect. Was all this some subtle ploy intended to influence him to stay? Hawk didn't think so.

He could see that some enterprise of consequence was in the process of organization here.

Besides the squat-toads, relatively easy to visualize when you knew how, a veritable crowd of other presences were waiting in the wings. The dim dungeon—as moderns would call this place, he'd rather simply call it a hole—crawled with powers, his own, Nimue's, who-knew-whose. All these were edging each other ominously, maneuvering for position, elbowing like basketball players under some evil backboard. Were such as these in fact spirits? Were they alive at all, or like the winds only the artifacts of some invisible force? He still didn't know, despite the long centuries of service he had received from some of them. The older he grew the less he knew with certainty. But when the ball flew at the backboard, things were going to happen. Of that he could be sure.

Anyway something of his own willed purpose must have been worked out amid the jockeying. A recent unspoken, almost unconscious wish of his was granted: another look at the coffee-colored man who had picked up Feathers on the street, and drugged him, and then drove him all the way out here from Chicago.

This abductor came through a door into the dungeon now. "What is it?" he demanded of Nimue, in the tone of one who has just heard his name called from an adjoining room. Then he looked in surprise at the old man's gown, and then he was distracted seriously by trying to aim a hard stare into the old man's eyes. Whatever the hard stare met there caused the kidnapper to back up a step, right into a corner where one of the demon-toads hung right above his head. Neither of Nimue's agents appeared, for the moment, to be aware of the other one's existence.

Now that her human helper had been maneuvered into the room, Nimue would go along with his presence gracefully. "Carados," she addressed him easily, "tell me why you picked out this par-

ticular old specimen? Out of all the wrecked men
who must have been available on that street." Her
tone was mild, but the speech was a display of ar-
rogance, giving away as it did the true name of
one of her people, throwing caution aside, daring
Hawk to make what use of it he liked. They both
understood that she could still dare him as she
liked. Because . . .

Carados shrugged. Insolently his eyes ran-
sacked his mistress's body, as if she had put that
brief costume on to please him. She was not only
in a swim suit, Hawk noted, she was actually still
wet. She must have been called from poolside for
the emergency. And again he wondered just what
the hell was going on.

Carados said: "Why not? He was just about able
to walk, so I didn't have to carry him, but too far
gone to put up any fuss. What's wrong with him?"

"Take a milder tone with me. Somehow you
were led, influenced, to choose this particular
man for the next sacrifice. I would like to know
who influenced you, and how and why."

"He been feeding you some kind of line about
me?" And Carados tried to look menacingly at
Hawk, but somehow the intimidating stare became diverted. Carados stared up uneasily into
one corner of the ceiling. Plainly he knew that
something was there besides the stones, but he
was having a lot of trouble even seeing what it
was. Nimue had to recruit whatever assistants
she could find, evidently.

And the jockeying in the background, below the
level of mundane reality, had grown more feverish. It was more than jockeying. Hawk could feel
the energies of magic, blind, immensely powerful,
all tensing steadily like the magnetic lines of force
wound tight within a generator, like land along an
earthquake fault. His first estimate had been
wrong. That little blowup of a few minutes ago
had really achieved almost nothing in the way of a

relief of tension. To hash the metaphor some more, that little blowup had only taken one key blockage out, and the logjam was now free to rearrange itself, which it was doing. When rearrangement was done, it would be free to move. There was likely to be another blowup down the road, and it was likely to be a bloody whopper.

His swearwords were becoming more English, he noted. He supposed that might count in some minds as progress toward elegance.

Nimue, he could see, was pondering, along with other problems, what best to do with her mad helper. The man must be very useful, very good at something, to balance the obvious difficulties of having him around. Hawk had now been near the man for long enough, and was now alert enough himself, to detect the dangerous madness radiating from him. The madman had received a bad scare, too, at some time in the recent past, a scare that would probably have disabled an ordinary citizen for some time. But he had hardly been affected once the danger was gone. Against some things madness could guard almost as well as powers.

Becoming aware of the scrutiny of the two sorcerers, and made uneasy by it, Carados became belligerent. "You're nothing special, old man. You're shit I picked up off the street. Hey, some cool threads you picked up there." And he muttered some garbage that was meant to be a pain-inflicting spell, and reached to grab Hawk by the robe-front.

Such manhandling of the old man had been relatively easy before the recent blowup and mobilization. Nimue understood that stage of things was past, and now Hawk could see her wince perceptibly in anticipation. But Hawk had already eased the trigger on his defenses somewhat, and Carados only pulled back fingers twisted in a sudden cramp.

Unnoticed by Carados, the demon above his head stuck out a foot-long tongue in mockery. Carados rubbed his aching fingers, glared at Hawk, and moved forward to try again. Hawk looked at him in turn, and Carados stopped, his eyes turned downward in disbelief. In his mind he had felt the solid stone floor of the dungeon crack, threatening to open up beneath his feet.

Looking at Nimue, Hawk put his question once more: "What're you trying to do here?"

Her smile was a touch broader than it had been before. Her teeth were fine, a little too perfect but otherwise very human. As she was, he reminded himself. She said: "Don't you want the wine before you go?"

He muttered something foul. He wasn't going to try to insist that she answer him, because . . . looking down at himself, he became distracted. When he showed up back on the Street, dressed like this . . . never mind, something could be done about that.

He spoke three more words, and was gone.

The woman in the yellow bikini looked up at the ceiling. All the toad-creatures were gone from its high corners.

Gregory, who must have been waiting, listening, just outside, came in. Fat Arnaud, still weak from the tearing of his werewolf's throat by vampire's fangs, followed cautiously behind him. Carados, understanding less and less of what was happening, looked at the three other people in the room with him, sneered at them, his mind retreating from the scene, superimposing its own reality.

The woman they called Vivian asked prosaically: "What time is it, Gregory? I must have a talk with our young visiting magician before dinner."

TWELVE

Marge was still sitting in the position in which she had collapsed, on the grassy flank of a lightly wooded knoll. She was facing a small lake framed in gentle hills, its nearer shoreline a little more than a hundred yards away. The sun was low in a clear sky, the weather a gentle fairness utterly unlike the scorch of the morning and early afternoon of the day on which Marge had closed her eyes a moment earlier. The air here had a pastel quality, touched with mist. It was all so different that Marge understood from the start, without reasoning about it, that her journey had been a long one.

Here it was either early morning or late afternoon, with no immediately apparent way to decide which. The long grass was damp, either from morning dew or recent rain. The air was moist and fresh. Between the foot of Marge's hill and the adjoining rise, a tiny stream murmured through tall rushes. The stream widened gradually into a small marsh at the place where it joined the lake. Immediately beyond the marsh, some high ground just along the lake shore held a string of crude, thatch-roofed buildings. Smoke rose tranquilly from a clay chimney. On the far side of the hamlet a single lane of road, unpaved and deeply rutted, followed the curve of shoreline for another quarter of a mile before turning away to vanish among more of the gentle, grassy hills.

In the opposite direction from the hamlet, to Marge's left, a few sheep were grazing along the flank of an adjoining hill. When she got to her feet the movement was slow and uncertain, but still it caught these animals by surprise. They *baaed* and turned in awkward flight.

The disturbance among the sheep triggered another. A great shaggy dog that had been dozing near the buildings now awoke, with a savage volley of growls and barks. The animal leaped to its feet and started toward Marge, to halt when it reached the edged of marshy ground between.

The dog's excitement in turn produced people. An old man and a young one appeared from somewhere to stand between two of the buildings. At first glance Marge thought that they were dressed very much like the servants at the party, but a second look showed that the clothing of these men was somewhat more varied and complex. They advanced slowly, with puzzled faces, to pause like the dog on the edge of the marsh. The young man spoke to quiet the dog, while the graybeard continued to study Marge from fifty yards away, then hailed her. Their language was not English, nor—and this seemed additionally unfair—did it even sound anything like the tongue that the other two men had spoken before Marge in the dungeon. That scene too had seemed perfectly real. Before the world blew up in a swirl of monsters . . .

The peaceful landscape before Marge now was

reassuring by comparison. Both men were calling to her now, but she could not understand a word.

She shook her head. At last she called back, in a tremulous voice: "I don't know who you are, or what you're saying. What place is this?"

The men looked at her blankly, then shook their heads just as Marge had done, and coferred briefly between themselves. Presently they advanced, wading the narrowest neck of the small marsh, to where Marge stood. Feeling uncertain and confused—but not really frightened—she smiled at them tentatively and waited. They talked to her a little more, uselessly. Then each took her by one arm, not unkindly, and they marched her back across the marshy land and up toward the buildings. These were somewhat larger than Marge had thought at first sight.

The door to one of the smaller houses stood open. As Marge was brought in by her escort, a worn-looking woman in a long, plain dress rose from a wooden bench beside the smoky fireplace, putting down her knitting. Or was it sewing? Marge had trouble remembering which was which. Anyway it was work of some kind, cloth and a large ball of snarled-looking gray thread or yarn.

The two men and the woman all talked together now about Marge, and took turns questioning her. They had only the one language, and tried it repeatedly. It was no easier to understand when they spoke slowly and clearly, or repeated the same question several times in a loud voice. She did her part by running the same experiments with English.

From somewhere nearby, Marge thought it was from inside one of the large buildings, there came at intervals a loud, determined clanging, as of heavy hammerblows on metal. The people with Marge paid this no attention but went on debating about Marge. Marge got the impression from their gestures that the woman thought they had better take the problem to someone who was over there, where all the noise was coming from, while the two men thought this not advisable, at least not right now.

Eventually they thought to offer Marge a place to sit down, a wooden stool that like everything else in the little house looked homemade. She had a cousin who had lived in one of those crazy communes once and had told Marge all about it. This must be, somehow, something similar. Now the woman was bringing her a wooden bowl, complete with wooden spoon, containing a thick substance that looked like unrefined oatmeal.

Marge said yes, thank you, and tried some. For oatmeal, it wasn't bad. Then the spoon rested idle in her hand for a while when she noticed two objects that were leaning against the roughly plastered wall just inside the open doorway. They were a short spear, and a shield of what looked like tough, thick leather. The spear's metal point was the size of a man's hand, its shaft was handcarved wood, straight and sturdy as a hoe handle. The shield was round, and bossed with metal decorations. But it was the functional look of both objects that impressed Marge.

Meanwhile the people who had been interviewing her had things to marvel at too. Her clothing, for one thing. They were not really surprised at the dirty rags her costume had become, but after she had given permission with a smile, they rummaged through her shoulder bag. One of the men held up the jeans against himself; evidently they were not considered women's garb.

Presently the men put her things back in the bag and went out together, leaving Marge with her porridge and the woman for companionship. The woman, who had gone back to fussing with her tangled thread, watched Marge closely, smiling now and then. Once she offered Marge a chance to try the knitting or whatever it was; her guest's helpless refusal came as a surprise.

Marge finished her porridge. Perhaps half an hour went by, with recurrent bursts of hammering from the other building. Men's voices could now be heard also, growing progressively more excited. At last there came a prolonged cheer. Maybe, Marge thought sourly, they were watching football.

Actually she knew better. There wasn't even an electric light in sight, or a radio, let alone a TV. And now the sun was getting ready to set.

The housewife crouched over her hearth, where a tiny fire was smoldering, and from the embers lighted a lamp of a kind Marge had never seen before, a clay bowl holding oil in which a mere shred of cloth floated for a wick. The smoky, flaring glow of it filled the little house unevenly.

Before the sun had gone completely, the two men who had found Marge on the hillside were back, their bulky figures darkening what light the open doorway still gave. And between them now was a third man, a little shorter than they. At first Marge could see him only in silhouette against the dying of the light outside, and then he came closer, into lamplight. He had a fair beard and mustache, and a large nose, and blue eyes that were hard to meet. He was dressed somewhat more richly than the other two men, and at his side was belted a sword in an ornate leather scabbard. The other two deferred to him, that was plain, and the woman of the house made a sort of curtsey at his entrance. Marge didn't know what to do, and so sat still.

The short man spoke to Marge, at first in the same language that the other folk had tried. His voice was light and clear, as if he could be a singer if he tried. When there was no response, he experimented with another tongue, that Marge thought might be French, and after that a third one, Latin-sounding. Was it the same the two men in the dungeon had spoken? Marge couldn't be sure.

At last the man of importance shook his head, and turned away, issuing orders to other men who had come up to stand in front of the house. Then the whole group of them moved away. Presently two young women came to the house, both robed in white as if for ceremony. With smiles and gestures they conducted Marge through the dusk to a larger building, set a little apart from the rest of the settlement.

Marge found herself in a lamplit hall, big enough to dance in, rows of posts set in the floor supporting beams with thatch above. A dozen other women were present, mostly young and all similarly dressed. As if, she realized, this were a convent of some kind. She supposed such places still existed. Obviously they did here. There were no crosses anywhere, nothing that she could recognize as a religious symbol.

Nunnery, sorority, whatever, Marge was too tired to care. The women showed her where the outhouse was, and went there with her. Yippee, just like summer camp. Then they gave her some water with a little wine mixed in, and some soup in another wooden bowl, and a piece of crude, dark bread. And, finally, when she'd begun to think they'd never ask, a straw pallet in a small back room. She had a roommate, who lay down in white robes on another pallet at Marge's side, and promptly went to sleep.

Marge collapsed on straw, utterly exhausted. She ought to try to think things through . . .

THIRTEEN

"What do you dream, vampire? Bad dreams ever keep you from getting any rest?"

Talisman stirred, groaned. He did not yet open his eyes, sensing muted daylight, dangerous daylight, in the air around him. He could stand some of it but not if it should grow direct and strong. Where was he? He remembered the rebuilt dungeon, the explosion of magical force. It had picked him up and dropped him somewhere else. He was immune to fear, his quick attempt at flight had been a coldly calculated effort at survival. But the flight had evidently not been an unqualified success.

"Vampire, vampire." The old man's voice, from somewhere, nagged him. "I knew one like you once. No way you could scare him, either, but you could drive him mad. Matter of fact I did. He kept dreaming of poisoned blood, you see, cold and green. I was the one who fixed him up with nightmares, after he once bothered a little girl I liked

147

. . . every day, in his trance, this dream about a girl would come to him. But when he tried to do his filthy trick and bite her throat—chilled emerald wine, that's what he got, hahaa."

It was certainly the old man's voice, though it was not speaking English now. It was speaking—what? Something very old, certainly, halfway familiar to Talisman though unheard for centuries. He stirred, forcing himself out of an incipient daylight trance, opened his eyes. He had to see where he was. The sun was low in the sky, behind some trees, and he saw and felt with relief that it was going down not up. That ought to boost his chances for immediate survival here—wherever here was.

He was lying right on the ground in the month of a shallow cave, a very different cave from the one in which the castle's secret tunnel ended. In getting to his feet, he stirred up rattling old leaves and straw, last year's debris dropped here by the wind. It was summer still, or summer again, to judge by the forest growth before the cave. The look of the flora and the smell of the air suggested strongly that he was in England.

The disembodied voice in his ear spoke English now. "You're in the land of cold green blood, bloodsucker. Still want to play with the big boys? See what happens when you do?"

"Bah." Talisman got out of the cave, where he had room enough to stand erect. He brushed himself off. "Is it your custom to play with boys, ancient one? Is it possible that you are sometimes able to frighten children?" He took a breath, to sniff the air again. Yes, England, at some early age. Interesting.

"You wanted to stop me travelling, didn't you, vampire? Well, I got where I was going anyway. I hope you enjoy your little trip. Hard to say how long it's going to last. You'll meet some interesting people along the way, though."

"I see now that I was mistaken about you, old man. I did you far too much honor, and debased myself by doing so. You are a clever peasant, nothing more."

"How can you debase a snake's belly? Babble on, bloodsucker. I don't give a damn if you can be scared or not—but I do hear they make some splintery stakes back there where you are now. They don't have any trouble at all believing in vampires, by the way."

"Tell me, you ancient peasant, ancient fool." Talisman's voice was still quiet and steady, but he had rarely in his life been angrier than he was now; never mind that in the cooler portions of his mind he knew that his anger really ought to be directed at himself. "Will this little trip of mine, as you call it, ever bring our two pathways once more together?"

"You better hope and pray it doesn't. Your bloodsucking ass is mud if ever we meet again."

Before Talisman could find a retort to this preposterous rhetoric, the voice, the mental presence, of the Disgusting One were gone. To Talisman's relief. If he could not get in the last word, at least he would no longer have to endure the gutter invective of . . . of . . .

Despite himself, the cooler portion of Talisman's mind was already starting to assert control. If age did not prevent rage, at least experience helped to moderate it at times when rage was plainly useless. At bottom Talisman knew that what had happened to him was not really the old man's fault. The quivering insults from the Disgusting One were a result of misdirected anger; a great enchantment kept the old man from properly identifying the proper target of his wrath . . . at bottom, Talisman knew all that. But still, right now, if the old man had been before him in the flesh, Talisman's arms, the strength of ten men in each, would now be reaching out to crush that wattled throat . . .

And doubtless before he touched it he'd find himself in a worse situation than he was now. Against the powers of that ancient one, Talisman knew that he'd be sorely overmatched. Ah well. Time enough to consider that point when it arose in fact.

A thin path ran through the forest near the cave, and Talisman could hear men's feet approaching now along the path. They moved lightly, with habitual quiet, yet not with the great caution of those thinking themselves in immediate danger. Two men, two breathing men, still too far away to have any idea that Talisman's silent unbreathing presence waited for them here. Should he confront them when they appeared, or seek concealment? It wasn't quite sunset, to shift to the form of mist or wolf or bat would be impossible, he'd have to slide behind a tree or bush. But no, he'd wait and face them. Let what was coming come.

The approaching feet were shod, in what sounded like soft leather. One of the men was half-singing, half-humming to himself, in what sounded to Talisman like some ancient dialect of French. There were subtle sounds to indicate that the two men had some burden slung between them, on a pole.

A very faint *pat*, as from the fall of thickening dead blood on a dry leaf.

They were bringing in a deer.

Talisman made himself ignore for the moment his hungry vision of fresh bood. He folded his arms and stood waiting calmly beside the path. The two huntsmen armed with bow and spear came into view, then came two steps farther into the little clearing before they saw Talisman, so still was he standing. There they halted in confused surprise. Not sure whether they ought to drop their burden or not, clearing the decks for

action, they didn't quite. One man gave his spear
a little flourish, calling attention to its existence.

Talisman, arms folded, hands empty, looked at
them broodingly.

"Who are you?" asked the man in front, shifting
the weighted pole slightly on his shoulder, so that
the dead deer. hanging swayed. The dialect was
hard for Talisman, but the meaning, in the context, plain enough.

"My name is Talisman." He led the word
through translation as best he could. "Who is
your master?"

"King Comorr."

"Ah." Could the vampire have known fear, it
might have touched him now. But as he began to
think about the name, it began to explain things
that had puzzled him till now. "You will bring me
to him."

The hunters exchanged glances. Then the one in
front motioned for Talisman to precede them on
the path.

FOURTEEN

In Simon's private bath electric light was his to command, and he was using it to get ready for dinner and then performance. If his appearance was good, reasonably convincing, in the modern mirror flanked by bright incandescents, then the soft candlelight below could only add romance and conviction.

The outfit he was putting on represented less his Chicago costumer's idea of how a medieval enchanter ought to look than what the costumer had readily available. There was a bulky jacket of blue and gray, what the man had called a doublet, worn open in front over an inner garment not too different from a modern turtleneck. There were pointy shoes much like those Gregory was wearing, tight hose, and another garment like a pair of bulkily padded swimming trunks, with an anachronistic but invisible zippered fly. All in all, Simon found the outfit reasonably comfortable, and probably as impressive as it had to be. He'd had the doublet fitted with some special pockets, useful for the special purposes of the conjurer. As a final touch, he now looped over his head the thick, brassy chain of a costume-jewelry medallion on which a lion and sword were shown in gold-colored relief. He thought that to a non-expert it would look classy enough to be convincing.

And now, before taking a last look at his image in the mirror, he reached out and switched off the bathroom lights. With just the light coming in from the bedroom, he thought he might be able to get a good idea of how he was going to look in the dim, soft illumination that would obtain in the great hall below.

Good enough, he thought. Quite good, in fact. Authentic.

His appearance was satisfactory, and yet for a little while he remained before the mirror. His reflected image was half silhouette against the brighter reflection of the lighted room behind him, as if he were standing in a doorway that led to the outside. He didn't know just what he'd expected to discover about himself, to prove to himself, when he'd started out on this day's journey into his own past. But certainly the day so far had been even stranger than he'd expected. First the series of visions, half-visions, hallucinations, whatever you might want to call them. And then, a blank of some three hours, including his arrival at the castle. He must have looked bad when he arrived, really out of it, so that someone had suggested he go up to his room and take a nap. It was probably fortunate that he'd agreed.

The soreness was almost completely gone from his throat muscles now. So nearly gone that he might have been imagining that, too. Hell, he must have been imagining it.

Simon rather surprised himself by the calm way he was now, after all that, getting ready to go on with the show. It was as if he knew, deep inside, basically, secretly, that all this strangeness was really nothing to be alarmed about. As if he'd really been expecting something of the kind to happen all along . . .

But now was not the time for introspection. Now was the time to go and put on a performance. Marge was ready, and he was too. One more check of the arrangements in his secret pockets, and Simon switched off his bedroom's lights and stepped out into the hall.

He had no more than closed the door behind him when another opened, two rooms down the hall, and Vivian looked out. She was wrapped now in a bulky beach robe of startling white, and her head was swathed in a towel with which she rubbed her hair.

"There you are, Simon." Vivian's voice was bright, energetic, still totally in control. "I was hoping to catch you before you went downstairs. That's a very handsome costume you've got there."

"Thanks."

Vivian took a step closer, a vaguely conspiratorial movement. Her eyes were innocent and eager; he'd seen them like that before; it might have been a warning to him now, if he'd been in the mood for heeding warnings. She asked: "I wonder if you could possibly spare me a moment before dinner? My brother's busy, as usual, and there's a bit of business to be taken care of."

"Sure."

"Great. Also I must admit that I've been hoping to get a little time with you alone, to talk about magic. It intrigues me, it always has. But so far today has been just one interruption after another."

"Of course. Any time." Simon moved down the hall (lit only by torches now; daylight had altogether faded from the high, narrow windows) and followed Vivian into her room. Her suite, rather.

It was a bedroom-bathroom-dressing room that made Simon's guest quarters look small, and in a movie would certainly have required at least one maid to go with it. Simon wasn't sure how these matters were usually managed in reality, but at the moment at least no servant was in evidence.

"Drink? There's a little bar there, fix yourself something if you like. And excuse me just one moment while I change. Things are running just a touch behind schedule." Vivian, still towelling her dark curls, vanished into the adjoining room.

"I'll take a rain check on the drink if I may," Simon called after her. "Going on duty shortly, you know. Can I fix you anything?"

"Not just now." Vivian's voice remained unmuffled by intervening doors. Simon looking into the adjoining room from where he was could just see one end of a folding oriental screen; presumably she was dressing behind that. Her offstage voice added, "You'll find an envelope there on the table. I trust the contents are satisfactory?"

Propped against a black electric lamp with a white dragon shade that shed a glow almost as soft as candlelight, was a small white envelope. Simon took it up. The flap was folded in but not sealed. It was thickly packed with hundred-dollar bills; with a quick finger-riffle he counted fifteen of them.

He cleared his throat. "Miss Littlewood?"

"Call me Vivian, please." From the other room came a prolonged rustling noise, as of some lengthy garment going on or coming off. "What is it?"

"Well. It's just that there's more money here than I was promised."

"Pardon?" Now her voice was somewhat muffled. Women's clothing and the rituals that went with it were still mystifying to Simon, despite the number of women with whom he'd been on dressing and undressing terms in the past fifteen years.

He moved a step closer to the doorway between . rooms. From here he could see a mirror on the far wall of the inner room, a mirror so placed that if he were to advance one more step it might show him the area behind the screen. It required some effort to refrain from taking another step. He spoke a little louder: "I said, you're giving me too much money."

"Really?" Cloth-rustlings continued, but now Vivian's voice was clear again. "That's a complaint one seldom hears."

Simon was staring at the envelope. "Gregory told me that the inclusive fee was to be one thousand."

"Gregory is an old pinch-penny. That's not exactly the instruction he had from us." And now, in a swirl of red-gowned energy, Vivian emerged from behind her screen, to enter the room where Simon stood and pose before him curtseying, as if his approval might be all the mirror she needed.

He usually had no trouble finding compliments for lovely women. But right now he was speechless. There had been no time for her to give the black curls any treatment except to dry them, and yet the curls looked perfect. There was as usual no sign of makeup on Vivian's face; it was hard to imagine any that could have effected an improvement. And as for her dress . . .

Unconsciously Simon had expected her to emerge in something very low cut, probably in flaming red. His imagination had been uncannily accurate about the color, but that was all. Vivian's gown was cut very high and full, with long sleeves and a floor-length skirt. It was of some material of gossamer fineness, yet perfectly opaque, and almost perfectly concealing. Only with movement was there any hint of the shape of the body underneath, and then the hint was subtle. This dress was in one way the very opposite of the yellow bikini. And yet . . . it crossed Simon's mind that an appeal to the imagination can some-times be more powerful than blatant advertise-ment.

Vivian was smiling; his hearty if silent approval must have been obvious. She said: "There's a thousand dollars in there for you personally, and five hundred for expenses. I wasn't sure what helpers or equipment you might want to bring along, or what that kind of thing costs. And I was sure that you weren't going to stint to bring us the best show possible."

"Oh, I wouldn't stint, as you say. But my ex-penses haven't been anywhere near five hundred dollars."

"But of course I insist on your keeping the whole amount anyway. Perhaps it's wrong of me to even mention your expenses." Vivian stood, as poised as a model, with tanned hands clasped del-icately in front of her. "What I should be doing in-stead, shouldn't I, is to prepare myself to undergo a convincing experience. Suspending my disbe-lief. Getting into the frame of mind that says the powers you are going to demonstrate for us to-night are perfectly genuine."

Simon waved the envelope in the air once more, slapped it against his palm, and then slid it into one of the inner pockets of his doublet. He spread his hands. "As I will of course claim them to be, as part of my patter during the show. But . . . well, I hope I'm misinterpreting your tone of voice."

"Why?"

"Because it sounds to me like you're saying you actually believe I might have some genuine . . . psychic powers."

Vivian remained standing very still. The smile with which she regarded Simon was one of sol-emn joy. "And that's not an attitude you fre-quently encounter?"

"Fortunately, it isn't. But, unfortunately, I do

run into it sometimes. I wasn't really expecting to encounter it tonight."

"Why not?" Vivian was still cheerful.

It wasn't smart to argue with the boss. Simon sighed. This was important. "I was assuming that tonight's audience would all be educated people."

"Education is good armor against the supernatural."

"It should be."

"You would prefer your audiences very skeptical."

Simon started to frame a serious answer, then gave up with a brief laugh. Vivian was in the mood for teasing, not serious discussion. "All right. Touché. Of course when I'm working I want people to believe—only what I tell them to believe. But not seriously. Not *really* to believe that what I'm doing is against the laws of nature. There's no fun, there's no art left in my profession if that happens. I'm just a—swindler."

"Oh, Simon." And now that he was trying to be light, Vivian suddenly was serious. Her voice was very soft, her eyes luminous and huge. " 'Fun' doesn't sound to me like the right word. Is there no such thing as joy in serious art?"

"I'm serious about what I do. But I'm an entertainer."

"And a good one, too. Never mind." Lightness prevailed again. "We'll have plenty of time later to talk some more . . . may I ask you one question now about your act?"

"Shoot."

"When I saw your performance at the dinner theater, you had a lovely young lady with you as assistant; I gather she was still with you when Gregory met you at the university. I hope he made it clear that both of you were welcome here as weekend guests."

"He made it clear." Simon considered. "The young lady's name is Marge Hilbert. She hasn't yet, ah, materialized, but I hope we'll be seeing her later in the evening.''

"Ah, a touch of mystery! Excellent. I just hope the young lady doesn't get stuck on one of our back country roads, if she's planning a late arrival. They tend to flood, and some heavy thunderstorms have been predicted.''

Vivian's eyes were very dark and very deep. Simon had drowned somewhere in the deepness of them, about fifteen years ago. The idea struck him as a fresh poetical discovery; that it was a cliché did not occur to him for several seconds, and even when it did occur it did not matter. The idea was too fitting, in this house of candlelight and centuries.

Vivian had taken his arm by now, and now, somehow, they were out in the torchlit hall again. "Shall we go down?" she asked him. Stringed music, on instruments that sounded as old as the walls, drifted up to greet them as arm on costumed arm they descended the broad stone stair. The past was far more than a feeling now.

As dinner began, the subject of time, in several of the word's meanings, was much in Simon's thoughts. He felt reasonably sure that the hour was a little after eight. But if for some reason he had wanted to make sure of this, he no longer had the means of doing so. His wrist watch was upstairs with his twentieth-century clothing. As far as he could tell, no one around him was wearing a watch either.

Saul took his place at the head of a great wooden table, a piece of furniture that Simon could believe was really centuries old. Eleven places were set, with earthenware dishes of a simple, handpainted design. The comparatively modern silver was anachronistic but not jarring. Saul sat alone at the head; the place to his right was empty, and Vivian sat to the right of that, with Si-

mon next, between her and Emily Wallis. Round
the corner from Mrs. Willis at the table's foot was
fat Arnaud. There was a second empty setting at
Arnaud's right.

At Saul's left sat Sylvia, wearing a low-cut Re-
naissance bodice, about the kind of thing that Simon had expected Vivian to wear. Jim Wallis was
at Sylvia's left, and at his left was Hildy. Seated
next to Hildy was the one remaining guest that Simon had not yet met, a coffee-colored, youngish
man introduced only as Mr. Reagan. "No relation,
man," he said, grinning, as they shook hands. Simon grinned back somewhat uncertainly. Reagan
was dressed up as a cowled monk, and when he
sat down with a swirl of robe and beads; Simon
got the impression that something was wrong
about the oversized crucifix hanging at the end of
the belted rosary. Getting another look a little
later he saw that the cross was fastened on upside
down. An attempt at a joke, maybe, or possibly
just an accident. Anyway Simon felt odder things
about Reagan than just that. And about Arnaud
too if he stopped to try feeling for them.

Enough of that. He was supposed to use to atmosphere to support the act, not be overcome by
it himself.

"I'm expecting one more guest, a very important one," Vivian told Simon quietly, as conversation got under way. "Besides your young lady, I
mean. I'm not sure if my friend will be able to
make it or not." And her gaze turned for a moment to the empty setting and chair at her own
left, between her and Saul. The quick turn was
the closest thing to an involuntary movement that
Simon had ever seen Vivian make, today or any
other time, and it conveyed to him forcefully the
idea of the guest's great importance.

"Then I hope he does make it. Or she," said Simon, wondering. Then he was suddenly sure,
without quite knowing why, that the expected one

was a man. He now observed belatedly that there were on Vivian's hands no rings that might indicate marriage or engagement. So far at the party she'd had no obvious companion except himself. He supposed she was between lovers and/or husbands at the moment. That she might really be without some male attachment for any length of time had not really occured to Simon as a possibility, though so far he had not the least evidence that any such attachment existed.

He added: "Will your important guest be here before I start the show? I mean, do you want me to wait for him, or—"

"Oh no." Vivian was quite positive, and for some reason lightly amused at the thought. "No, you must assume that your audience is now complete."

"Okay," said Simon, and turned to answer Emily Wallis, who had just spoken to him from his other side. Old Emily looked a little lost, he thought; she probably hadn't found much in common with Arnaud, who sat at her right hand.

And where, mused Simon in the next interval without chat, where is the promised show business connection? Not that he had all that much hope for it, but he was curious. Could Reagan, if that was really the man's name, be in the business, some kind of an oddball performer? The more Simon thought about that name, the more he became convinced that it was false, only an evening's joke. What about Arnaud?

He looked more closely at the fat man, who, garbed elaborately enough to be a king, sat at the foot of the table beside the empty place reserved for Marge. Marge would be glad that dinner was over when she popped out. Arnaud's costume covered his neck where it was presumably still bandaged; he looked steadier and stronger now than he had a little while ago. His face was still somehow as familiar as it had seemed when Simon first saw it at poolside.

And in a moment Simon had it. Arnaud's face was that of the news photographs of Prince Something-or-other, the renegade from the royal family of the tiny middle eastern country. The exile, the one who had been called the latter-day Farouk. A year or so ago he'd been a star of the jet set and the sensational press, trailing denunciations and photographers behind him around the world. In this case Simon had no trouble understanding the use of an assumed name. If this was supposed to be his contact with the big time, forget it.

On the other side of the table Saul's bride Hildy was chatting comfortably with old Jim Wallis. Saul, meanwhile, did not give the impression of presiding at the head of the table, so much as sitting where he had been told good form required him to sit. He continued to look much as he had looked at poolside: mildly bothered, mildly bored. As if he'd really rather be off in his study or his office and taking care of business. Several times his sister caught his eye with what must have been a meaningful look, for each time Saul roused himself and with an evident effort brought himself back to the job of playing host.

The second time this happened, Saul revealed a hitherto hidden talent for entertaining discourse, by turning the conversation to medieval things and customs. He apparently knew much more on the subject than Simon would have thought. For example, how, if an effort had been made for real authenticity at the dinner table tonight, there would have been no forks, and each pair of people would have shared a plate and bowl between them.

Just as this juncture, Simon felt Vivian's hand touch his, as if she were demonstrating privately to him certain advantages of a shared dish. And for a simultaneous moment her knee brushed his thigh under the table. The lower contact had the subjective effect of a spark of electricity.

It wasn't the first time their legs had touched . . . but he wasn't going to think about that now. He was here on business. There was a performance to give in a few minutes.

Courses came and went. The service was extremely skillful, in what appeared to be a practiced compromise between antique ways and modern. The skillful servants came and went on swift and silent feet. None of the servants' faces that he saw now were familiar.

Had he ever paid the kid who'd rowed him twice across the river? He must have. But the trip back, like the paying, was still lost in utter blankness.

The medieval music, played offstage somewhere, had stopped about the time dinner began. Were these people now waiting on table the musicians also? There was a strangeness about them, as about so much else that Simon had seen today. They were all physically small, to begin with, which was a bit odd. And all costumed for the occasion, of course, but it was more than that. Simon thought they all looked . . . well, servile-looking, as perhaps real medieval servants ought to look. And it wasn't acting. Or, if it was, they were all wasting great and subtle talents on menial jobs.

The more Simon looked at the people serving dinner, the more he thought that all of them were quietly, desperately, and deeply frightened.

"I see you are observing the staff."

Simon almost jumped. "I didn't mean to."

"Of course you did. And there's no reason why you shouldn't. They're quite well trained, wouldn't you say? I've borrowed most of them for the occasion. Try a glass of this wine."

The staff was well-trained indeed, for the glass had appeared on the smooth wood of the table, right at Vivian's fingertips, without Simon being aware of any servant bringing it. He wished his own sleight-of-hand could match that.

"I think I've had enough," he objected uncertainly.

"But not of wine like this. This isn't going to hurt your concentration. If anything it'll enhance it. In fact, it's just what you need before a performance, to give you the clearest possible vision." Was Vivian laughing at him? No, she was happy but deadly serious. "If this wine should prove too much for you, if it doesn't actually help, or harms, the fault will be all mine."

The wine was ruby red in a small crystal glass. Simon picked up the glass and sipped. This, then, was the kind of thing the very rich could afford to enjoy. Simon, no expert, couldn't place the wine as to type, but it was quite simply the best he'd ever tasted.

The dinner went on, with conversation flourishing cheerfully around the table. Everyone had his or her own little wineglass, though the colors of the contents differed. Simon sipped his own glass again. He certainly wasn't taking enough to get drunk on, but all the same he was beginning to feel a little odd. Not drunk, no, not at all. His mind was very clear.

He leaned back in his chair and briefly closed his eyes, while behind his lids a parade of the day's strange visions came and went. Yes, anyone who saw the things that he had seen today really ought to seek help, medical assistance. The thought came, but there was no urgency in it, and very little worry. Actually, if he'd been having strange visions off and on for most of his life, they couldn't very well indicate a brain tumor or anything of that sort, now could they?

Oh yeah, he'd been bothered by visions for a long time, all right. At least since adolescence. Sometimes he'd had them right on stage. It was just that he'd taught himself to recognize them as outside of ordinary reality, and to ignore them once he knew what they were. So the reason he wasn't worried now about going for a medical exam was that he knew he really wasn't going to have one. He'd considered having checkups before, at various points in his life, for similar reasons, and in the end he'd never had them. Because he knew they were unnecessary.

Ruby wine before him. Even with eyes closed he could see the glass, how much was left in it, its exact position. The clearest possible vision: maybe Vivian for once had told the truth.

A couple of hours ago Marge had signalled him that all was well. And Marge was probably watching him right now from her vantage point behind the wall, ready to do the act. Was it really credible that Vivian didn't know about the passage? Anyway she was pretending she didn't know. Too late to worry about all that now. Now it was almost show time.

Eyes still closed, Simon reached for his wine again. His fingers, with perfect sureness of the position of the glass, closed on it gently. He drank all that was left.

Surrounding the great house were all the sounds of summer night in rural northern Illinois, sounds well-remembered by Simon from the visits that he'd made to the country in his childhood. He'd dwelt then not in the castle but in one of those huts . . . little houses . . . over there across the river. Those little dwellings were, if you could discount the water, almost at the castle's foot. Like the huts of peasants. Land-bound creatures who were once owned, body and soul, as part of some great lord's dominion. Maybe that was why, when Simon was growing up, he'd never thought of the castle in romantic or adventurous terms. It wasn't his castle, and he knew it. It sat on him.

Clear seeing indeed came from this wine. The

others round the table were sipping their own assigned vintages. The talk was lively but not noisy; through it Simon could hear, barely audible, the hiss of a torch burning in a wall sconce. From outside there drifted in the sounds of low, distant thunder, the night-noises of insects and an occasional bird. A very occasional something else, perhaps. All this was not particularly reassuring, even though it was familiar. Even as a child Simon had spent most of his life in the city, and the country had never quite lost its strangeness to him, though he'd come to know his way around it well enough . . .

A great howl, somewhere outside, made him open his eyes. Had that really come from a dog? But no one else appeared to have noticed it at all.

"A small coin for your thoughts," said Vivian beside him. She appeared totally relaxed now, the model of a relaxed and confident hostess, with nothing on her mind, for the moment, but chatting with one of her guests.

"Sorry. You'd never guess. I was trying to remember my grandmother." And it became true as he said it; that would have been the next turn his thoughts had taken. Today was for, among other things, probing his own past. His parents had died before he could start remembering them at all. That happened to a fair number of kids, sure, but . . . the more he looked back on his childhood, the more he realized its strangeness.

"You're right," said Vivian calmly. "I mightn't have guessed that. Was your grandmother fond of parties like this one?"

The question struck Simon as supremely irrelevant. The odd thing about this party, as it had turned out, was that all the disparate guests appeared to be enjoying each other's company more and more.

Simon sighed, really trying to remember Grandmother now. A firm, sallow face. Nondescript gray hair, small frame. She'd died when Simon was away at his one year of college. He couldn't remember having any important feelings when he heard the news. He chuckled. "I don't know what Grandma thought about parties. I don't know that the subject ever came up."

"Maybe she gave you birthday parties when you were little?" Vivian was probing, as if she were interested.

"I guess. I guess they were routine, as those things go." And now Simon noticed, without any particular surprise or concern, that Marge was not going to be the only exotically costumed entertainer of the evening. There were more acts than he'd been told about. Someone in an excellent, highly realistic toad costume was squatting in a corner, amid thick shadows at the far end of the great hall. Probably getting ready to do some kind of jester's number as soon as he was noticed. Well, Simon wasn't going to be the one to point him out to the other guests.

"I don't remember my parents at all, you see," he explained to Vivian. "And I don't know much about my aunt and uncle either, come to think of it, though I lived with them for a time." Now stop it, he warned himself, you're going to give your identity away.

But Vivian only said: "Oh?" politely, and turned to speak to someone across the table.

Now, how could she fail to identify him sooner or later as her own second cousin, or whatever the hell the exact relationship was supposed to be? The boy from across the river, the one she'd once let . . . but maybe she had as little inclination as he did to keep up with relatives—and old lovers. He hadn't been the first for her, that in hindsight was obvious enough.

Simon had never made any effort to keep up with relatives, or childhood friends. And now, whenever he tried to visualize any of the people

he'd grown up among, their images came to the
eye of memory with an odd, faded quality, like old
photographs.

Except, of course, for the image of Vivian herself.

Now, on the other side of the table, the smooth
rounds of Sylvia's inflated breasts were more
than half exposed to candlelight. Yet Simon had
scarcely noticed, because Vivian sat beside him.

The night-sounds of the surrounding countryside beseiged the castle, came in through the narrow windows piercing the enormous thickness of
the walls. The dinner went on. Thunder grumbled
louder. If rain now drummed on the roof that was
so far above, in here no one could hear it.

Someone had just spoken to Simon, and he
opened his eyes (when had he closed them again?)
to see Vivian regarding him. The expression on
her face was one of utter, almost worshipful intentness; and one of her little hands was raised in
the shadow of a gesture, that must have been
meant to warn some third person against
interfering.

Simon began to speak, in a loud, clear voice: "If
we must find something, an obstacle to be removed, then the place to look for it is—" And having got that far he stopped, listeing to himself in
utter amazement, with no idea at all of what he
had started to talk about.

Vivian was leaing forward, concentrating so intensely on Simon that for the moment she seemed
to have stopped breathing. The flicker of a reflected candle was the only motion in her eye. The
folds of the shapeless kirtle did not stir across her
breast.

"Yes," she urged Simon when he paused.
"Where is it?" Her voice was quietly solemn.

"I don't know yet." The answer felt like something forced from him. He had the feeling that it

was true. Then he blinked and with an effort recovered something like normal control over his
speech. "Sorry, what are we talking about?"

Vivian sank back a little in her chair. Disappointment had struck her but she was very brave
and still hopeful. "We're having a party, Simon.
We can just relax and talk as our thoughts lead
us."

Thunder crashed again, this time even closer
than before. A puff of wind somehow got into the
great hall, to make the flames of torch and candle
flicker. The dinner was almost completely cleared
away by now.

Wallis down the table imitated thunder, with a
laugh. The imitation was not too well done, but
everyone, except for the silent, frightened servi-
tors, seemed to enjoy the effort, and some ap-
plauded. "Good night for some ghost stories,"
Willis told the table in a loud voice.

It's showtime, folks, thought Simon. Vivian was
now looking at him keenly, as if to make sure that
he recognized his cue. As he could hardly fail to
do.

Simon drew a deep breath, and tried to will
himself back toward an ordinariness of mind and
of perception. It was not to be, not now. But still
he felt that he was ready to perform, more than
merely ready. His vision was very clear, his hands
supremely steady.

He got to his feet smiling, silently running
through the last items on his mental pre-per-
formance checklist. He noted that the toad-
costume was no longer to be seen. Good, no immediate competition. Establishing the proper atmosphere for magic? In tonight's special setting that
wasn't going to be a problem; quite the opposite,
in fact. He was going to have to be careful to keep
it light.

The servants, presumably at someone's signal,

had already ceased activities, and most of them were out of sight. All eyes were on Simon as he stood up.

"Ladies and gentlemen," he began, looking up and down the table. "Our charming hostess tells me that she's expecting one more guest—" Vivian was nodding, smiling lightly. "—and as on many occasions of this kind, when one more guest arrives, the hostess is somewhat upset to find that the balance of male and female guests has been upset." Simon was ready here, should Vivian show the slightest sign of social distress, for the quick switch: *But this is not one such occasion.* There was no distress signal from her, and Simon moved smoothly on: "So I'm going to find out first what sex our impending visitor is. Vivian hasn't told me. Am I right?"

She nodded encouragingly. "Right."

"So my intention now is to summon up one of the fay, the fairies of the old world, to help us find out some more about this potential visitor. Maybe even to help him—or her—to find the way to get here."

Vivian, enthralled, was nodding with great intentness. This wasn't at all the way that Simon had planned to open, but once he stood up the stunt had just seemed to suggest itself. He could see, as in a flash of inspiration, how it was going to work. If the visitor then failed to arrive, Simon would have a way out; if he did arrive, so much the better. Marge was quick-witted, she'd pick up quickly on what he had in mind, and work along. "Would you all join hands, please?" Simon asked. "It'll help the vibrations."

With merriment, and a minimum of delay, the folk at the table all brought themselves into a hand-joined circle. "Now I need just a little more room," said Simon, backing away a few steps from the table. He was standing now, as he had planned, with his back only a few feet from the fireplace, to which another log had recently been added. The blaze was up moderately, and he could feel the warmth of it, welcome in the damp coolness of the castle's interior night. He had another reason to be glad for having his back to the fire now; when he'd first stood up he'd started seeing faces, real faces, in the flames. He could do without that kind of a distraction just now.

Simon's audience would be seeing him backlighted now, but the firelight gave him a good look at their faces, and he noted with professional joy that they were receptive to whatever he was going to do. They watched him happily. They were already a little high on the wine, or whatever had been added to the wine. They were calmly certain that he was going to show them wonders. And indeed he was.

The object that he meant soon to throw secretly into the fire was already concealed in Simon's palm. Ten seconds, approximately, after he threw it in, the fire would flare up dramatically and in exotic colors. In that moment when everyone but Simon himself was looking at the fire, Marge would be able to slip through the dark hidden panel in the dim far wall of the great hall, and close the panel after her. She would have appeared in what looked like a doorless and windowless corner, inaccessible except by passing within a very few feet of the dinner table itself. Simon expected that the effect would be tremendous.

But before he threw anything into the fire, he would puzzle the audience first with Margie's voice, seemingly coming out of nowhere.

He made wild passes with hands and arms, he rumbled his made-up words of magic, "Sprite of the woods and waters, princess of the summer night! I summon thee to questioning!"

There was a quavery moan, from . . . somewhere. Oh, beautiful, Marge. Simon called out peremptorily: "Are you there? Answer me clearly, please!"

"Simon . . . I'm here." It was a very eerie voice, from very far away, from everywhere and nowhere. For a moment it even raised the hair on the back of Simon's own neck.

Vivian watched, calm but utterly intent. The rest of the people at the table marveled, more or less quietly.

Simon called softly: "The guest that our hostess is expecting. Can you see him or her from where you are?"

And the disembodied voice: "Yes, Simon. Yes."

"A man or a woman?"

"A man." Margie from her secret observation place had perhaps learned something; otherwise there would have been no need for her to be so positive.

"Is he going to be able to join us here tonight?"

"He will try."

Vivian did not take her eyes from Simon. The rest of the audience looked everywhere, under the table, up among the distant rafters, for the source of the voice. Simon heard someone mutter about ventriloquism.

"Will he be here soon, do you think?"

"Either he'll be at the castle very soon . . . I think he will . . . tonight or tomorrow . . . or . . . if not soon, then never . . ."

"And are you going to join us too?"

"I'll try . . . Simon." There followed a soft, heartrending cry, from what sounded like an enormous distance. Oh beautiful, Marge! Beautiful!

Simon faced the table. "Our sprite is going to try to join us. It will help if we all concentrate intensely. All of us, even the old gentleman up there on the wall. I've been watching him. Now if I were to tell you that I've seen the eyes of that portrait move, you'd tell me that I've been seeing too many horror movies."

And in beautiful obedience to suggestion, all eyes, even Vivian's, swung together to regard the portrait high on the dim wall above Margie's secret door. And in the second of time he had thus obtained for invisible action, Simon's wrist flicked gently, tossing the object already in his hand behind him at the fire.

He and Marge now had about ten seconds to wait, if all went well. If it didn't, if his toss had missed the actual flames, then he'd have to distract the audience once more, and try again. But so far tonight everything was going so smoothly and so well that Simon was absolutely sure he hadn't missed.

And now while the count (five) was going on in his head (four), he kept the patter going (three): "To bring our guest among us, we call upon the powers ruling space and time, the strength of Astarte and Apollo, the oaths of Falerin—"

Where had that last name come from? There was no time to wonder now, for behind Simon the fire *whooshed* up most satisfactorily, smothering his words. The faces round the table all swiveled right to left, tennis-watchers startled bright green in the eerie new glow of a conjurer's chemistry set. Saul, under the surface of his mild surprise, still looked bored and worried; the man who called himself Reagan looked almost childlike in the openness of his wonder. Only Vivian's gaze did not turn all the way to the fire, but came to rest again on Simon himself.

This was the second of time in which Marge should be halfway through the panel. Simon of course was not looking toward the panel now, but it should be now, this very second—

It struck like some monstrous aftershock from the puny stage-explosion in the fireplace. Ten thousand times as loud, it came with a deep crack sounding through the timbers overhead, and a si-

multaneous flat concussion of the stone floor, as
if the castle's foundation of bedrock had been
struck by some earthgod's hammer from below.
All Simon's sureness of body and mind was in an
instant brushed away. From a corner of his eye he
saw one, two, three of the fear-struck dinner servants vanish, go out like blasted candle-flames. Simon staggered on the vibrating floor and almost
fell. Voices round the table, Vivian's among them,
were raised in fear and incomprehension. And
now a brightness, a fishbelly glare the equal of
midday, struck in upon them all from the place
where the secret panel had been sealed into the
wall.

In the first instant of shock, that secret door
had been burst from its hidden hinges. It spun
now toward Simon as if hurled from some giant's
hand, and he watched it coming with the sense
that everything in the world around him had been
shifted to slow motion. There was a blast of wind,
bearing a strange smell. Trying to dodge the flying door, his own body seemed capable only of
very slow movement, feet stepping awkwardly
and off balance.

The door missed him, somehow. It missed
everyone, to crash with splintering force against a
distant wall.

Vivian, breaking the hand-held circle, was on
her feet, her arms spread wide, her head thrown
back in what appeared to be a paroxysm of triumph. She looked past Simon, into the cold fur-
nace of light beyond the once-secret doorway.
Then she screamed a name.

And now, from that glaring, howling world beyond the blown-in door, someone was trying to
enter the great hall, someone very different indeed from Marge Hilbert. It was a man, tall and
powerful, handsome and richly robed. The young
and evil king of Simon's afternoon dream. He was

about to burst in and claim them all.

And Hildy was screaming, on and on, in utter terror.

FIFTEEN

When the soldiers who held Talisman in charge at last received the necessary signal from inside the building, and motioned for him to go in alone, he found only four people waiting for him inside. The building was a great hall, built of timber and thatch, and no bigger than some of the bedroom suites would doubtless be in the reconstructed castle on the Sauk. Behind a long trestle table, three men and a woman sat perched upon tall stools, the nearest thing to thrones, probably, that could be found in the whole island. By now it was deep night. A fire in the clay hearth smoked the air, and there were a pair of torches. Stray gleams of light caught on the slender gold or silver circlets worn on the heads of all the four.

No one spoke immediately. From the invading army camped about this building on all sides there drifted in some sentry's call.

Comorr the King—*a* king, rather, within a hundred miles of here you might find a dozen men calling themselves king of this or that—Comorr, Breton invader of what would one day be England, Comorr, mass murderer, bluebeard, sat watery-eyed and ineffectual-looking upon the highest stool, his by reason of claimed royal rank. He held a piece of fruit, on which he chewed with difficulty, as if his teeth were bad.

At the right hand of Comorr there perched in fine robes the foul magician Falerin. In his countenance he was as handsome as a god, and there hung about him the sense of devilish evil. At the left of Comorr there sat Medrat, the bastard son of Artos. Medraut was short and burly, wearing fine chain mail, and though he was very young his eyes were a haggard pale blue, a traitor's haunted eyes.

At the other end of the row, at the right hand of the handsome magician Falerin, there perched the woman who was his aide in magic.

As soon as talk began, it was apparent that there would be a language difficulty. The conversation proceeded only slowly back and forth, with many repetitions and rephrasings on both sides. Comorr for the most part only waited, listening, watching with watery eyes, gumming the fruit, content to let those who could apply a touch of magic to the translation do the talking. Medraut for the most part waited too, more dully.

Talisman began by bowing to them all. "My Lords Comorr, Falerin, Medraut. My Lady—?"

Her red lips parted, "Nimue."

Thus Talisman addressed them all: "My lords and lady, I do not know that I am here at any summoning of yours; and yet for all I know it may be so. I do know that there is enmity between myself and a certain old man who is a friend of Artos; and that that old man has cursed me, that I must wander far from my proper land."

There was a shade of alarm in the lovely dark eyes of the Lady Nimue. "He launches curses still? I thought that I had well disabled him."

Talisman looked at her. For the barest instant the look was purely sexual. "And so you have, my lady. The launching of this curse was many years—away in time." He did not say in which direction.

Falerin smiled at him; the teeth of Apollo. "You are obviously of high birth, Sir Talisman, wherever you are from. Let us get down to cases. What can you do for us? And what rewards do you expect in return? While some fighting remains to be done, our battle against Artos is virtually won, now that old Ambrosius is, as you say, well disabled."

Medraut roused himself from silence with a cough, and leaned forward to point at Talisman with a thick forefinger. "You are———," he said, concluding with a word that Talisman did not know. But from the way they were all looking at him now he knew it meant that in some way he was not human.

"As much human as any of you, dishonorable scum," he replied, smiling, in modern English that no one would understand. "Nay, more." And then he bent and took up the dead deer from where the reporting huntsmen must have left it on the floor. It was as heavy as a child nearly grown, and Talisman lifted it casually in one hand, as a man might hold a mutton chop. Before the four pairs of watching eyes he bit surely into the great blood vessels of the deer's neck, neatly piercing hair and hide with his very adaptable teeth. He was hungry, and the deer's blood would start to spoil if it were left much longer in the body. Even now the blood was not as good as it would have been when the heart still pumped; but it would do. The good taste was reassuring; half a doubt had been raised in his mind, about chilled emerald wine.

The eyes of Medraut widened to see this feeding; he'd have a tale to tell his fellow swordsmen, over wine. To the watery eyes of Comorr, it appeared that all marvels were about equally uninteresting. The eyes of Falerin—they had seen it all already, seen everything at some time in a long past; he was obviously much older than his face would indicate, his youth and beauty maintained by means of magic.

The eyes of Nimue ignored Talisman's peculiarities, and subtly promised much. They said that perhaps nothing would be too good for Talisman if he were her close friend and ally. But he was too old and experienced by far for such a casual seduction to tempt him seriously against his will; even so he knew a pang of regret on deciding that it would not be wise to accept the challenge.

In a minute Talisman had finished taking nourishment, and tossed the drained meat casually upon the table. "This share in your dinner for tonight is the first part of the reward I claim. As for the rest—" Oh, it was impossible to try to be witty and subtle, when everything had to be repeated, and at best he and his audience could barely understand each other. "—to see my enemies suffer. That will be enough."

Falerin leaned forward. "But what can you do for us, to earn your gorge of blood?"

Talisman had learned here all that he needed or expected to learn. "I go this very night to scout the camp of Artos. Your men tell me that it lies within two hours' walk."

Medraut: "And if we do not release you, to go anywhere?"

"Consult with your wizard colleage here, Sir Swordsman. He might not be able to prevent my departure from this camp before dawn. Or, if he could, he might see why the effort would be unwise."

"You know then," asked Medraut, "in which camp my father is?"

"I can discover that."

"I know," said Nimue. "Beside my lake. I am, I was, the Lady of the Lake."

SIXTEEN

Up on the third floor of central headquarters on South State they had a few special cells known informally as VIPs, along with a couple of specially equipped interrogation rooms nearby. The man called Feathers was already lodged in one of the special cells before Joe Keogh got to see him for the first time. Some patrolmen indoctrinated by Charley Snider had been alert to the fact that the old man was wanted for serious questioning in the Carados case, and had picked him up almost as soon as he'd got back to the Street.

He hadn't been hard to spot.

The patrolmen had picked up Feathers at about eight-thirty in the evening, and it was only a little after nine when Joe arrived at headquarters with Charley Snider. Fortunately the two of them had been together, working not far away, when the word about Feathers reached them.

The old man, still wearing the gaily decorated robe in which he'd come back from somewhere to

Skid Row, was sitting in one of the interrogation room's comfortable chairs, staring at nothing, when the two police lieutenants arrived. There were two or three other chairs in the room, and a sort of desk, and some other more special equipment, most of it not visible.

"Yo, Feathers," said Charley Snider easily. The instant he entered the room he slowed down enormously from the rush he'd been in to reach it. "Looks like somebody's been givin' you a hard time the past few days."

Actually, thought Joe Keogh, closing the door behind them, the old man waiting to be questioned by them looked quite hale; apart from his bizarre garment he looked very good indeed for a supposed Skid Row bum.

The gray blue eyes, wary and weary, looked up at both detectives. "I'm through with that name," the old man told them in a raspy voice.

This is no long-term wino, Joe thought to himself again. This old man was too healthy. If the overall physical description were not so completely different, he could more readily have believed—from something about the eyes—that this was Carados himself.

In one wall was a small mirror, actually a one-way glass through which an observer in the next room could watch this one; and Joe shifted his position by a step, enough to catch the old man's reflection clearly in the glass. That, as he understood the matter, was a simple and foolproof test for one exotic oddity at least, one which he was not going to try to discuss with Charley Snider. The old man was not a vampire.

Charley meanwhile had seated himself casually on one corner of the desk. "Okay," he said cheerfully to their prospective witness. "What name would you like?"

An expression flickered across the old man's face, come and gone again in a moment; Joe had seen something like it on the faces of prisoners who were being offered some kind of a deal that they knew was really too good to be true.

In this case the real wish was not to be attained. "Hawk will do," the old man said, in a voice of compromise.

"Hawk. Okay, then, Hawk. *Mr.* Hawk, is it?"

A shrug.

"Any complaints about the way you been treated here?"

"Just about the fact of being picked up. Since you wanna know. You guys didn't have any reason at all to pick me up."

"For your own good, Mr. Hawk. Your protection."

"Huh."

"And then, you see, that garment you have on there, it sort of suggested to the patrolmen that maybe something a bit unusual was going on. I'd even be inclined to think that way myself."

"Huh. I wasn't drunk," the man who used to call himself Feathers insisted. "I'm not drunk now. You charging me with that?"

Charley appeared to take a careful, judgmental look at the old man's condition. "You're talking sensibly so far. Maybe you ain't drunk. I don't s'pose you're gay, either, but that is quite a fancy getup. Want to tell me where you got it?"

The ancient one flushed faintly. "I didn't steal it."

"Didn't say you did."

"A man wants to be decent, to try to keep from gettin' busted, well, he's gotta wear something."

Charley's large brown hand was now cupping a photograph of Carados. One of Charley's favorite tools in questioning was the sharp change of subject. "Seen this man recently?"

Hawk appeared to be grateful for the sharp change. He gave the picture some deliberate thought. When he looked up from it he was obviously making some mental calculation, one in which fear did not appear to have a value; as if, thought Joe, this business of being in jail were only a kind of game, that tomorrow would be over with and forgotten.

"Yeah," said Hawk at last, surprising both policemen by cooperating at once like the prince of solid citizens. He nodded deliberately. "That looks a lot like the guy who picked me up on the street a couple days ago. I'm pretty sure it's him."

"Pretty sure? Or sure?"

"It's him."

Joe and Charley exchanged a glance. "Where is he now?" There was a controlled tightness in Charley's voice.

When Hawk shook his head, conveying ignorance, Joe put in: "Where and when did you see him last?"

"I'm not clear on what day it was." Hawk pulled at his own beard, as if the length and feel of it were a matter of surprise and some distaste. "This's what?"

"Friday night."

Hawk shook his head again; the blur of time in the eye of his memory was all too visible. "Anyway, I know where." He named a street intersection deep in the inner city. "He picked me up there, took me into a tavern a block away. It was late in the afternoon. Then he fed me something in a drink and I passed out."

"And where were you when you woke up?"

Hawk looked at them both, not the way a street bum ought to be looking at detectives. "Next thing I can tell you I was back on the street, and your man was busting me for being in drag, or whatever. Ask him what for. And now I'm here."

Charley was tapping the photograph with one big finger. "This man's name is Carados. That mean anything to you?"

"Name? I don't care anything about his name."

"You say he picked you up. Why'd he do that? What did he want?"

"Said he wanted to buy me a drink. I said sure. We had a drink and I passed out, but not just drunk. He drugged me, like I said."

Charley was silent for a moment, trying to choose which way to go next. It had to be as obvious to him as it was to Joe that this was not your ordinary wino. But if Hawk wanted to play that part, they would go along with him, for a while at least.

Joe chimed in: "You're looking good, Mr. Hawk. Like maybe you've been off the booze, resting up for a couple of days?"

The blue-gray eyes considered him fearlessly. "Like I said, I can't really remember anything since I passed out in that tavern."

"But you could try to remember something. How about this—when you woke up, how were you dressed?"

Charley flicked the photo. "You don't want to do this man any favors, do you? After the way he treated you?"

Hawk was thinking again. They let him take his time. At last Hawk said: "All right, I'll give it to you for what it's worth. The way I remember it, I woke up in a castle."

"Castle," repeated Charley. Under the circumstances the flatness in his voice had to be taken as courtesy.

Joe Keogh's reaction was different, fortified as he was with the memory of a certain phone conversation. He took a long shot now. "See any swords in that castle, Mr. Hawk?"

The old man flared at Joe silently; he'd hit home, though in exactly what way Joe wasn't sure.

"Whadda you mean by that?" Hawk demanded

at last.

"Just wondering. Swords, castles, they go together. Describe the place for us."

"Don't think I can," the witness muttered sullenly. "About all I remember is the inside of some
stone walls."

"You mean," said Charley, "you were in a big
house with stone walls when you woke up?"

"All right, yeah, that's what I said, a big house.
Listen, you guys, can you get me some clothes besides this?"

"We're gonna take care of that right away. Did
you see Carados in this house? The man who
picked you up?"

"It's kinda embarrassing, sitting here this
way."

Joe stuck his head out into the corridor and
called. Presently he came back in and shut the
door again. "Some clothes are on the way," he
said. "Just jail issue for now, okay? We'll work
out something else later."

"Okay."

"Now tell us," said Charley, "some more about
Carados."

Somehow he never did, although the interrogation session went on for about an hour. There
were a lot more sessions planned, Hawk was sure,
but meanwhile he was at least dressed in some ac-
ceptable clothes again. There had been a time,
long ago, when he would have thought nothing of
wearing a gaily decorated robe as his sole garment; one adapted to the times one lived in. Unfortunately, in periods of rapid change, one sometimes found one's learned attitudes lagging by a
few decades.

The face of the little girl who'd kindly given him
the absurd robe stuck uncomfortably in his memory, even now after the garment itself was gone.
She wasn't his responsibility, of course. He hadn't
meant her any harm. He couldn't afford to get in-

volved with her situation.

So he got through the first session of questioning, playing dumb, then acting weaker and more tired than he felt. It wasn't that he'd made a decision to tell the police nothing more of substance about Nimue and her friends. The decision had somehow been made for him. He *couldn't* tell them anything more, certainly not that Nimue was up to something involving murder, because . . .

He had got as far as identifying Carados, his kidnapper, for the police. Beyond that point he could not go, because then Nimue would start to become involved, and . . . and that was not something Hawk could do.

In a little while, he thought, alone in his comfortable little cell again, the cops would slacken their vigilance, give him a chance to depart the slammer without being too spectacular about it. Of course as soon as they realized he was gone they'd be out looking for him on the street again. Well, if he had to move on to some other town, okay, he'd move. Sooner or later they'd catch up with their important murderer, or else move on to some other problem, and then no one would want to bother much about Hawk. But catching Carados for them wasn't Hawk's job. That coffee-colored one was crazy, badly and sickly crazy, and he was going to have a short life and a miserable one no matter what. No special powers were needed to see that. Hawk wasn't going to go out of his way for revenge, just to give that crazy one more trouble.

If he were to go looking for revenge on anyone, it would be that damned insulting vampire. Hawk's temple was still a little sore. Thinking about the vampire. Hawk started to get angry again. Then he chuckled, imagining the hard time the vampire would have trying to get back to the twentieth century, if he got past Nimue and her bunch back in the sixth.

Nimue.

There was a cop posted about two steps from Hawk's cell door. Hawk was going to wait a while before he decided how to go about trying to get out. To sit in jail for a little while wasn't really suffering, not in a cell like this one anyway, not in comparison to the kind of life to which he was trying to return.

He paused in his thoughts to ponder that point. If life on the Street was really so bloody awful, as it undoubtedly was, then why was he . . . why did he . . . ?

Just because.

Hawk's thoughts wavered, sought a new tack. The coffee-colored madman's face came again before his imagination. He returned to the idea that if the cops had Carados, they wouldn't care any longer about Hawk. He'd be free to fade away.

The cop two paces from his cell door was sitting in a schoolroom chair, one of those things with one broad flat arm, for doing paperwork. He was working away at some kind of record or report, and meanwhile keeping an eye on the few occupied VIP cells. Hawk wasn't left unobserved for more than a minute at a stretch. It would just be too damn spectacular, it would draw too much attention to him, if he simply vanished now. Sooner or later, though, this close surveillance was going to flag.

Then, if he knew where Carados was . . .

Hawk cleared his throat, and made himself as comfortable as possible sitting on the edge of the jail cot. These cells were sure a great improvement over the drunk tanks downstairs.

Now . . .

His vision went farseeing, through the concrete wall that was not much more than an arm's length in front of him as he sat on the cot. He stared for a little while into the mists that he saw beyond the wall, then shook his head in puzzlement. He was having a hard time locating Carados. Was that because Nimue needed Carados in her plans?

Hawk really didn't want to think about Nimue. Dark and extremely ugly things were going on round her, as usual. Meanwhile there was a young woman whose welfare somewhat concerned him. He'd find her, and also take another look at the insulting vampire. It was good to be doing *something* again, at last, after all the centuries.

The centuries of what? Just what *had* he been doing for the past thousand years? Nothing, it seemed, but rolling in an alcoholic fog from one gutter to another. He didn't want to think about it.

He started over, by rubbing one horny thumbnail reasonably clean on the sleeve of his new blue jail shirt. Then he oiled the nail as shiny as possible by rubbing it on the side of his nose. Whispering a few words, Hawk settled down to stare into the dull mirror thus provided.

"Oh," he added a moment later under his breath. "There you are." He tried to chuckle wickedly at first at the girl's predicament, when he saw where the backblast of his own broken transportation spell had tossed her up. But instead of chuckling he moaned inwardly, in sympathy. Then he cursed inwardly, at himself, knowing himself, knowing how even an unconscious appeal from an attractive young woman could twist him from his purposes, force him into doing madly dangerous things.

And then Hawk drew breath with a gasp. Of course he ought to know, even without farseeing, where this particular girl was in the sixth century. Because he'd once met her there . . . oh God.

It was all the vampire's fault, the goddam bloodsucker, the—but later he'd worry about the vampire.

He gazed into his thumbnail at the young girl's face. "Thanks for giving me the nice robe, pretty one," he breathed, wheezing. "Now I have a little something for you in return. Send you something that you'll find useful, where you are. That's about all I can do for the moment. Later maybe I can do more. Now here it comes."

Hawk spoke the words of sending, and watched with satisfaction. Then he turned from the past and looked into the future, just a little. He marveled. And felt a deep and fundamental chill. The laws of magic were inexorable. It wasn't only the girl's life that was in jeopardy. It was his own as well.

SEVENTEEN

On her first night in the past, Marge tossed and turned on her straw pallet, and had bad dreams. Simon was calling her, from some vast distance, and she had to go back to him at once, but her arms and legs were paralyzed and it was impossible to move.

"Are you there, Marge? Marge, answer me clearly please."

She couldn't see Simon but his voice was coming to her clearly, drifting from beyond massive dream-walls and squat towers of timber and earth and stone. And there were also tall stone castle walls, and wooden screens of maze-like fretwork.

"Simon, I'm here, I'm here." Now Marge was able to stand, but the ground was very slippery and slid out from under her feet whenever she tried to move, and if she fell it would mean her total and eternal ruin. She had never wanted anything more than she now wanted to get back to Simon, and yet she knew that was impossible.

His voice still drifted to her over parapets, under a starless sky. "Marge, I want to know about the guest that our hostess is expecting here. Can you see him from where you are?"

Marge was about to call back *no*, when in dream fashion the question arranged its own answer. "Yes, Simon, yes," Marge called instead. A presence was standing near Marge now, a man. He was dressed somewhat in the manner of the man of the village who had taken her in, only his clothes were richer than any of theirs. He was at least a head taller than the short leader who had questioned Marge. She could not really see the tall man's eyes. His lightly bearded face was very handsome, but Marge could feel a sickness radiating from it like a glow of ugly light. The man moved past her, starting up the same slippery slope on which she struggled for a foothold. His hands were raised before him, holding things that she knew were magically powerful, though she could not see them clearly. He totally ignored Marge as he passed her.

Simon's next question came distantly: "Is it a man or a woman?"

Whether it was a man or a devil was the only real question. Sickness and hatred played from it like the beam of a dark searchlight. But Marge had no way to cry a warning. It was as if she and Simon were performing a version of their mentalist act, but one in which the warning codes had been proscribed. She had no power of speech except to answer questions truthfully. "It's a man," her voice said carefully.

Simon's voice drifted to her again, in tones of careless ignorance. "Is the guest going to be able to join us here tonight?"

Marge uttered a silent, agonized prayer that he could not. And the handsome man, as if he were able to read thoughts—or hear prayers—turned his face to her and now she could see his eyes.

They rested on her only for a moment, but inside
her skull a silent scream went up. Her voice, independent of her control, called calmly back to Simon: "He will try."

"When will he be here, do you think?"

The slippery slope was not high. But near the
top, opposition waited for the would-be guest. Out
of a small mound, made of something Marge
could not see clearly, there rose the broad,
straight blade of a shining sword, topped by a
cross-like ornate hilt. Light pulsed from the
sword, and the jewels of its handle winked like
small glowing eyes. The radiance of it forced back
the man who tried to climb.

Marge answered Simon: "Either he'll be at the
castle very soon . . . I think he will . . . tonight or
tomorrow . . . or . . . he may never get there."

"And are you going to join us too?" Simon
sounded so cheerful, so totally ignorant, that
Marge felt her heart was going to break. She had
opened her mouth to try once more to scream a
warning in anger and despair, when a great
soundless explosion tore the world of the nightmare to bits. She knew that this time the radiance
of the Sword had repelled the man who tried to
climb the hill of time, and she awoke sobbing with
the relief that knowledge brought.

Marge did not wake in her own bed, or even in
her own world, but for the moment even being in
an alien world did not matter. The part of the
world she found herself in was bearable and live-
able; it was not yet a part of *his* domain.

She was still in the building that housed the
white-gowned women. On the second pallet in her
small chamber her companion was still sound
asleep. The nightworld around them was one of
utter peace. Through the single window, too narrow for a man to enter, the moon looked in,
nearly full and pale as cream. The small slice of
the night sky that Marge could see was alive with

stars.

But she had only the briefest glance to spare for them. On the moonlit grass a few paces outside the window, a man was standing silently. Marge recognized Talisman with relief. What she had seen of him before suggested strange things indeed, but he still represented a link to her own world.

Somewhere nearby a dog wined in its sleep, dreaming its own terrors. And Talisman, looking up and in at Marge, conveyed with an imperious motion of his hand that he wanted to be invited in.

Marge glanced at her roommate, who was snoring faintly, then leaned forward close to the unglazed window. "Come in, if you can," she whispered cautiously out into the moonlight. "But this window's too small and I don't see—"

The figure standing on the grass vanished before her eyes. She had the sensation of a trailing garment brushing lightly across her eyes and forehead. As she turned her head in reaction to this she muffled a little cry. Talisman was standing in the middle of the small room, between the two straw beds.

He bent down at once, to touch with two gentle fingers the forehead of the sleeper at Marge's side. To Marge he said quietly: "She will not awaken now, if we are reasonably careful. What have you discovered?"

"Discovered?"

Talisman hissed impatiently. "I am making allowances for the shock you have experienced. But it would not do for you to abandon your brain to permanent paralysis. Our situation requires that we cooperate, whenever we are able. I have made an enemy of a deranged wizard of immense power. And your circumstance while not exactly similar, is near enough. On top of that, our real enemies will sooner or later notice us; or at least begin to take us seriously."

"Our real enemies?" Talisman *sounded* as if he were reasoning sanely, at least if you didn't pay too much attention to what he was actually saying. And it gave Marge's sanity a welcome boost, just to hear another human being calmly addressing her in English. Talisman intended to cooperate with her, and whatever else he might be, he was powerful. She was no longer alone.

He nodded. "I have stood before them, within the hour, not many miles from this village. Comorr the Cursed, Medraut—and the wizard Falerin, the one most dangerous to us. I was able to speak a few words that they could understand, and I understood more than I allowed to show of what they said among themselves." His eyes were fixed on Marge. "There is a woman there who . . . well, that is important, but no need to go into it now. I have come here to tell you that these evil folk are planning a military attack on this village. They hope to catch a certain leader here, away from the bulk of his army; with him out of their way, their conquest of the whole island will be easy, or so they think."

"The island?" Now stop echoing, Marge told herself fiercely; it sounds so dumb.

Talisman informed her softly: "We are in what is called, in our own time, Britain. I thought you had grasped that much at least."

"I knew I'd landed in . . . someplace different. I can't understand the language of these people at all, and they don't speak mine, so we just haven't been able to communicate. Look, we're a long time in the past, aren't we? From where we ought to be?"

Talisman nodded gravely.

"I thought so." Marge quickly outlined what had happened to her since her arrival, then added her speculations on the white-garbed women, and on the building they were in. "So what do we do

now? I have no intention of spending the rest of
my life here."

"My own sentiments exactly; I rejoice that we
are in agreement. Our situation as I see it is dangerous indeed, but far from hopeless. These matters of magic have their own logic, you understand, even as dreams do. When we have grasped
the logic of the situation, we ought to be able to
do something to help ourselves."

"Great."

He nodded briskly. "You cried out in your sleep
just now, before you woke. You were dreaming?"

"Yes."

"Describe your dream, please. It could be of
great importance."

Marge told him of the slippery hill, and of the
voice of Simon that had drifted to her from somewhere beyond it. She described as well as she
could the evil man, and his losing conflict with
the Sword.

Talisman listened carefully, nodding. "The hill
is of course, among other things, an obvious pun
on your friend's name. But the evil young man, as
you call him—I wish you could show me a photograph. Never mind, I think I know him anyway.
The Sword thwarts him, do you see. Perhaps the
Sword is also the key to our passage home."

"God, if you can think of some way to get us
home . . ." Marge leaned forward, putting her
hand on Talisman's arm; beneath his sleeve it felt
as hard as wood. "Speaking of swords, yesterday
the men here were forging something. At least
there was a lot of hammering on metal, just after
I arrived."

"Ah." Talisman's eyes were fixed on her in spec-
ulation, and what she hoped was new hope. "If
the Sword itself were forged here yesterday, that
would provide the connection, the logic of magic
that we need to find. If—" He broke off suddenly,

with his head cocked listening. His raised hand held Marge silent.

She listened as hard as she could. In a few seconds the still night air brought her the sound of hurried hoofbeats, as of a single animal running at a fast pace.

The sound grew closer rapidly. There was a new uproar among the village dogs. Presently an exhausted horse with a youth riding bareback came cantering up to halt among the buildings.

"Hello the village! Men of Artos!" the youth cried out. In Marge's state of mixed excitement and weariness it took her a few seconds to realize, with mixed feelings, that she could understand him perfectly, though he was speaking in the same tongue that she had listened to uncomprehendingly for hours before she fell asleep.

Armed men were running out of huts and houses to confront the messenger, demanding to know his name. Talisman, frowning, started to say something, but it was now Marge's turn to gesture him to silence. "Wait," she ordered. "Let me listen. I can understand them now."

For the first time she saw Talisman truly surprised. "You can? What do they say?"

"The messenger says there is an enemy army advancing—he gives names, the same ones you mentioned, Comorr, Falerin, Medraut the Traitor. Everyone here in the village is going to have to pack up and run right now, without waiting for morning. To something called the Strong Fort, wherever that is."

EIGHTEEN

In the ears of Simon Hill that last scream of
Hildy's seemed to go on echoing endlessly. The
echoes escaped the castle, they fled down corri-
dors outside of time, passages that he had not
known existed. The blast that provoked the
scream drove Simon to his knees, his face averted
from the small, broken little doorway that had
once been secret, through which the sickly light
now poured into the great hall. At last that pale
glare abated. And at last the inward echoes of that
scream faded to a tolerable level.

Then Simon could raise his eyes. When his gaze
fell on the fireplace he saw again the faces in the
flames. The faces were even more distorted now,
as if they writhed in pain.

So for him there was to be no easy escape, no
calm pretense that magic did not exist. He'd tried
that for most of his life, and it wasn't going to
work. In a way, he was almost glad.

He made himself look back toward the doorway

that had once led to a secret passage. The bizarre light that had come pouring out of it was fading steadily, was now almost gone. The wind that had seemed to blow through it from another world had dwindled to a faint draft, was hardly more than imaginary now.

Marge was in there, somewhere. At least she had been there. He, Simon, had got her into this, pretending to himself that no real danger existed here at the Castle. Feeling responsible, he rose unsteadily to his feet and moved toward the little doorway, a jagged opening now with stones and wood torn from its edge. He glanced in passing at the group still gathered round the dinner table, a few steps to his right. Some were still seated, looking stunned, some now stood beside their chairs. Voices rose in a moaning jumble. Someone was muttering something about lightning. And now Vivian's voice was speaking, plainly, loudly, reasonably, enforcing calm. But a few moments ago she had been screaming too, Simon was sure of it. Just before Hildy's outburst, Vivian had screamed in hopeless agony, something that might have been a name. A word that sounded like *Falerin.*

Simon faced forward again, toward the shattered wall. What was that howling that he could hear now, coming from outside the castle? Wolves, in the 1980s, in Illinois?

Reaching the blasted doorway, Simon supported himself in it numbly, with a hand on either side gripping the edges of the broken wooden screen. It sank in on him now that the door had been literally blown away, as if by a charge of high explosive. Traces of strange odors reached his nostrils. He put his head forward, into the passage.

When he looked down the narrow, stone-walled passage to his left, what little the darkness let him see appeared normal. But to his right, the darkness and the light were both different. There was brightness, somewhere in that direction, but the source of light, whatever it was, was far off now and still receding. A faint but savage howling persisted, as of a remote wind. Simon wondered, with a sudden chill, if it could be a man's voice that made that noise, if a human voice could be distorted so by superhuman agony and hatred.

Even as Simon watched and listened, the light and the sound continued to recede. There was no clue in the passage of Marge, or indeed, except for the distant howling, of any living thing.

A hand fell on Simon's shoulder, startling him. From the touch there flowed into his body a trickle of some force that felt like electricity. He turned, knowing he would see Vivian. Her eyes looked into his.

"The roof may have been struck by lightning," she said quietly. Her tone shared wih him the knowledge of how widely that statement missed being a real explanation. "So I'm going up to take a look. I wish you'd come along."

"Sure," said Simon automatically. He paused to look around the great hall, where the flames of torch and candle were once more burning peacefully upright. The vanished servants had not reappeared.

The Wallises, he standing behind his wife's chair, were clutching at each other's hands in shock. Emily Wallis' face was white and she looked ill. Saul, his expression that of a man who has been through all this before, was also trying to comfort and calm his wife; Hildy was quiet now, but silent sobs still racked her sturdy body as she clung to her husband. Thin Sylvia stood alone, studying the others as if for some clue as to what her own behavior ought to be. Arnaud was nowhere to be seen, nor was the man who had been introduced as Reagan.

"This way." Like a guide conducting a private

tour of some disaster, Vivian led Simon diagonally across the great hall toward the elevator. He
let himself be led. But he was gathering his
determination.

"What happened?" Simon asked when they
were alone in the elevator, going up, and Vivian
had released his arm.

"I don't want to tell you what happened, Simon.
Instead I want you to tell me what you saw."

"I saw . . ." He broke off, swallowing. "Vivian,
wait."

"Tell me what you saw." Her voice had become
a coaxing caress.

"Listen. I want you to tell me a few things first.
I'm missing about three hours out of this afternoon. I want you to explain that. I feel sure you
can. And then tell me what we're going to do
about Margie."

Vivian seemed to find it hard to believe that he
could be so difficult and argumentative. "All
right, Simon. We had to help you to your room
this afternoon and put you to bed. You arrived
here in a confused state. It's not the first time in
your life, I'm sure, that your special powers have
given you a hard time. But now you are with those
who want to help you."

"Special powers?"

"Let's not go on pretending. Yes, special
powers."

He sighed. "All right. No more pretending. But
about Marge, my helper. The girl you saw working with me at the dinner theater. She was here,
hidden in that passageway. She was going to pop
out; that was the big effect I had planned, why I
was going through all that mumbo-jumbo with
the fireplace. I think you knew all along that she
was in there. Where is she now? What's happened
to her?"

"Yes, Simon dear, I knew." Vivian took him by
a hand, which suddenly lacked strength to pull

away. "Not quite soon enough, unfortunately. So there's been some trouble. But we'll do what we can to get Marge out of it. Just as soon as you've finished helping me in what I want."

"Marge . . ."

"As soon as you've finished helping me." Vivian patted his hand firmly.

Simon had made his effort. There was only so much of an effort that he could make. Now he obediently forgot—whatever it was that Vivian wanted him to forget. He went back to the moments in which his act had started to go wild, and told Vivian what he had seen and experienced then. She listened, hanging on his words as if she thought them of great importance.

The telling was finished before the elevator reached its highest level and eased to a stop. They got out of it and Vivian guided Simon along a short, stone-vaulted corridor and through a door. He realized that they were entering the tower; what must be its highest flight of stairs curved up before them. A wavering, eerie glow from somewhere above let Simon see the stairs clearly as they climbed.

The highest round of the stair was thickly littered with loose stones, fragments of mortar, singed bits of wood, unidentifiable debris. Cool night air, carrying misty rain along with a whiff of acrid smoke, was blowing in through a jagged hole in the tower wall. Up here the walls were much thinner than those of the lower levels of the castle, and the hole was big enough for a man to climb through. Above it, the normal door at the head of the stairs was closed.

When Simon reached the hole, he found himself looking out with his eyes at the level of the flat roof. Solid, physical forms were moving on the roof, people were at work in the near-darkness of the eerie outdoor light. There was the shift and thud of heavy weights being moved.

Vivian gestured, and Simon climbed out ahead of her, bracing a foot on an ancient, newly-exposed timber that hissed and smoldered in the light rain. The smell of bitter smoke was stronger now, mingled with the dankness of old wood and old stonework freshly wet. Gregory, hatless, but still in his medieval servant's garb, was working in the rain, heaving chunks of stone away from the place where the new hole went down into the interior of the building. Working with Gregory at his command were the twins from the antique shop. The girl looked at Simon helplessly when he caught her eye—it was the same look he'd seen on her face in that bedroom scene that he'd thought was a dream. In a moment she had moved away. She and her brother were scrambling about, taking Gregory's orders, helping him shift debris, as if in a panic of fear. Illuminating the scene was an unearthly glow clinging to the top of the tower. St. Elmo's fire, thought Simon, he'd heard of it; it sometimes accompanied lightning, but he'd never seen it before.

Climbing up after Simon through the blasted hole, Vivian took Gregory by the arm; now for a moment it was Gregory who looked frightened. "Have you seen Carados?" she demanded of her servant, while Simon, not knowing the name, looked puzzled. Then Vivian added another question in another language. Simon thought that it was French or Latin, but he could extract no meaning though he had a smattering of both.

Gregory shook his head, and in the same tongue began what might have been an explanation. Meanwhile the two young people continued to work as if the penalty for slacking might be death, turning back torn edges of roof, lifting stones away, exposing more of the smoldering fire to the rain that would not let it grow.

"Simon." Vivian had him by the arm again. "An enemy of ours has been here. He may still be here, nearby, on the castle grounds somewhere. He is a very unusual man, and he is calling himself Talisman. I met him once, a very long time ago . . . I should have remembered. I shudder to think of what might happen to Margie if he should find her. He likes to drink girls' blood."

"Talisman. I don't know that name."

"Rather tall, on the thin side. Dark. Age uncertain. If you can see him anywhere, anywhere at all, it's important that you tell me."

Somewhere out there a presence moved. In the rainy woods around the castle, pitch-black now except for passing smears of lightning? No, farther away, much farther. Simon wasn't going to try to determine where. To be able to withhold the sight of it from Vivian was a small victory.

He said: "Your house seems to be on fire."

"The fire itself is nothing. Gregory will manage it. But come, we should reassure the others." Then she guided Simon back over wreckage into the tower again, as if he might be incapable of making his own way. The power of her touch burned at him, sapping his will. Her own physical movements were as certain as her will, her plans. "Now you've seen where the lightning struck, Simon. Now tell me, where is the thing that drew it down?"

He could have protested that there was no way for him to have that knowledge; but somehow he knew that Vivian knew better than that. There was an answer to her question; he didn't want to look for it.

"It's very important, Simon. More important even than Talisman. Never mind if you can't find it for me just yet. I'll have a way soon to make it easier." Vivian was smiling at him, talking to him in the tones of love. Her small hand, irresistible, drew him back down the littered stair, along the passage to the waiting elevator. "But right now you can tell me this much at least: you saw *him?*"

He couldn't pretend not to know who she was talking about. Not Talisman. "Yes. He tried to get in, through the passage. But he couldn't."

There was a soft intensity now in Vivian's voice that Simon had never been able to imagine there, not even in daydreams when he'd made her image speak to him. She said now: "His name is Falerin. His real name, just as your real name is Simon Colline . . . oh, I know, of course I know that too. He is a real magician, more than you are, more even than I am. I learned from him, you know. He is going to come to our world, and he will be the king of the world someday. Oh yes, oh yes, with his power, and the power that we can develop for him here. The science we can add now. One day the whole earth will be his domain, and mine. And yours too, Simon, if you help us . . . of course you'll help us." Simon had never seen Vivian so happy. She went on: "That's what this is all about. He couldn't live through all the centuries between his time and now. But I have, for this one purpose, to bring him here. He was about to come through, but the Sword blocked him and he had to retreat. It's hidden here in the castle somewhere, or nearby. And you are going to find it for me, Simon. Then he'll be back, he'll come again."

Downstairs in the great hall, Hildy's husband was calmly refilling his wife's little crystal cup with wine. She picked up the cup, and drained it, and put it down again, and sat there looking steadily at Saul. In keeping with the other strange things of this strange night, the wine, which was like no wine that Hildy had ever tasted before, had the effect of making her thoughts clearer instead of clouding them. Problems to be solved were not blurred but sharply delineated. Hildy was no longer hysterical. She was not even much afraid now, in any physical, immediate sense. And now while she was alone with her husband she meant to get some explanations from him.

Emily Wallis had had to be helped away, her husband going with her. No one else was left at table. The dinner had never been cleared away; the remaining servants, so efficient earlier, had obviously been ordered to tasks judged more important.

Saul was smiling faintly at his wife. But then, as if bothered by her close, silent scrutiny, he turned away from the table and moved a few steps to stand near the fireplace. The flames, though unattended for some time now, were prospering cheerfully.

"Where are all the servants, Saul?"

He turned from gazing at the fire to regard her mildly. "I don't really know, m'dear."

"The truth is that they're not really *our* servants at all, are they? They don't really work for us."

"Afraid I don't quite . . ."

"I mean they belong to Vivian. Don't they?" Hildy paused. Her husband was waiting. She pressed on: "Like everything else here, no matter what it says on the legal papers about who owns this place."

Saul considered that in his calm way. "Vivian is the leader of the family, yes."

"Why does that have to be? You're older than she is."

Saul was going to answer, then decided against it. He waited calmly.

"Saul, you've been lying to me about a lot of things, right from the start. Haven't you?"

He turned away again, picking up a long poker, stabbing experimentally with it at one of the burning logs. "I'm sorry you look at it in that way, Hil. I've been meaning to sit down with you sometime, and try to explain it all."

What was really chilling was that he wasn't even trying to deny her accusation. Hildy discovered that perhaps her hysteria wasn't as thoroughly exorcised as she had thought. She definitely wanted to scream again. But she was still able to hold her voice calm. "I'd like to hear the explanation now."

"To begin with, you're quite right, of course. We're not an ordinary family."

"Is that how you describe this . . . what's going on? Are you trying to be funny?"

"I'm sorry. No, I'm not trying to be funny at all." Saul put down the poker, but continued to stare into the flames. Hildy rose from her seat at the table and gradually moved toward him, as he went on: "Let me try again. To begin with, as you've noticed by now, I'm sure, there are a number of interrelated families living here in the area of Frenchman's Bend. There are other members of those families living in other places around the country, around the world, but this locale is a sort of—focal point. The Littlewoods, of course. The Wedderburns, Collines, Picards. They have a continuous connection that not only extends back over generations, but maintains and renews itself."

"Go on."

"There's a certain—well, purpose, that unites these families, as well as ties of blood and marriage. There are connections that don't appear on the surface. That go much deeper than outsiders realize."

Hildy was standing close beside her husband now, looking up at him, confronting him. "All right. Go on. Tell me all about it."

"Well, I will." The look Saul gave her was judicial, but there was something else in it too, something that Hildy could still hope was love. "I just can't explain the whole thing all at once."

"Then you should have started explaining it before now. Long before. You would have, if you really loved me."

Saul's eyes were wistful. Was there anything

left of him now, Hildy wondered, but this sad observer, who puttered around keeping himself occupied with his airplane and with business that didn't really matter? It struck Hildy that the man she'd married had been going downhill pretty steadily ever since that first wonderful day when she had met him. Very slowly, but steadily. It wasn't something that she wanted to let herself realize, but she no longer had any choice.

Saul said: "I do love you, Hil. At least as I understand the term. I love you the only way I can. The word means different things to different people, you know."

"It means a lot to me."

"And I can't always be eloquent, or whatever, as I was on that first day. I'd like to be that way always, for you, Hildy. But I can't."

She could feel how close she was to breaking down again. "I understand."

"No, I don't think you do understand. Not yet. You can't. But you will in time. I want to tell you everything as gently as I can, so you'll see it isn't so bad."

"Tell me what, Saul? What isn't so bad?"

"I've grown up with this. But when people marry into it, as you have—well, it's just not something that you're able to grasp fully all at once."

Hildy couldn't speak. She was afraid that if she tried, nothing but screams would come from her throat, ever again.

Saul went on: "I do love you, Hil, as I've said so often. But the truth is that our marriage was in part arranged."

"Arranged? How? What does that mean?"

"Vivian always has an interest in bringing new people into the family. Selected people, with something to contribute, like special abilities. It generally works to the person's advantage, of course, very much to their advantage in fact. But it's not something that can be explained to them ahead of time."

Hildy was shaking her head, unable to find words. A horrible truth was right in front of her but she couldn't see its whole shape yet. Dimly she was aware that on the other side of the great hall the elevator was returning from upstairs, its door was opening. She looked that way as Simon the Great emerged from the elevator. He appeared to be in a daze, a trance. Vivian had him by the arm, she was guiding him, manipulating him. Another slave, another toy for Vivian.

Hildy said: "Saul, at least tell me one thing right now."

"If I can. What is it?"

"Just now, right after everything seemed to blow up, I saw this young man. I don't mean the magician, someone else. That wall blew open and there was a doorway, an opening, with light streaming out . . . and he was there, and he was very handsome, and at the same time his face was the—the most hideous thing I've ever seen in my life, I don't know why—"

"Shh!" Saul hissed it fiercely, at the same time darting a glance toward Vivian. But Vivian was fully occupied with whatever she was doing with Simon, leading him toward the door of the once-secret passage, and whispering in his ear meanwhile.

Hildy would not be put off. "I want an answer, Saul. Who was he? He was trying to come through that doorway, and then something stopped him. It was an object like a cross, I couldn't see how it was being held. Except that it wasn't a regular cross, it was more like the hilt of a sword. Who was he, Saul?"

"Hildy, I said there was a purpose uniting the family, remember? I'm afraid he's what this is all about."

Her lips soundlessly formed questioning words.

With gentle seriousness her husband said: "He's Vivian's lover. He has been, for more than a thousand years."

NINETEEN

Being out on the street wearing jail issue was better than walking around town in that damned flowered gown; but it really wasn't, when you came right down to it, a whole hell of a lot better. In the shadowed mouth of an alley, Hawk leaned against a dingy brick wall, considering things.

He'd had to wait around in his tiny VIP cell until nearly midnight, when things at headquarters started to get really busy, as he'd surmised they would. As soon as that happened, surveillance necessarily slackened. He had remembered to turn the lock in the cell door open before he left, which he thought would perhaps make his disappearance at least a little less memorable. There was still going to be trouble for the guards in charge of seeing to it that cell doors stayed locked, but Hawk wasn't running any charitable organization. He hadn't asked anyone to arrest him in the first place.

He considered that he'd managed his departure

very smoothly, for a magician long out of practice. He'd appeared on the street not many blocks from headquarters, got his bearings at once —Chicago was an easy city to do that in, with its logical grid of street numbers—and then he'd started walking, heading without any conscious plan back toward his old stamping grounds on Skid Row.

If any of the passersby he encountered on the first leg of his hike had recognized his clothing as jail issue, they weren't about to make an issue of it. HaHaa. A wise decision on their part.

He couldn't help noticing as he began to walk that physical movement was a lot easier for him now than it had been a few days ago, before Carados picked him up. Involuntary defensive powers, long dormant, had been mobilized. It would seem that Carados had actually done him a favor. He paused before a darkened plate glass window, to look at himself in the half-mirror inside its steel grill. Yes, his figure was straighter than it had been for some time—for a long time. His pants were zipped. Danger and abuse had served as tonics. It puzzled him that he had been so terrified a few days ago, cowering away from the hunters of helpless old men. He didn't have to take that kind of crap. Not from the likes of them, at least.

No good answer suggested itself. Next question, obviously: Where did he go from here? But he didn't want to try to think that through just now.

Hawk had walked on until he'd covered half a mile, then ducked into the mouth of this alley, as if to take a leak. Actually he just wanted to be able to close his eyes and concentrate for a minute or so. If he couldn't answer questions at least maybe he could do something about his shirt. He figured that the shirt was the clothing item most conspicuously identifiable as jail issue; the shoes were plain, the pants could be any new workpants of medium blue.

He spent a couple of minutes with eyes closed, leaning against the dirty brick wall, mumbling. After a couple of tries (this kind of thing had never been his specialty) Hawk's plain blue jail shirt was a muddy brown, crisscrossed by an ugly pattern of thin pink stripes. Not quite what he'd been aiming for. But, come to think of it, just the kind of inelegance that would fit in perfectly on Skid Row.

Hawk left the alley and moved again along the midnight street, borne quickly by his new, healthy walk. The shirt was all right. Actually he felt a little proud of it; and anyway it felt good just to have done *something* again. Maybe later, if he felt like it, he could work on the colors a little more. Meanwhile . . .

Meanwhile what was he going to do now? He had been putting off making a conscious decision, but the Street, Skid Row, was drawing near. It appeared that by default he was going back to his old haunts, but what was he going to do when he got there?

. . . anyway if he made the shirt look too good, somebody would try to roll him, no, mug him was the proper word, now that he was standing up on his two feet again. By bloody hell, he wished they'd try. He wished he had that vampire, the stalking butcher, in front of him for just five seconds now. He wished he had that smirking, contemptuous kidnapper, Carados.

Now if he were to go and collect Carados somehow, and deliver him to the cops, that would get the cops off his own tail. But Hawk didn't really want to go after Carados, because . . .

Because if he did . . .

Because, because. He just got a train of thought going, starting to make sense, and then it stalled. Every time. There had to be, there *had* to be, a damned good reason.

He had the feeling that his life was being steered, controlled, by some will not his own, to some hostile purpose. It was not a good feeling to have.

At one o'clock in the morning, with his mental state increasingly perturbed, the man who now called himself Hawk (and how long would *that* name be usable?) was leaning against a streetlight not two blocks from where Carados had picked him up. He craved wine, there was no doubt of that. But somehow while he was off Skid Row the craving, like so much else, had altered. The animal urge to drunken oblivion had become entangled with older and nobler things—wine as symbol of elegance, wine as rare privilege, wine as a way to spiritual (no pun intended here) enjoyment.

And even as Hawk thought of wine, and of how he might provide himself with some, he was gazing at a half-dead wino stretched in the gutter just a few paces away, and he knew in his heart without having to argue the point with himself that there was no way in the goddam world he was ever going back to being *that*. God, how could he ever have—?

Just *because*, that's why. Why he'd been condemned to spend most of his life lying in a gutter. A thousand years of gutter, just *because*. And he mustn't ever try to find the underlying reason, *because*—

This *because* was hammering him to death, with every mental step he tried to take. He couldn't move an inch now without colliding with it, and at the same time he knew he had to move. What made his situation all the more desperate was the fact that until this moment it had never come really clear to him what bad shape he was in.

Looking up into the starless city sky, Hawk gasped a few deep breaths. He clung fiercely to the thought that he was making progress against

. . . against whatever was oppressing him, whatever had kept him in the gutter for a millennium. At least he now understood that there was a fundamental question that cried out to be answered. And experience assured him that when something like this had a man in its grip, when a life was totally screwed up as his was, for no visible reason, then the invisible reason most likely involved . . .

It involved . . .

It had to do with . . .

He couldn't make it. He could grunt and groan, struggle any way he liked, but he could not complete that simple thought. He was gasping, on the point of fainting, ready to kill someone for just one drink. But he wasn't going to drink. So, if he couldn't go after Carados, then how about the vampire? That would be fine, that would be fun. Already he had tentatively planned on bouncing the bloodsucker around from one century to another, as long as that game could be kept going; but that was more prank than serious punishment. And sooner or later the victim of the game was more likely than not to wind up back in present time. Where Hawk would be able to get at him in earnest . . . or, indeed, where he would be able to get at Hawk.

That thought was enough to somewhat curb Hawk's yearning for a drink. Not that the prospect inspired him with anything like the terror it would have a few days ago; Hawk no longer felt particularly afraid of anyone or anything. Still the probability of being confronted by an angry vampire, one as tough and smart as that old one had been, tended to clear the mind and concentrate the attention.

Before he could really concentrate, though, there were other nagging questions to be thought about. Example: That young cop, hopelessly mundane if anyone ever was, had asked Hawk if the castle contained a sword. Imagine a question like that, just asked out of the blue. Where would a mundane young Chicagoan have got hold of that idea?

Until now, Hawk had managed to keep himself from thinking about the Sword at all. It wasn't forbidden him to do so, it was just too painful, it was rooted in memories that he didn't dare stir up for fear of the anguish they would inflict upon him. But it was *possible* to think about the Sword, at least as an alternative to that subject about which he could not think at all.

And once he had allowed himself to start to think about the Sword, why then he knew right away just where it had to be, at least its general location. It was right in Nimue's way, interfering with whatever it was that she was offering blood sacrifices to accomplish.

In his mind's eye, now probing his own dark future to the extent that he was able, Hawk could see himself beginning to be surrounded by swords. From them flowed danger, and breath-taking opportunity too, possibilities not quite visible as yet . . .

First a small plastic blade, held in the unknowing fingers of Carados, juxtaposed unwittingly with the clear liquid held up inside a vodka glass, so that the hilt seemed to project above the surface ready to be grasped. By one who dared . . . and then the other Sword, the great iron cross-hilt held up in a dream, throbbing out of concealment with a beneficence of power . . .

Swords . . . and there were pentagrams too in the future to weight upon him. There for a long, long time he'd been sure that all the business of magic was in the past for him. But it was not to be.

Tears gathered in his eyes, spilled slowly into the upper furrows of his aged cheeks. Lord God, Lord God, so this world is not yet through with me. But I am crippled, have been crippled for a

thousand years. Bound and deformed by . . . some
. . . great . . .

Enchantment.

There. His uglified new shirt was soaked with
sweat, and he was gasping. But he'd got that far,
at last, at least. Now weariness and awe were
transmuting slowly to fresh rage. The damned
bloodsucker must be even older than he looked.
He was the enemy. It was all his fault from the
beginning.

TWENTY

Simon was aware of himself riding down in the elevator, of the elevator doors opening, returning him to the great hall. After that, he began to lose track of his physical location. Vivian's electric touch was on him steadily. He could hear the murmur of her voice, he saw her eyes. And then he could see nothing but her eyes.

Vivian had not changed from when she was fifteen, he could see that now. She was still fifteen, or rather she was ageless. Nor would she ever change. She would never be any different from what she was. And Simon knew that to have her would be to possess the world.

Under Vivian's careful guidance his body walked, going he knew not where. And, also guided by Vivian, his mind drifted, entering a secret, pleasant, mysterious place. In that place there was nothing to see but Vivian's eyes, nothing to think about but what Vivian might want.

Your powers are real, Simon. That was Vivian's

voice, the only voice that could reach him now. *They always have been real. You shouldn't be afraid of that.*

Yes, all right, they are real. I won't be afraid, if you tell me not to be afraid.

I do tell you so. Now. Do you remember the day when you were tested? I want you to remember that day.

Tested?

The day, said Vivian, *when I let you lie with me. Did you see the Sword on that day, Simon? I think you may have seen it.*

He wanted to keep silent, but it was hopeless, his thoughts burst out. *Oh, damn you, damn you, Vivian. All I've ever been able to remember is how you let me fumble at your body. All I've ever really wanted since then is to have you again. To have what you wouldn't give me even then.*

But what he wanted did not interest Vivian. *I'm going to send you back to that day, Simon. I'm going to send you wherever I must, to find the Sword. We must discover where it is now.*

Simon didn't ask what Sword. He had seen it in one vision already.

You are going to walk what you call the secret passage. With my help it can take you to many places, many times. If we must, we will follow the Sword forward through the centuries from the day when it ws forged. But first we'll try that day just fifteen years ago. You can do it, for me. We must find where the Sword is now.

I'll try, Vivian. Vivian.

You must do more than try. When you have found the Sword, Simon, then I will tell you my true name. And then I will give you the secret thing that you have always wanted. The secret thing, most precious and intense, that lies behind the door of sex.

Oh, I want you, Vivian. For a moment Simon saw only the vision that was always with him, that one day had been reality, Vivian as a young girl naked, inviting him, beckoning him on. He tried to reach for her.

Not yet, dear Simon. I want so much to love you, but not yet. First you must find the Sword. Magic that you must penetrate conceals it. No one, not even I, not even Falerin, can find things, see things, as well as you can. In that magic you have the potential to be supreme.

In a momentary flash of clear physical vision, Simon knew that he was standing again in the blasted doorway that led to the once-secret passage. His attempt at a performance had been used by Vivian to key the forces that had torn it open to the mundane world. And now Vivian was about to send him into it.

Find the Sword for me, Simon. Here begins your search, in your own past.

And he was drifting on the Sauk in the old rowboat, the almost paintless hulk that in all the childhood summers he could remember had been tied up at the old willow stump at Frenchman's Bend. The boat wandered with the motion of an almost lifeless current between two jungled islands. Simon was alone, lying on his back in the bottom of the old boat, with a little sunwarmed leakage water flowing and ebbing gently around him. He was wearing the old remembered green swimming trunks and nothing else. His feet were up on the middle seat, and a clear warm summer sky was over him. Insects droned from the island shores, and there was an almost fleshy smell of mud.

When he was back in the city between vacations, going through the dull routine of school, Simon's memories of Frenchman's Bend grew in color and interest. But the glamor applied by his restless imagination tended to disappear quickly when he returned to the real place. The river had shrunken, every time he saw it again, turned muddier and dirtier than the Sauk he thought that he remembered. And most of the people appeared somehow shrunken too, even if months of growth had actually made the young ones physically larger. When reality seemed inadequate Simon's imagination tended to come back into play.

He was letting it take over now, as he lay on his back in the heat of the sun with his eyes half closed. He was thinking, as he so often did, about Vivian. He was concentrating, as he usually did when he thought of her, on that day last summer when Simon and her little brother Saul had tried to talk her, dare her, into going into the river naked while they watched.

The effort had been a tantalizing near-success. Vivian had waded in in her bikini—watching her play around in that was maddening enough, for Simon at fourteen—and then, once up to her shoulders in the opaque brown water, she'd slipped quickly out of the suit, holding up the two pieces of it for them to see, and laughing that she'd won the bet. Simon had rowed his boat toward her, but before he could get very close the suit was somehow on again.

The whole business, of course, had really been Vivian's idea from the start. No one ever talked or teased or bet her into doing anything but what she wanted to.

Simon sunning in the bottom of the boat at age fifteen couldn't let this memory dwell on that scene for more than about two seconds without a physical reaction starting. That was okay. Pretty soon he'd pull down his trunks and do something about it. But there was no rush.

He'd closed his eyes now fully against the sun, and was letting his imagination work on the remembered image of Vivian laughing at him, shoulder-deep in water. It was coming clearer and clearer. She held up her suit, panties in one hand, bra in the other. Her smile in the image was becoming inviting, beckoning, not the taunting expression it had been in reality. And now she was starting to wade towards him.

Simon sometimes felt a little frightened at the things his imagination could do for him. He'd never, for example, seen a real live girl completely unclothed. But when in a hundred hot deliberate dreams since last summer he'd brought Vivian out of the water naked, every detail of uncharted anatomy was as clear as something from a motion picture frame. And Simon couldn't resist doing it that way, usually, seeing more and more detail, even if it did tend to get a little scary.

Now he brought the image of Vivian wading into water only knee-deep, smiling at him, displaying herself. He hooked his thumbs in the waistband of his trunks, and then immediately worried that maybe he ought to row over to an island first, get among bushes where he could be absolutely sure of a few minutes' privacy. Not that anyone was likely to see him where he was now, but—

A high-pitched voice shattered his daydream, calling from some distance away. "Yeeoh, Simon!"

Vivian vanished, reality returned with a rush. In confusion Simon sat up in the boat, tugging his trunks as straight as he could. A craft he recognized as Gregory's white canoe was sixty yards or so downstream, being paddled up toward him by one person. In a moment Simon recognized Saul Littlewood.

She's here, was Simon's first thought. *If Vivian's little brother is here in Frenchman's Bend today, then so is she.*

Saul was waving a greeting. Simon waved back, then took up one of his oars. Using it like a paddle, he made slow headway to meet the canoe's advance.

"Yo," Simon called back, when the canoe with the younger boy in it was closer. "I didn't know you guys were here."

Now Saul with a delicate touch of paddle brought canoe sideways against boat; and Simon with his stronger hands gripped both gunwales, holding the two craft clamped together.

Saul was wearing cutoff jeans, and a new, expensive-looking T-shirt with an elaborate pattern. He was dark-haired, of average size and chunky build. As was to be expected for a twelve-year-old, he'd grown considerably in the nine months or so since Simon had seen him last.

"We ain't gonna be here long," Saul said now. "We're driving home again tomorrow morning."

"Oh." *Then I've got to see her today, before she leaves.* Vivian and Saul lived most of the year with their parents in one of the far northern suburbs of Chicago, closer to Simon's home in the city than either place was to Frenchman's Bend. Yet Simon had never seen them anywhere but here. In fact he had never met them, had known only vaguely of their existence, until just last summer.

Saul, watching Simon closely, said: "So why don't you come up to the castle now? Vivian's there. She was saying to me she wished you were around."

"Yeah?" Simon swallowed. "Okay, I will. Who else is there?"

"Our parents were, but they had to go back into Blackhawk. Some kind of a meeting or something. They won't be back till after dark."

"Is Gregory there?" Simon knew that the dignified-looking man intermittently lived in the castle, as part of his caretaker duties. For various reasons he didn't like Gregory, and thought that Gregory felt the same way about him.

Saul shook his head. "Vivian's up there all by herself right now. She's out by the grotto, you know? She's painting a picture of one of those statues. She was telling me she thought it looked like you."

"Me? Jeez. Which statue?"

Saul looked for a moment as if he thought that a dumb question, but he answered without comment. "The big naked guy standing there holding the stone and the slingshot. Well, he ain't quite naked, he's got a figleaf on."

"Jeez. I haven't got muscles like that."

"You got a lot more muscles than you did last summer. Vivian was saying she bet you had."

"Jeez." Simon couldn't think of anything to say to that. He hoped that if he was blushing it didn't show through his tan. And the uncomfortable bulge in the front of his trunks had eased abruptly when Saul startled him, but now it suddenly gave signs of coming back.

If Saul had noticed either of these reactions he was being diplomatically silent about it. The joined boats had drifted out from between islands, and now it was possible to see the relatively distant shore on both sides. Saul was gazing toward the shabby house where Simon stayed during vacations. "Your uncle's car's not there," he observed.

"My aunt and uncle had to go into Blackhawk. Just like your folks. Said they prob'ly won't be back till late."

"Your grandma go with 'em?"

"Yeah."

Saul was silent, with the air of one who has just made some kind of subtle point. The hot, humid air seemed to be somehow supporting the suggestion that somewhere in Blackhawk, population about one hundred thousand, there was a gathering today of the adults of the clan, and that gathering might have a secret importance.

It might be true, thought Simon, and so what, and anyway Vivian was throbbing in his blood.

He said: "Look, how about it we both go over there in the canoe? It'll be faster. I'll tie up the rowboat first." He released his grip, letting the two craft separate.

"Okay." Saul wielded his paddle again. Rowing and paddling, they worked their respective vessels toward the landing at Frenchman's Bend.

As if returning to a dropped subject, Saul asked: "What do your aunt and uncle do in that shop all day?"

"Jeez, I dunno. Putter around. Sometimes they get a customer. Why?"

"I bet they don't have too many customers."

"I guess not."

"But they make enough money to get along. Or they get money from somewhere else."

"I guess so. Why?"

Saul paddled, looking straight ahead. "Does your grandma have a job?"

"Yeah, in an office down in the Loop. Some days she works at home. Why?"

Saul shrugged. "Just that some of our relatives have a lot of money, and some don't."

"Which ones have a lot?"

Saul just shrugged again.

They were nearing the shore. "I guess," said Simon, "your folks are some who do."

Watching Simon closely again, Saul said. "They're my step-parents, actually."

Simon nodded at this information, then did a double take. "Both of 'em?"

"Yeah, both. The way they tell me it happened was that my real father died before I was born, and then my mother married again. Then *she* died, when I was still real young, and my stepdad got married. So I got a full replacement set."

"You and Vivian both did, then."

Saul never answered that straight out. The prow of the canoe grated gently at the shoreline, and he braced his paddle against the river bottom to hold the craft against the gentle current. He said: "Our whole family's kinda crazy, you know? I mean the way it's organized. There's about a couple thousand people all related to each other. Like you and me. And the funny part of it is, almost nobody has any really *close* relatives. Except for husbands and wives."

Simon grunted, rowing one last hard stroke, driving the old tub of a rowboat firmly into the shore. Then he shipped oars and hopped out into the muddy shallows, grabbing a length of chain to tie up the boat at its usual place, the ancient willow trunk. He said: "There's not really a couple thousand."

"All right. Maybe there's really about a hundred people. Littlewoods and Collines and Picards and Wedderburns. Hell, old Gregory's actually some kind of a cousin to both of us." Carefully shifting his seat in the canoe, Saul made ready for Simon to get in. "You wanna do the paddling?"

"Sure." Simon had learned to use a canoe the previous summer. He was in a hurry now to get across the river, and also eager to see how fast he could paddle, with another year's growth of muscle to call upon. Jeez, Vivian was thinking about his big muscles. "I guess you're right, about the family." But he wasn't really able to think about the family now. Not now, when Vivian wanted to see him. Maybe there would even be some way that Saul could be got rid of for a while . . .

Saul, relaxed now, sat in the bottom of the canoe, watching the water go by as Simon swung the craft downstream and headed it out from shore. "Yeah," Saul said, "maybe my folks will be the ones who own the castle someday, and we'll be rich."

Simon paddled. To have something to talk about, to relieve his mind from Vivian, he asked: "So just who owns the castle now?" He felt sure it was someone in some branch of the family.

Saul sighed faintly, as if he didn't much care about that point. "They say it's all tied up in the courts and things. We can come and stay in it whenever we want. There's a little furniture and stuff." Pause. "That room still looks burned, and screwed up, you know, where old man Littlewood blew himself up. He was like our great uncle or something."

"Yeah." After using the old rowboat, the sleek canoe was a joy to handle. Simon drove the paddle fast and hard, angling between islands, taking advantage of quicker current wherever he could. Between strokes he asked: "Gregory don't mind you using the canoe, huh?" He'd asked for its use himself and had been turned down; he knew his aunt and uncle went out of their way sometimes to do what Gregory wanted.

Saul shrugged again, as if what Gregory minded or didn't mind was no concern of his. "He don't use it much himself. Hey, Si?"

"What?"

"You ever see Gregory outdoors in the day-time?"

"In the daytime?" Simon repeated mechanically. He yearned to ask Saul what Vivian was wearing today. On a hot day like this, it wouldn't be much, probably. "In the daytime? Hell, I dunno. I guess, sometimes. He usually comes around at night. Why?"

Again Saul's shrug; it was a superior gesture, as if he had too many pressing things to think about and had already had to go on to think of something else. Saul and Vivian were basically among the castle-owners, not the dwellers in the huts below.

Simon said: "I dunno what part of the family I'm really in. The poor part, I guess."

"I dunno either." Saul meant about himself. He sounded suddenly worried about it.

Now Simon was past the islands, he could see the castle landing dead ahead. There were no boats at the tiny floating dock. There usually weren't. "Hell," said Simon. "Go start up your own family. That's the way I feel about it."

Saul's expression seemed to say that it wasn't that simple, but he didn't want to argue about it, at least not right now.

Simon stepped out on the floating dock, after bringing the canoe neatly alongside. To his surprise, Saul only changed seats once more and reached for the paddle.

"I'm just gonna goof around in the canoe for a while, Si," the younger boy said. "You go on up."

"Oh," said Simon, not knowing what else he ought to say. He was going to be alone with Vivian. A pulse inside his head began to tap, lightly and quickly. Inside his trunks he could feel himself shrivelling up completely, as if with fear.

When Saul had paddled out ten yards or so from the dock, he turned the canoe and let it drift. Now he regarded Simon with a look in which he let some wicked amusement show. "Hope you're ready," he called back. "She had a kind of funny look today. Like maybe her pants were a little hot or something." And he continued watching Simon carefully for some reaction. Watchful, that was the word for Saul Littlewood at twelve.

Simon was past caring about, or even knowing, what reactions he might display. He turned dazedly and started along the lightly worn path that wound upward from the shoreline, into the trees that covered the face of the bluff. Mosquitoes greeted him as he entered the shade. Even nearly naked as he was, he hardly noticed them.

The pulse in his head tapped on. Halfway up the switch-backed path, he scraped a toe raw, stumbling on one of the carved stone steps, and barely felt it.

Saul had said that she was at the grotto, and

when Simon came to the branching path he turned that way. His breathing was shallow and quick, and sweat trickled under his armpits newly grown with adolescent hair. He was distracted from other difficulties by something in the way that Saul had delivered that last remark. It had begun to raise a horrible suspicion in Simon's mind: suppose Saul was screwing his own sister, or wanted to? Looking back on certain things that had been said and done last summer hinted at confirmation of the grotesque thought. Ugh. Of course he, Simon, was some kind of a cousin to her too. But that wasn't like a brother and sister. God.

On silent feet Simon rounded the last shoulder of limestone rock before the grotto, and there he stopped. The thought came, almost calmly, that imagination had taken over completely, that his mind had at last given up reality. Vivian was sitting totally naked on the edge of the stone table at the center of the little paved court before the grotto. Her back was turned to Simon, and, as Saul had said, she was working on a painting. One slim, tanned arm was extended, holding a small brush to an easel set up just beside the table. Beyond the easel was the tall, pale stone statue serving her as model. There was a set of paints beside Vivian on the stone table, as well as two parts of a discarded green bikini and a crumpled red garment that might be a beach jacket. She was sitting sideways on the edge of stone, right foot on the lower paving, left leg raised and bent on the tabletop. In the faint breeze, leaf-shadows slid over her bare back.

This was not imagination. Suddenly the pulse in Simon's head was pounding hard. His heart and lungs were laboring as if he'd run up the whole hill. His hands and his knees were trembling violently.

Saul had known she was sunbathing, he'd set

this up. Or else Saul hadn't known. It didn't matter. Simon turned for an instant to look at the ascending trail behind him. He couldn't see Saul on it, and Saul couldn't have sneaked up through woods and underbrush without Simon's hearing him before now.

Simon stared at Vivian again. She was real, not imaginary. He had to try to see her from the front, see everything. In a trembling frenzy he tiptoed off the trail, then went down into a crawling crouch, heedless of occasional sharp twigs. If he could move behind bushes and the low wall to the other side of the court, then look up over the wall carefully, he'd be able to see Vivian from in front. Heart in mouth, Simon made a scrambling, desperate progress. He was as silent as he could be, but still things crunched and snapped faintly under his hand, his knee, his foot. She had to hear the noise he was making, oh God, she had to be alarmed. But when at last, with enforced slowness, he raised his head beside a tree to look, Vivian was still calmly painting, she gave no sign of having heard a thing.

He had a perfect view of two small breasts, their tan softer than that of the surrounding skin, imaging a bikini top. The nipples were richly brown, exactly as his imagination had formed them for him a hundred times. He saw her spread thighs, the left knee raised and sharply bent. The foot was placed on the table exactly where it prevented his observing the central mystery. But he could see that that enigma was surrounded, just as his solitary dreams had shown him, by dark curls like those on Vivian's head. Oh God oh God. And she was still intent on painting.

He couldn't approach her while she was naked, he couldn't let her know he was here watching. He couldn't turn and leave. One thing he could do, would do, must do now. In desperate haste he stripped down his trunks, letting them fall

around his ankles, then pulling one foot free of
them to keep his awkward balance on the slope.
Now he would go to it hard and quick. But he had
no more than touched himself when Vivian suddenly stood up. Simon crouched, agonizing in fear
of discovery, bending his body in a contortion to
seek all the concealment possible. The world
would end if she should see him now, the way he
was. But she had turned away. Stones had printed
faint red marks on her rump. Ignoring her discarded swimsuit, she reached for the red robe or
jacket. She'd seen him after all, and was about to
go tell everyone. No, that was unthinkable. And
turned out to be a false alarm. It was still her
painting that absorbed her attention. She frowned
at it unhappily as she tied the cloth belt of her
jacket, covering herself loosely from neck to mid-
thigh. Then a moment later she turned and strode
impatiently away, heading for the single path
where Simon had come up a few moments ago.

Again he crouched low, limbs tangled in an
aborted effort to get his trunks pulled up again.
But Vivian never looked in his direction. When
she reached the main path she walked up it
briskly toward the castle. Simon could easily
mark the passage of the red jacket behind screens
of green growth. Then Vivian was gone.

Simon stood up, feeling more than half insane.
He was dripping sweat all over, his nerves totally
shot. What next? If she was clothed at all, he
could approach her; he'd follow her up to the
house, say he'd just come up from the landing. He
got his trunks pulled up, his congested maleness,
feeling like dull toothache, more or less housed
again. Through bushes whose little scrapes and
pricks he now could feel, he worked his way out
onto the sunwarmed stone pavement of the court.
He stared at the table; that very stone, right there
at the edge, had been pressed moments ago by
Vivian's warm ass. The easel and the paints were

there, the small brush, tip wet, just where she'd thrown it down. Speaking of wet tips . . . he ached. And there were the two parts of her bikini. She'd worn them this hot day, and they would smell of her. He imagined himself raping her bikini now. But the possibility paled before one infinitely better if still discouragingly faint; he'd catch up with her, up at the castle.

Crossing the stone-paved court toward the path, Simon passed beside the abandoned easel. His eye was caught by the painting, and he paused momentarily in surprise. Even at the age of fifteen, even in his present state, he could see that the painting wasn't very good. This was a surprise in itself, because Vivian always gave such an impression of overwhelming competence. But the main thing that stopped Simon was the painted face. Clumsily as it was done, he could see it wasn't supposed to be the same face that the statue had. And for just a moment of wild conceit he thought that the face depicted might be modeled on his own; but no, that was supposed to be a short beard under the chin, not just a shadow.

The pathway brought him through the tall, thick hedge, into the half-tended back lawn of the castle. He stood beside the weed-grown tennis courts, with the great brownish stone face of the reconstructed keep rising broodingly before him. Afternoon shadows were lengthening. That didn't matter. Saul had gone off somewhere with the canoe, probably. That didn't matter a whole lot either, it would be easy enough for Simon to wade and swim his way back across the river, in the dark if he should stay on this shore that long. There was no rational reason for the sudden urge he felt to turn and hurry away.

He moved to stand beside the disused, empty swimming pool, looking up at the face of the keep shaded by tall trees and by its own west wing. Just ahead of him, at ground level, one of a pair of

French doors stood slightly open. Otherwise the whole building appeared unoccupied, deserted.

Everything was silent, but he knew that she was in there, somewhere.

"Vivian!" It came out as a booming, grown-man's shout.

Only silence answered it. And then a cicada in a tree somewhere, keening loudly, as if in a mocking pretense of amazement.

Simon went to the Frech doors and entered. It was dim inside the castle; at night it would be pitch black. He supposed Gregory must have electricity turned on in some of the rooms at least. He paced silently from one unfurnished ground floor room to another. They looked just as they had when Simon had seen them briefly in summers past, when he and his cousins had run through them in play, sometimes taunting, daring Gregory to chase them out. Which the caretaker had done, effectively enough, without seeming to try very hard. He had a way about him, that seemingly could turn on fear like an electric light in the cavernous dim rooms. The game did not last long, nor had it been frequently repeated.

"Viv?" He still said it loudly, but this time it was not a shout.

But this time his calling got response—of a kind. So faint that Simon wasn't even really sure it was a physical voice, or of what it said. But he was sure that it came from Vivian. He was standing in the great hall when this answer came floating to him from upstairs.

On the stone stairs his bare feet whispered almost silently. Now his scraped toe had begun to hurt. Jeez, but he was a mess, Vivian wouldn't want to come near him, no one would. In the interior coolness of the castle, sweat was drying clammily on his skin. He ran a hand through tangled, dirty hair, dislodging a small leaf. His mosquito bites had started itching, his frustrated balls reproached him with dull swollen pain . . .

At the first stair landing, he was distracted from this unhappy internal litany by . . . something. A nagging urge to turn aside here, explore a particular side hallway. The summons, whatever it was, was not from Vivian this time. But it was there.

At the end of a short hall he opened a thick wooden door, and was surprised to find that it gave onto a circular gallery that went at balcony level around a stone room at least thirty feet across. Enough daylight to show the general configuration of the chamber found its way in through small windows at a level a floor higher than the balcony. In the middle of the stone floor below was a low dais, much resembling the outdoor table near the grotto. This place reminded Simon of something else too, and in a moment he understood what—a medical operating theater, something he had never seen except in movies and television. A small central stage with not much audience space around it, what little there was provided safely out of the way of the performers.

But the most striking thing about this theatre was that the floor and the lower walls were blackened, scorched, in a pattern of streaked radii extending from the central table. The top of the dais itself was darkened too, solidly and in a different shade, as if exposed to repeated hard use and damage. It was quite clean now, as was the whole empty room, empty except for shadows.

This had to be, Simon thought, the room in which Old Man Littlewood, whom Simon had never seen, had burned or blown himself to death five years ago, Simon had never been told just how. And now there were only shadows . . .

For just a moment Simon thought he saw a man, someone standing at the edge of the floor, against the lower wall on the side where the blurred daytime shadows presently were thickest.

But when he looked closely there was no one. Even when he closed his eyes, in an unconscious effort at the proper kind of concentration, his inner vision could detect no one.

It was a spooky place and he wanted to turn and leave. But there was some important reason, still undiscovered, why he should not do that just yet. Instead he started walking round the gallery, like a small child trailing the fingers of his left hand on the stone balustrade. When he got about halfway around, he could see what was directly under the part of the gallery where he had been standing when he first entered. A cot was there, in shadows but with enough indirect light on it for Simon to make out the recumbent figure of a man. The man lay partly on his back, partly on one side, with the pale outline of his face turned directly in Simon's direction.

Gregory.

It was very difficult to distinguish any features forty feet away, in the dim light, but Simon was sure. Gregory's eyes were open—how could he really be sure of that?—and they might even be following Simon as he walked.

Feeling a chill of fright and horror compounded, Simon walked on quickly, keeping his eyes on the man's face as he moved. He told himself that Gregory had to be asleep, despite the impression of open eyes that tracked Simon as he walked. If he was awake he'd certainly sit up, say something, yell at Simon for intruding. Something about the way the man just lay there, as if he were watching Simon in his sleep, was horrible in the extreme. It brought to a focus all the strangenesses that Simon had seen or imagined about Gregory in the past. It forced Simon to begin to see him clearly.

When Simon had got far enough round the gallery's circle for the man on the cot to pass from his field of vision, he broke into a soft-footed run.

Sweating again despite the coolness, he trotted quickly back out through the gallery's single entrance, and closed the thick door behind him, as quickly as he could without making noise. And then even as he moved on he began to tell himself that the pale face and dark eyes following him must have been some kind of an illusion. Seeing something was one thing, and making sense out of what was seen was something else entirely. It wouldn't make sense for Gregory to simply lie there and watch . . . as if he were in some kind of trance.

And Saul had said, hadn't he, that Gregory had gone with the other adults to Blackhawk; of course for Saul to lie, or be mistaken, would be no big surprise, but . . . Simon yearned to leave the castle as quickly as he could, running, wading, swimming, to get back to the other side of the river. But it was a hopeless yearning, like that of a soldier who knows the war must be finished before he can go home. Vivian was here. He couldn't leave while there was a chance of finding her.

Simon went back to the stairs, and up again to the next landing. Having got that far he paused, hearing somewhere—was it behind him?—a sound like the faint closing of a door. He listened but there was no other sound. To find Vivian, the direction to go was up and forward.

When he came to a landing that felt right, he paused again and softly called her name. Then he slowly made his way along a dim hallway lined with doors, listening for an audible response that never came. It never came, yet he had the feeling that it *had* come . . . Simon couldn't really explain it, even to himself. But he did feel sure, very sure, that this was the way to take to find Vivian.

This was a part of the castle where Simon had never been before. He went down the hall looking into one bedroom after another, most of the rooms disused and unfurnished, with doors standing open. When he came to a closed door he tapped on it, not really trusting his sense that the room beyond it was unoccupied. He called Vivian's name softly, and looked inside, and went on to the next room.

Simon held his breath when he came at last to a room whose closed door held the feeling of something different shut up behind it. When after tapping and calling he opened this door, he discovered furniture, including a made bed. But there was no one in the room.

He stepped in and looked around. To judge by the few items of clothing hanging in the closet, an adult couple was staying here, and logic said it must be Vivian's and Saul's parents. They hadn't brought many things, so they weren't staying long. So, if their important meeting was really in Blackhawk, why not a hotel there? It must have been important to them for some reason to establish a presence in the castle too.

Out in the hall again, Simon looked back toward the stair he had come up. He saw nothing, heard nothing, but there was . . . something . . . back there now, somewhere just out of sight in that direction. The shadows would be deepening on that stairway now, as the sun lowered outside. He'd take some other route when the time came to go back downstairs. He'd already looked for Vivian in that direction, and in that direction maybe Gregory . . .

Damn it, he wasn't going to let himself be all that scared of Gregory. Sure, the man might yell at him angrily if he found Simon here. But he knew Simon and wasn't going to shoot him for a burglar, so Simon wasn't going to be scared . . . his hands were shaking slightly, and his knees. His mouth was dry, and he had to fight with himself to keep from running in the opposite direction from the stairs.

Come on, he told himself fiercely. This is ridiculous. He was fifteen, not the age to start having hysterics over nothing, over one little odd experience, like some little kid who'd just watched his first horror movie. And what had he actually seen? Not a ghost, not a skeleton. A man, lying on a cot. What was so bad about that?

He moved along the hall, walking normally, in the direction away from the stairs. The next room he came to also showed signs of habitation. Judging by the spare clothing visible, the occupant must be Saul.

The door of the next room after Saul's was also shut. The pulse in Simon's head came back as he called softly, and tapped on the door, then opened it and went in. Vivian wasn't here, though the clothes indicated it was her room. She wasn't in the bathroom either. She wasn't even (and here Simon felt silly bending down to look) hiding mischievously under the bed.

What now? Having led him this far, his instinct seemed to have faltered. He could go out in the hall and search for her some more. He could wait in her room for her to come back. Neither of those courses felt right.

He'd left the door to the hall open. Out there it appeared to have got darker rather suddenly. Or had it really? Looking that way, Simon blinked. One thing for sure, he suddenly didn't want to go out into that hall again. He didn't want to because . . . there was a presence out there now.

Not Vivian. It could be Gregory, yeah, he thought it was Gregory, but . . . Gregory with something added, something taken away, something odd.

It was not that Simon, looking out from Vivian's bedroom, could see or hear anything physical out in the hall. Even the greater darkness was perhaps not physical. But it was there. Whatever shadowy presence he'd awakened in the scorched circular room had followed him up the stairs, and was out there, in some form, now. If Simon were to stick his head out into the hall he might well see it with his eyes, and what he saw might well be more than he could bear, though he didn't know just what his eyes would see.

Was it Gregory out there? Yes and no. Simon knew Gregory, to the limited extent he knew him at all, as a man, a human being, and this did not quite fit those categories. It felt like an *it*.

The it/Gregory out in the hall hadn't followed Simon right into Vivian's room. It wouldn't, or it couldn't. Simon thought he could see how, in some half-conscious way, it had thought that it had better not. But if Simon went out there now, he'd have to confront it directly and rather closely. It might be no more than twenty feet down the hallway, listening, trying to think, struggling against whatever power kept it from thinking clearly right now and acting forcefully . . .

Simon could, if he dared, if he hurried, rush right out into the hall this moment, without looking to his right, and then hurry along it to his left. If he hurried along, never looking back, then somewhere he'd find, he'd have to find, another way to get himself back downstairs. Although, as he thought about it, he got the distinct impression that in that direction there wasn't a whole lot of hallway left.

Simon stepped forward, teetered on one foot for an almost paralyzed moment. Then with a sound like a sob he sprang for the door and slammed it shut. The moment of possible escape had passed, because he'd been too scared to seize it. There was a huge, old-fashioned bolt near eye level on the massive door, and Simon reached up and shot it home, then sagged in relief against the wall beside the door. The it/Gregory had moved forward suddenly. Simon was all right now, he was safe for the moment at least, but almost he had waited too long.

The presence he feared was now just outside the door. Simon could hear no sounds of breathing, he could hear nothing in fact, but he had not the least doubt that it was there. It moved, a little, and he sensed the movement by some means that was not hearing. It was waiting with great patience.

Was it waiting for him to come out?

The realization came to Simon that he was in a trap.

There ran through his mind, like the litany of some prayer memorized but never quite believed, all of the scientific, rational, logical opinions that he had managed to accumulate during his fifteen years of life. But to try to call on science and logic now was useless. Simon could no more open that hall door now than he could have leaped from the castle roof.

Maybe he could get out of the room through its window . . . but the window looked pretty small.

A quick check in the bathroom showed him that the window there was absurdly tiny, and filled with little stained glass panels. If he were a cat, maybe. Back to the one window in the bedroom.

Here, standing on a chair and pushing his upper body into the deep embrasure, he could manage to stick his head out easily enough. It was something of a surprise to see how full the daylight still was outside. Tall trees but not the horizon were covering the sun. Simon could have wriggled his body out through the window too, if there were anything at all nearby to offer a good grip, anyplace at all which he might reasonably hope to reach by climbing. Maybe, if he balanced on his toes on the sill here, then leaned far to the side, he might grasp that small ledge . . .

He could see, if he tried, that this wasn't really the way out.

Standing on the floor inside the room again, the half-seen way to Vivian, to freedom, was as hard to pin down as ever. Once again Simon had the impression that it might be the window—but no. He could expect nothing but a fall to his death if he tried that.

If he couldn't find any way to get out of this room, then he'd have to wait here. Sooner or later, Vivian would come back, or someone . . .

Unless it got dark first.

With the evil, infallible logic of nightmares Simon understood the worst in that one phrase. It was an axiom without support and needing none. When the sun had set, the room's closed door would no longer hold.

Oh Jesus. Oh Jesus God. Some hand of human shape outside was trying the doorknob now. This was not only a feeling, Simon could actually see and hear it move. He stumbled away from the door and sank down on all fours on the thick bedside rug, stifling fear-whimpers in his throat. He could feel his bowels quivering, threatening to let go.

The knob was still. Now there was a brushing sound, very faint, against the door. It reminded Simon of someone holding a corpse's arm, manipulating it so that the dead fingers tipped the wood with excruciating delicacy.

Minutes of daylight still remained, the barrier still held. Simon made it to the providential toilet, dropped his trunks and squatted there. He could void the sickness of fear to some extent, but not the fear itself. When at last he stood up and worked the handle that brought a prosaic rush of water through the pipes, terror was exorcised enough to let him once again approach the door to the hallway.

Fearfully he approached the barrier, sensing now emptiness beyond, a deserted hallway. This time he put his ear right to the thick wood of the door and listened.

He could detect no one, nothing, waiting for

him in the hall outside.

Choking on peculiar sounds, Simon unbolted the door. He pulled it open, like one reaching for air after near-suffocation. He stepped out into the hall.

The it/Gregory had tricked him, just round the corner it was coming back in an utterly silent rush from the direction of the stairs—

Simon screamed. He hurled himself back into the room and slammed the door and bolted it. Pride, logic, and science had been utterly routed from his mind. He threw himself toward a far corner of the room, floundering diagonally across Vivian's wide bed that lay in his path. With his feet under him again, standing in the corner of the room, he sent his fingers groping behind knurls on the dim wall's elaborate wood paneling. Small, hidden catches yielded to his fingers' pressure. An almost door-sized section of paneling swung gently out into the room, just clearing a night table by the bed. Gasping, Simon stepped into the opening, down and into the passage hidden in the wall.

He could have run through the dark passage if it had been necessary. So clearly did his mind now see the way ahead of him despite the physical darkness. But he did not run, for his vision showed him with equal clarity that he was not being pursued, and was not going to be. Instead of running he paced steadily, discovering and ignoring the spyholes and the other secret doors. They did not lead to a way out for him today. The way out was still somewhere ahead. He discovered, and bypassed, the lower, branching passage. A few moments after that he was standing inside the grotto looking out with a certain amazement at the paved court. Its stones were in shade now though the sun was still not really down. On the central stone table Vivian, now wearing her bikini, was stretched out napping with the red jacket folded under her head for a pillow.

The door of iron grillwork was secured with a chain and padlock. But there was enough play in the chain so that Simon was able to open the door just enough to slide through. It cost him a painful moment, but he made it.

He walked over to stand beside Vivian, looking down at her.

He thought that he had made no noise at all approaching, but still she awoke. It was a graceful, not at all startled, stirring. "I see you found me," Vivian said, smiling faintly. "You should be very glad."

"Yeah," said Simon. His throat wasn't working too well. Sweats of lust, exhaustion, terror, had dried on him in layers, mixed with a little river mud, powdered with the dust of long-forgotten passageways. He knew that he must stink. But that was no longer relevant. Emotionally he was too mangled to worry about or plan for anything.

Vivian moved, stretched, got up. Her motions were luxurious, catlike. When she turned for a moment to again study the picture on the easel, her bikini bottom was pulled low in back, showing the top of the cleft between her buttocks. Simon stared at it, just stared, not aware of feeling anything. Whatever happened next would happen, that was all.

Meanwhile Vivian was considering her work with evident dissatisfaction. "Maybe I should give up. It's hard to paint from a statue. I don't suppose you've ever tried."

"No."

"And to do a face from memory. Never mind." And Vivian undid her bra and pulled it off. "Someday you'll do much greater things than paint." The panties fell, and Vivian held out her arms. "Now. Don't you want your reward for finding me?"

* * *

And yet she made him wait a moment while she arranged the red jacket into a pad on the stone table, to ease her back when Simon's frantic weight descended on her. She held him tightly and competently, and if she was uncomfortable, as she seemed to be, she certainly didn't have to hold him very long. As he grasped her, Simon became aware that Saul was watching them from behind some bushes. But even being watched could not distract him now. Frenzy dissolved in joyless spasms. What pumped from him into Vivian burned heavily, bringing a mental image of molten lead. The convulsions of his body went on and on, draining him completely. They emptied the last reservoir, then died away, mechanical as functions in a plumbing system.

Exhausted, void, he rolled free of Vivian's body to lie stickily on stone. The stone was chill beneath its surface warmed by the day's sun. Simon thought to look toward the bushes, but Saul wasn't there any more. If he ever had been.

Simon had trouble thinking. Or feeling. He couldn't find anything inside himself now but emptiness.

Vivian lay on her back almost primly, knees raised together, as if after all she might have enjoyed it, and her body was seeking to absorb what his had given. She raised an eyebrow at him now. "Simon?"

"What?"

"I thought I heard a car drive up. My folks will be here, and Gregory, and you look awfully guilty. Suspicious. I think you'd better be moving on."

TWENTY-ONE

Talisman paced in darkness.

The woods were thick, and muted sound to some extent, but half a mile or so ahead he could hear the undeniable sounds of an army breaking camp and setting out on a night march. In his breathing days, campaigning against the Turk, he had done it himself too often to be mistaken about it now.

He had come directly back here from his talk with Marge Hilbert, wondering what the sudden offensive move by Comorr and Falerin portended. He wondered also if his own presence and Marge's, intruders from the future, was going to be allowed to alter the course of history. He thought that would not be allowed but he could not be sure. Anyway he was going to put it to the test tonight. The leaders of the invading army ahead were the allies in time of the evil folk in the twentieth centry of the *nosferatu*—reason enough to attack them, but there was more. Talisman did not mean to spend any more time as an inhabitant of this antique century than he was forced to spend, and attempting a violent alteration of history here seemed to be a good way to bring matters to a head.

He was rapidly nearing the camp. There was a lonely outpost forty or so paces ahead, beside the forest path. A single sentry leaned against a tree. Start the attack here, then. When they came to call the man in, they'd find a corpse.

Talisman shifted to mist-form when he was within a dozen paces of the sentry, and drifted closer. It was almost impossible that a mundane eye should see him in this mode, but being mist dulled his own senses inconveniently as well. When he was only an arm's length from the soldier, he regained human form and simultaneously reached out—

The man's head turned, an instant before Talisman could grasp his throat. The grinning face under the crude helm was unexpectedly familiar.

"Think I'd forgotten you, bloodsucker? This is the land of cold green gore, remember?"

It was certainly not the land Talisman had been inhabiting a few moments ago, that of Artos and Comorr. Even though Talisman had shifted his body out of mist-form, yet the mists round him persisted. Night forest had been replaced by gray nothingness. And Talisman's reaching fingers never did find the throat they sought, though he redoubled his efforts when he saw who now confronted him. In vain. This was the land of magic now, like that of dreams outside of normal time and space.

His foe vanished from his grasp, reappeared behind him. The old man chanted triumphantly, an incantation. Then he cried: "Go for a little spin, bloodsucker! Keep going until someone calls you back!" And with that a mighty force swirled Talisman away.

He traveled timelessly through a pyrotechnic world. The lack of physical orientation was sickening, even for him; one not immune to fear, he thought, might well have been driven mad. Is this then the end for me? he thought again. Where will my body—?

There was once more stable light, dependable substance. Talisman was standing upright, but on what? He discovered himself still—or again—in mistform, and he willed himself out of it, to manshape, to get a better look at his surroundings. Still there was some difficulty in doing that.

Sound clarified first: the voice of a man, chanting something in medieval French, a language that was almost as familiar to Talisman as his native tongue, though a long time had passed since he had heard it spoken. The teeth of the man who spoke it now were nigh-chattering with fear, his tongue was on the verge of stumbling with every consonant.

The words made sense, of a sort, though Talisman could not immediately see what they had to do with his present situation: ". . . bound to my will, Sathanas, by Apollonius, by Proteus, I adjure thee by Thutmose and Din that ye do us no harm but rather be constrained to serve us as we may command . . ."

Bemused, Talisman muttered: "At least I know now where I am—still in the land of magic."

And now—some kind of smoke was swirling heavily about him, slowly dissipating—he began to get a look at his new physical surroundings. He was standing on cleared ground on the edge of a forest, beyond whose low trees a portion of a sizable castle was visible against a cloudy night sky. Lights as of torch or candle showed in a couple of the small windows. It was not the castle on the Sauk, nor, thought Talisman, was it any castle that he had ever seen before.

The dissipating smoke, or part of it at least, came from two bonfires, that were about equidistant from the spot where Talisman found himself standing. The chanting voice was that of a pudgy man in robes that fit very well the role of a medieval alchemist-sorceror; Talisman had known one or two such in his breathing years. This man was crouched in a would-be protective circle chalked or painted on the ground, with his arms outflung in what was evidently his idea of the way a wizard ought to gesture. Nothing, or almost nothing, of real power was emanating from him. A few feet from the wizard another man, dressed in the rich garb of the higher nobility, was standing on one foot as if he had almost decided to run but did not know which way to go. The faces of both men were turned toward Talisman, displaying a rich mixture of terror, triumph, greed, and sheer astonishment.

"Hah!" said Talisman, experiencing a powerful blend of feelings too; he understood suddenly that this pair must think him a demon that their spells had succeeded in calling up out of hell, doubtless in some desperate pursuit of wealth.

The wizard had not ceased to speak; ". . . I charge thee, make obeisance before us; submit thy fortunes and thy powers to our will . . ."

"Bah." Talisman took a step toward the circle. "Whose castle is that yonder?"

"Mine," said the nobleman. And now there was a scramble between the pair of them, the lord trying to push his way into the protective circle with his magician, a mutter of hissed argument and imprecations back and forth.

". . . I told you you'd need a circle, told you it would work this time . . ."

". . . never worked before! Move over . . ."

"Watch out! Sathanas, I adjure thee—
damnation, quit shoving—I charge thee to reveal . . ."

Talisman gave them another moment or two to
pull themselves together. Even a power as weak
as this fool's, caught by good fortune at the
proper moment, must have been enough to rescue
him from the timeless spaceless spin in which the
old one calling himself Hawk had set him danc-
ing. Very good luck for Talisman . . . or something more. In magical matters there was rarely
such a thing as simple luck, good or bad.

"Gold," said the nobleman at last, plainly and
boldly. He evidently felt himself secure now,
clinging to his wizard's back and looking over his
shoulder, with the white circle snug about them
both. "That is what you are to bring to us." He
was addressing Talisman, in the imperious tones
of one accustomed to obedience.

"Indeed? And what is the name of that river
yonder, behind the trees?" In moments of relative
quiet, between outbursts of the others' babble,
Talisman could hear far rapids murmuring. He
wanted to know where he was, and he asked
about the river first because rivers, unlike coun-
tries, duchies, domains of all human kind, rivers
tended to retain their names throughout the
centuries.

"It is the Loire," the wizard said. "Now you
must bring us gold, or tell us how to find it or
make it."

"Bah." Talisman scowled at the magical gim-
cracks, debris of diabolism, items used in their
wretched spells, that lay scattered in the firelight
round about. There were bones. He wondered if
they had been led to murder children to add
power to their spells; such was not unheard of.
"And the Year of Our Lord is now—?"

They looked at him with changing faces; plainly
they were puzzled as to what kind of devil they

had caught, who rolled the Lord's name so trip-
pingly off his tongue. "One thousand," said the
nobleman. "Four hundred, and twenty."

"Aha. And the nearest city?"

Puzzlement grew, and a new wariness.
"Enough," ordered the magician, emboldened by
success and continued survival. "We are not here
to answer your questions, but you ours. How are
we to obtain wealth?"

Talisman strode closer to them, while they
shrank down within their circle. He extended one
foot, still shod in a dark twentieth-century shoe,
and deliberately scuffed a generous arc of the
white circle into oblivion.

"Those who lust for wealth as you do," he said
softly, glaring at them both with intent to
frighten, "will no doubt eventually obtain more
than your just share of it—provided only that you
live long enough. How long do you intend to
live?"

"Th-th-th-the nearest city is Orleans," the lord
of the castle got out. His voice was somewhat
muffled in his robes, as he was now down on all
fours, head below rump, definitely in a state of
collapse. That he could achieve this posture without getting any part of himself out of what was
left of the circle struck Talisman as remarkable.

"Orleans!" Talisman mused aloud. "In
fourteen-twenty. The Sword . . . I might have
guessed. The Sword acts through the centuries. If
I could find it here . . . which way to town?"

At last the wizard, still more or less upright
though speechless, pointed with a shaking arm.
Talisman without another word turned his back
on the pair and strode off into the night. Once
away from the fires he paused, sniffing, listening,
then shifted into wolf-form for quick, keen-
scented travel.

He had not gone far in this mode before he
gained two new perceptions: the Sword was some-

where near, as he had thought, though magically protected. And the old man was somewhere nearby too, not far ahead of him.

The sight of a wolf entering a medieval city would not be all *that* much of a surprise to the human inhabitants, but it would certainly draw unwelcome attention from them. Walking in as a man in twentieth-century clothing might create something of a stir also. It would be mistform or batform then. The latter would provide keener senses, and be virtually no more noticeable.

Talisman thought it would be pointless for him to search directly for the Sword, protected as it was. So, knowing what he knew, and guessing what he had guessed, he sought confrontation with the old man by seeking taverns. It took little effort to discover three of them, not much more than spitting distance from the brooding cathedral of Saint-Croix. Halfway between two of these establishments, on a guttered but unpaved street, his perception of his foe's presence grew very strong.

Talisman came down out of the night on small bat's wings, then extended human legs to find a footing in the mud, and bear a man's full weight. He was sure of the identity of the sodden figure collapsed at streetside even before he turned it over on its back. When he saw the old man's face, stupefied and ugly, he felt his own fingers talon and go reaching for the throat; but with an effort of will Talisman mastered the impulse to kill. No doubt the powers guarding this fifteenth-century version of the old man's self were dormant, but they would still be very powerful and capable of being roused by real peril. Instead, Talisman spoke a soft, compelling order to awake.

The man who would one day call himself Hawk stirred, sat up at last, then tugged drunkenly to free himself when Talisman would have pulled him to his feet.

Grimly, Talisman heaved him erect anyway. The old man staggered, wiped his face with a sleeve of filthy medieval rags, then leaned for support against a wattle-and-daub house wall.

"What are you? Don' tell me you're a man." The old man's French was perhaps even a little better than Talisman's.

Talisman, wondering how best to proceed, almost despairing, growled at him.

"Speak up. You know, when I wake up tomorrow, I'm not gonna remember any of this. Are you perchance acquainted with the Lady?"

"Lady?"

"The Lady of the Lake. Didja know she was my lover, once? Well almos'. These fingers right here . . ." The old man held up a gnarled claw. "I once almos' got these very fingers right on 'er little . . ." The alcoholic bass voice dissolved in a chuckle, half agony, half gross obscenity.

"I know about that, old man. Or I have guessed. But right now something else is more important. I am looking for a Sword."

"But whooinell are you, anyway? Tell me, are you from my past? Or my future? I have days, guess this is one, when the creatures of either may come 'round to 'flict me."

Talisman clenched his hands, to keep them from reaching out again. "You have made me a creature, as you put it, of both, you son of the devil and a whore. Now where is the Sword? It's near here somewhere, else why are you here now, and why am I here to meet you? Yours is the magic that concealed it, am I not right?"

"Dunno any sword."

"You lie. This is Orleans. Will not the Maid herself have the Sword in hand, nine years from now, when she comes here to lift the British seige?"

"The Maid? Who—?" The old man, appearing honestly puzzled, shuddered. "No, I'm not looking ahead tonight. Jus' gimme another drink, that's all I want. Safer that way. Wish I could still feel good when I wake up again, but I can't. Can't even remember feelin' good."

"Then it will be hidden again. As it was hidden before. But you can tell me where it is now. And you shall."

"Tell you nothin'. What are you, anyway?"

"Tell me, you ancient madman, tell me—" Talisman's taloned hands reached out.

Effortlessly the old wizard's defensive powers struck out at him. Talisman was swept back into the pyrotechnic swirl, outside of space and time.

TWENTY-TWO

In pastel sunlight the paved road was a flow of stone that had been moving for hours in a hypnotic rhythm, almost without pause. The surface that flowed backward underneath Margie's stride was for the most part of flat paving stones. Underneath them was another layer, that in the frequent unrepaired breaks showed as some kind of rough concrete. Beneath the scuffle of marching feet, these surfaces gave up dust. The dust tended to drift up in a fine cloud, and by midmorning all of the trudging Ladies were white with a layer of dust on top of the flaxen offwhiteness of their dress. The dust grayed the clothing of the other villagers who trudged with them, and added a touch of stage makeup to the faces of everyone.

Artos had got this march, this flight, started well before dawn, just as the lad who'd brought the warning to the village had advised. When the House of Ladies was aroused (overhearing speech now with new understanding, Marge had soon learned that was their proper name) they had, like well-trained troops, mobilized themselves at once. There were about a dozen of the Ladies, mostly young, but led by a First Lady of strong middle age. Under her direction the evacuation of their House had gone like clockwork. A few belongings were packed on backs, some loaded on a donkey. The remainder were left behind without a second glance.

The couple of dozen other people who inhabited the village had been just as brisk in getting ready to hit the road. If the road was narrow, the column of refugees was narrow too, and short. There were fewer than forty people in it altogether.

At the first indications that people in the House of Ladies were waking up, Talisman had vanished back into the night, leaving in Marge's ear the whispered hope that he'd be able to rejoin her later, probably at night. Meanwhile he was going to learn what he could about the enemies of Artos.

By now, midmorning, Marge herself still hadn't been able to find out much about the enemy—or very much about her companions, either, except for noting a small collection of unfamiliar names. Among the feared and detested leaders of the foe were people called Falerin, Comorr, Nimue, and someone whose name sounded like Medrow, the last especially despised as traitor.

She puzzled continually and uselessly over where her newfound ability to understand these people's language had come from. She had not yet revealed her new understanding, though she felt intuitively that she would be able to speak as well as understand, whenever she chose to try. And, without appearing to listen, she continued to absorb the talk of those around her, picking up what information she could. She learned less than she would have thought, for the people who spoke to each other were always assuming background knowledge that Marge simply didn't have.

And Marge was tired. A little lightheaded, not at all confident that she was thinking straight. She had retired early to her pallet last evening, but sleep had been uneasy and interrupted. And now she'd had to keep up for hours with what she considered a damned hard hike. It was a good thing that she'd been in shape when this whole crazy experience started.

There were three or four donkeys, used as pack animals. The only horses were carrying half a dozen fighting men. These were all evidently leaders, and there was no chivalrous nonsense out of them about offering weaker folk a ride. This small cavalry squadron, wearing chain mail over regular clothes, was led by the short, forceful man, Artos—that had turned out to be his name and not the name of the village. Armed with short spears, knives, shields, and the only two swords that Marge had seen since her arrival, the cavalry since dawn had been maneuvering in and out of sight of the trudging foot column. Sometimes they went trotting ahead to scout the way. At other times they dropped back, or vanished along hedgerows to one side of the road or the other, Marge supposed to look out for ambush or pursuit. Among the people on foot, ten or a dozen men and boys were carrying spears and short blades, serving as immediate armed escort.

Marge had heard frequent mention of something called the Strong Fort. It was the place they were trying to reach, and she gathered that they might possibly ge there sometime tomorrow. She supposed that meant at least one night spent in the open, in what promised to be an uncomfortable camp. Marge wasn't looking forward to the night.

A distant whistle, intended as a signal, broke in on her thoughts. Everyone around her was galvanized by the sound.

"They fight!" one of the Ladies near Marge gasped. The whole small column, men, women, and children, had already quickened its pace into a run. The whistle had sounded from somewhere in the rear, where a few minutes earlier the cavalry had dropped back out of sight.

Marge, surrounded by grim, whitedusted, gasping faces, ran with the rest. The pace was not an all-out dash but a long-distance lope, and so far she was keeping up. Somewhere far in the rear, the men of the cavalry shouted, going about their warriors' trade. Now already the older people in the column were beginning to lag helplessly. No one was going to wait for them. The younger adults pressed on, dragging the smaller children with them as best they could.

Before Marge was totally winded, another whistled signal overtook the refugees. Stumbling with relief, the fleeing column straggled to a halt. Some sat down where they were. Heads turned back. Within a minute, Artos rode into sight at the head of his tiny squadron, all of whom had apparently survived the skirmish in good shape. Artos had his sword in hand, and when he waved it briefly, signalling the walking people to move right on, Marge could see that it was stained. The horses of the cavalry, skittish now, snorting, walking quickly, brought their riders forward, overtaking the pedestrians.

"And the new sword?" an old man, walking, asked Artos anxiously. The speaker had fallen in beside the leader's horse, on whose saddle Marge now noticed there were no stirrups. None of the saddles had them, she assured herself, looking around. How did the men manage to stay on?

Artos nodded in reply to the old man, who had powerful, gray-furred arms. "Excellent. You forged well."

The First Lady, hiking nearby in white gown and well-worn sandals, put in a few words grumpily: "There was no time for a proper consecration of the sword. And at the Strong Fort there's no lake big enough to do it properly."

"Then, mother," said Artos, clapping hand to the hilt of the weapon he had just wiped and resheathed, "the consecration will have to be in the using of it. Forward!" He kicked lightly at his mount's flanks with his heels, and led his squadron cantering ahead.

One of the ladies murmured: "Oh, if only Ambrosius were still around. Artos needs his help, his magic. We all do."

"Ambrosius is dead, girl." The First Lady spoke bitterly. "Save your breath for walking."

Near midday, with the sun as high as it seemed likely to get in the mild sky, there was a halt beside a brook, for which the paved road made way in a simple ford. All the land that Marge had seen here so far was green and flat, except for occasional soft hills, and well-watered with streams and lakes. As they traveled she had seen increasingly more forest, less cultivated ground. What cultivation there was looked to her extremely crude, confined to patchy, stump-studded clearings, fenced if at all wth makeshift wooden rails. The land of Hansel and Gretel, she had thought to herself. And then sure enough by God they had passed the woodcutter's cottage. thatched roof and all, looking not only poor but deserted.

The edged weapons she saw all about her, the stains on the sword of Artos, were impressively real. But this brand of reality only left her all the more deeply embedded in the bloodthirsty world of fairy tales.

The march resumed after a short rest. Soon it overtook livestock being driven in the same direction, by more people with meager belongings packed on their backs. Some of these cheered aloud for Artos when they saw him, all looked relieved when he rode by. First they passed a gaggle of geese, persecuted by children with sticks. Then, presently, a couple of dozen sheep, in the care of armed but not mounted shepherds. The trudging villagers passed up the herders, exchanging a few news items as they passed.

A little later, with Artos and his half-dozen horsemen again scouting ahead, there was a new outburst of whistle-signalling from that direction. Marge was startled out of a state of near-hypnosis into which the rhythm of the march had brought her; but her new talent for understanding let her recognize the signal at once as one reserved for announcing good news. The people she walked among made the same interpretation; there were smiles, and an outburst of chatter. Shortly Artos reappeared ahead, a score of mounted warriors with him now. Obviously contact had been made with some larger, friendly force.

Friendly infantry also came drifting in, equipped much as the villagers were. Amid notable relaxation, another rest stop was decreed. There was a faint smell in the air that Marge recognized as that of wine, and she saw men drinking out of skins. But none of the Ladies were being offered any. She allowed herself a sigh.

At least there was no prohibition against the Ladies relaxing and mingling socially. Marge gratefully unburdened herself of her assigned pack, and drifted closer to where Artos, now seated on the grass, was talking things over with some men of the newly arrived group.

As she approached, she could hear the short man saying: "Would that we had him here; we sorely need his magic. Would that he had at least sent a final message before he met his doom. But evidently he did not. So we must just manage without Ambrosius as best we can."

"My lord?" Marge broke in impulsively, the first words she had spoken with the aid of her new power. She had framed them in modern English, her mind intending something like *Excuse me sir but*—What came out, however, had been translated automatically into the language of her hearers, and sounded in Marge's own ears like, "My lord?"

Faces everywhere turned toward her. The blue eyes of Artos, like those of others round him, showed surprise; in his case, it was a reaction that lasted all of two seconds.

"So," he asked Marge then. "Whose agent are you?"

"I am the agent of Ambrosius, lord." Marge spoke confidently, following a plan that was taking form in her mind, fully developed, as she went along. "It is only by his magic that I now have power to understand and speak your language. When I arrived at the village I truly could not."

Artos was studying her carefully. "And his magic has touched you since then? For what purpose?"

"Truly. There is a message I am to convey to you from him."

On all sides a babble of excitement rose. Some people were expressing doubts, others were hopeful, ready and waiting to believe. It all quieted when Artos raised a hand. "What then is the message?"

"He wishes you well. He is now—in a place of relative safety." And Marge, listening to herself, knew sudden inward terror. *Where are these words coming from? The First Lady said a little while ago that Ambrosius is dead, but still so many here seem ready to believe what I'm saying.* "He bids you to be of good cheer, despite —despite your traitorous son." She saw pain cross the face of Artos.

Marge drew breath. "And Ambrosius warns you that the Sword—" *I don't understand this at all.* "—is to be returned, when you can no longer use it, to the lake."

Artos, to Marge's surprise, was nodding at her thoughtfully, at least half inclined to accept the message at face value. "Very well," the short man said. "If what you tell me is true, I rejoice that Ambrosius is again able to help us with his advice. We'll see. When we get to the Strong Fort I expect we'll be able to talk to him in person."

TWENTY-THREE

Hawk was sitting on a fence, and it wasn't very comfortable. Actually there were two fences, one physical, one metaphorical, bothering his backside. The physical barrier enclosed a small parking lot on the north side of Chicago. It was about two feet high, with a metal top that was sharply enough angled to discourage sitting by any Skid Row bums who might wander this far from their own turf a few blocks distant. The metaphorical fence, though, was the one that pained Hawk the most: pretty soon he was going to have to get up and go back to Skid Row, or else he was going to have to make a definite decision about what else to do. To make himself start walking in some other direction, into an unknown and therefore frightening future.

It was early morning again, the sun up somewhere, though still out of sight for most of the dwellers in the city's artificial canyons. It had rained on Hawk a while ago, but he was used to that, and now it had stopped raining. All he knew for sure was that he couldn't sit on this damned fence for the rest of his life.

Since getting out of jail he found himself unable—or unwilling, the distinction was frequently blurred—to get a look into his own future. He found himself now trying to imagine it instead. It was an odd thing—or maybe, if he thought about it, not so odd—but he supposed he'd never had much real power of imagination. It seemed to him marvelous that the human beings who thought of themselves as ordinary could sometimes wield such an eldritch power without even thinking twice about it. Hawk strained his own resources when he tried to imagine things, and even then he suspected that he couldn't do it very well.

Right now, for example, he was trying to imagine what would happen if he decided to go back to Skid Row. He could, with some effort, just picture himself sitting there in the gutter again. His ugly new shirt would be stained here and there with puke and grime, and he would be doing a trick—now that he could do tricks again—for his old coin-pool buddies, to produce some wine. He'd get good stuff that way, of course, probably wouldn't be able to conjure up anything less than a fine vintage even if he tried.

Hawk sighed. He could imagine one of his old acquaintances going *blahhh*, spitting the fine stuff out—not the kind of wine they were accustomed to tasting on the Street. Hawk sighed again. He knew he wasn't ever, if he could help it, going back to that.

At about this point his reverie was interrupted by the realization that two men were approaching him. The pair were coming along the broad sidewalk from the direction of his old haunts, slowing gradually toward a stop as they drew near. Neither of them was the parking lot attendant he'd been halfway expecting to show up to shag him off the fence. One of the men was Carados, halfway expected also. The second was a stranger to Hawk; a second look at this stranger set off alarms all up and down the picket line of Hawk's defensive powers. Hawk beheld the shape of a fat man, whose throat under its present turtleneck covering had recently been injured, and was now healing at a speed not consonant with pure, breathing humanity. Not, by God, another vampire—? No, not this time.

The two came confidently close to Hawk before they stopped in front of him. "Mr. Hawk?" the plump werewolf inquired formally, being mock-courteous in English whose accents the old man could not immediately place.

The old man could feel the fierceness of the glare he gave them in return, the tension in his own beetled brow. "I've just decided I don't want to use that name any more."

"Oh?" Chubby monster was doing the talking, while Carados smirked silently at his side. "You are now to be known as—?" It was humoring, almost mockery.

The old man gravely took thought. "Falcon. You may call me Mr. Falcon."

"By whatever name you wish, then. Mr. Falcon, you are to come with us. A certain great Lady wishes to consult you, on a matter of importance to her."

"Ah. All goes not so well with Nimue. Could it be that she wants me to help her find something?"

Carados, showing anger, spoke at last. "She got you right where it counts, old man. Whatever you got left there, she got hold of it. You know that, we know it, so don't try to give us no problem. Just get up and march where we tell you."

That was almost right, Falcon reflected. If Nimue had condescended to come after him herself, there would have been no question about it. He would have had to get up and go with her at once, probably without even arguing. But she hadn't. Perhaps, not long ago, her power over him had been fully transferable, but he could feel that it wasn't any longer. Perhaps in general it had started to wear a little thin.

Falcon dug in his mental heels. It was time to see how far resistance could be carried. He couldn't, or at least he didn't think he could, go so far as turning these two into turnips or the equivalent, thereby thwarting some of their mistress' no doubt rotten plans. Now she wanted the Sword, she thought for some reason she had to have it. Well, time would tell. Maybe, just maybe, Falcon could manage to arrange matters so she didn't get it. The thought had a deliciously forbidden, wicked feeling; but he could think it now.

Ah God, but she had been, still was, so beautiful . . . that was only a memory for Falcon now. He had been immunized. At what expense.

Looking hard at Carados, he said: "You're from Haiti. Your accent tends to come and go, that's what threw me off. Older than you look. Aren't we all? Friend of old Papa Doc's, I bet."

Carados glowered at this mild display of spirit. "You get up and march, I said. Else when we get you there, we'll use you as I first intended."

Falcon stood up, moving more slowly and creakily than was really necessary. It was a considerable relief to be off the fence. "Where's your car?" he asked, trying to sound reluctantly submissive. He meant to try a thing or two while they were riding.

Then he paused, looking at the fat figure in manshape. "What's your name, by the way?"

"Call me Arnaud," replied the werewolf cautiously. More alert than Carados, he sensed changes in the old man. Arnaud stood straight and watched the old man carefully.

Carados said: "Move, old one. This way, across the street. Just a short walk, no car this time."

Falcon, who had been ready to walk, let himself slump a little. "No? What then?"

"We simply walk the tunnel," explained Arnaud. "Nimue can extend it a long way now. We've created a temporary entrance in that alley across the street. It's being held open for us."

"Nimue's power is high." Falcon nodded to himself. "The sacrifices." And then he saw the car that was pulling up quietly behind the others, and was aware before they were of what it meant, and allowed himself a twisted little grin.

The car's doors were opening on both sides. "Police officers! Stand right where you are!"

Falcon doubled over slowly, went down in a crouch-and-fall like a man already shot, except that he reached out with his hands to save his face and body as he sprawled his whole length out on the sidewalk that was still faintly warm with the heat of yesterday. *Get yours you bastard*, he thought with pleasure, seeing Carados turn toward the police, drawing a gun.

Chicago cops were not at all slow about getting down to the nitty-gritty, not when armed-and-considered-extremely-dangerous turned at bay with metal glinting in his hand. A fusillade was already rambling in the air not far above Falcon's head. The nearest auto in the parking lot behind him swayed on its wheels, squealing like a hurt animal as it took a bullet's full energy in frame or engine block. Fragments of brick wall sprayed down on Falcon sharply before he got his personal protective spell in gear, tuned against the heavy threat of leaden bullets. Should have done that sooner, but it had taken him precious seconds to remember how.

Carados must have been getting similar help, from Arnaud or more likely from Nimue herself, or he'd be down in bundled bloody rags by now instead of sprinting after Arnaud for the alley beside the parking lot. In the dark alley's mouth the dark man turned, heedless of more bullets harmlessly puncturing his clothing. Grinning, he aimed his own weapon carefully, pausing long enough to add one more cop to his list of victims, before he turned again and ran back into darkness. Quite probably, Falcon realized, by now the mouth of the secret tunnel had been shifted from the alley across the street to this one. It could be almost anywhere. Falcon could see the potential connections in his mind, almost without trying. That magic tunnel was web-centered at the castle, and now it went on across the world as far or almost as far as did the Street of Failure.

There was another squad car partially blocking the street at each end of the block, and still more cop cars were now screeching to a halt nearby. The police wouldn't have forgotten the alleys either, of course. Not that thoroughness was going to do them much good against Nimue. They must have spotted Carados some minutes ago, to give them time to close in like this from all sides.

Their prey had fled—no, it hadn't. In a moment of silence Falcon could hear two voices bickering. Arnaud was remonstrating with his companion about something, trying to get him to hurry along. Carados after one reply ignored Arnaud, and raised his voice to call a fond farewell to the police, adding a few terms of endearment of his own invention. As far as Falcon could tell now, the voices were up in a second-story window in one of the nearby buildings. The cops hadn't been expecting magic tunnels, any more than anti-bullet spells. Falcon, still holding himself face down on the pavement, smiled bitterly.

His faint hopes of being left alone, forgotten now, were dashed. A pair of hardrunning feet came zeroing in on him. Hard hands seized him under the armpits, began to drag him around a corner. Falcon's dragging feet kicked feebly, and he protested, mumbling curses—not really *aiming* them at anyone. Whoever was dragging him muttered them right back at him, in a voice strained with fear and physical effort. There sounded a shot, whose leaden burden whizzed the air close by.

Once round the corner, he was propped in a painful sitting position against a building. Glaring close into his was a young man's face that he ought to be able to recognize—in a moment he did. It was that of the mundane young cop who had once talked to him of swords.

"Are you hit?" It was a fierce demand.

"Hit? Hit? Shit no I'm not hit. I got sense enough to know when to go down and stay put."

The cop's mumbled obscenities conveyed mingled exasperation and relief. "Come on. I want to get you into a car. There are things besides Carados that we have to talk about."

Like how I walked out of jail so easy, thought Falcon. Now the cop had him on his feet. Which car were they going to get into, though? Two, three more were braking to a halt, brakes squealing, sirens silent. Here came the—what the hell did they call it? the Mash team?—the men with fancy helmets and body armor, cradling firearms of elegantly devious design. In a sudden near-silence Falcon could hear their little handheld radios rasping at each other cryptically. Another single shot sounded, and someone yelled, hit. Carados was contemptuously pushing his—no, it wasn't luck at all. There were bursts of activity as uniformed men scrambled this way and that, climbing buildings, ducking in and out of doorways. Joe—Falcon suddenly recalled the name, from their long interrogation session—pulled his charge back into the sheltering mouth of another alley.

This alley proved to have unpleasant occupants.

The plump hand of Arnaud, at the moment sporting neither fur nor claws, closed gently but firmly on Falcon's right wrist. "Nimue bids you come with us," Arnaud chided softly. "It is her command, and you have no choice."

Carados stood just a few feet distant, aiming his gun point-blank at Joe; Falcon saw the young policeman turn pale to his lips. The promise of death was very plain.

Joe started to say something, and at the same moment he reached quickly for his own gun, inside his coat. Carados deliberately tilted his aim slightly to one side and shot Joe through the right arm. Joe's gun, half-drawn, fell to the alley floor.

"Come on!" urged Arnaud softly. Ten feet now from where Carados and Joe were locked in a hideous confrontation, Arnaud tugged almost tentatively—as if he were wary of being rough—at Falcon's wrist.

"You can't do that," Falcon muttered under his breath. He was speaking to Carados, even if Carados couldn't hear him, wasn't paying him the least attention. When Arnaud tugged again, this time growling lightly in his throat, the fingers of Falcon's held hand made a small gesture, as if he were spinning away a little top. An image of Falcon separated itself from Falcon, like a detachable shadow, as Falcon himself simultaneously became invisible. The image, head down and shuffling, moved off down the alley, one wrist gripped by its captor who appeared to be quite satisfied.

Carados had backed off another step or two from Joe, teasing, as if he might really be willing to walk off and leave a live cop looking at him. In the streetlight Falcon could see the harmless bullet-tears in the dark man's clothing. Joe stood in shock, holding his shot arm, swaying a little as if he were continually trying to brace himself against the next bullet, the one that it seemed must hit him with every passing second.

If Falcon was not completely invisible to both of them now, he might as well have been. He felt choked up. He groped for words that just were not available. If Nimue herself had been here . . . but she wasn't. So something ought to be, had to be, possible. Falcon could fight her helpers. He could try at least, he could . . .

"Just reach for it, pig," said Carados softly, backing away one more slow step. "Or don't, I don't care. It's good night either way."

A police radio rasped; it was half a block away, and it might as well have been on the moon for all the help it was going to be. Outside the alley the teams were going into action with professional care, all facing in the wrong direction. From deeper down the alley, Arnaud's voice called impatiently for Carados to come on.

"In just a second," Carados called back in a low voice.

Falcon tried to think of, come up with, what he needed; grunting aloud with the effort. He couldn't, couldn't, couldn't smash Carados down, not directly anyway. Nimue's grip, like some network of ancient ropes, still bound him too tightly for that.

Joe's body started to bend in several places. Then he fell to his knees. Obviously having to summon all the control he could, struggling just to stay conscious, he reached left-handed for the gun.

"Beautiful, pig, that's beautiful. Just the way I want you." Carados started to make a slow, careful aim, then paused. "I'll even give you the first shot. Fair?"

Falcon's right hand, unseen by anyone but him, pointed in a double-fingered gesture toward Joe's pistol, as the policeman fumbled the weapon up from the alley floor. The old man muttered half-forgotten words. He had to strain hideously against the constraints that Nimue had laid on

him an age ago. But he got out the words: ". . .
balle de plomb . . . le balle argent . . ."

Joe's arm lifted suddenly, and sharp bursts of
thunder filled the alley. Falcon hunched down,
cursing himself for having let his protective spell
lapse in the concentration of his other effort. The
gun-explosions seemed to go on past any reasonable number, echoing, reverberating. At the end
there came a crashing as of hollow armor, and
from down the alley a howl as of a hurt wolf.

Cautiously, his own defenses once more in order, the man whose public name had once been
Ambrosius lifted his head to look. Joe was on his
feet again, looking dazed, gun swinging in his left
hand. There was movement at the other side of
the alley too; one dangling arm, pistol hanging by
one finger through the guard. The body of
Carados lay across a row of garbage cans, where
it had been flung by silver bullets.

TWENTY-FOUR

Simon was fifteen years old when he stumbled away from Vivian and her stone table, and started back down the bluff, blindly following the trail. After taking only about twenty steps—or so it seemed to him—he was thirty years old again. He began to remember that he was only reliving events that had happened to him years ago.

Only?

He slowed to a stop, looking round him and trying to orient himself. Yes, he was in the same woods, outside the castle. Though he tried to shake it, the vision of his experience in the past persisted strongly. In one part of his mind he was still just fifteen. He was going to swim and wade his way back across the river, letting it do what it could to cleanse him of the dirt and sweat of the day just past. When he got back to his aunt's and uncle's house, the adults wouldn't be back from their meeting yet, and he'd go right upstairs to his small room and fall into his narrow bed. He knew that the image of Vivian was coming with him as never before, and that it would draw him back again and again to the deserted grotto, where he would never have to worry about Gregory appearing in the bright daytime. Where, on the stone table, Vivian's shape could be brought bursting out of Simon's imagination with intensity never before realized, to be made to do exactly what he wanted her to do . . .

At last it faded, his vision of that exhausted fifteen-year-old walking through the twilight. Simon was thirty, and though he stood in the same woods it was now dawn not twilight, and he was no longer on the trail that wound so familiarly down the bluff. He raised a hand to his face, assuring himself of beard-stubble on his cheeks. He was dressed in the pseudo-magician's costume he'd put on for the night before—

Ah, yes. The night before. The last thing Simon could remember before the strangely realistic memory-flashback was himself in the castle, entering the hidden tunnel again at Vivian's urging. It could lead him, she had said, to many places, many times. It had looped him back into his own memory, and then . . . somehow it had delivered him here outside the castle? Through the grotto again, he supposed. He couldn't remember.

Vivian had ordered him to find an object. She'd called it simply the Sword, without explanation, as if there were no possibility of his not understanding. And on some deep level of his mind he did understand what he was commanded to look for. He hadn't found it yet, just because it was hidden with superlative magic. But he would find it in time, if he kept on looking. He knew that the power existed in him to see, find, anything.

Unconsciously he had slowly started walking again, slowly shuffling rather, through the woods. And now he halted once more, trying to orient himself. Just where *was* he? Somewhere not far from the castle, certainly. The wooded land was quite limited in extent.

Gradually increasing light assured Simon that the day was coming, if it was not already here behind the clouds. During the night it had rained heavily, and the air was still full of mist. Last year's dead leaves made a thick sodden carpet on the ground, else he'd probably be ankle deep in mud. Every leaf and twig in sight seemed to be dripping steadily. But the sky no longer really threatened, and innumerable birds were up and being cheerful. The show must go on. Oh God. At least he'd tried his best, last night, to give a good performance. That was something that they could carve on his tombstone.

The sky was solid with light cloud or high fog, pearly gray and almost featureless. Simon was standing at the top of a deep, tree-grown slope. Of course it had to be the familiar bluff, though now with the odd light and the surface fog the decline appeared somewhat too gradual. Downslope, where the fog naturally was even thicker, the river remained completely invisible. Somewhere on the far shore a heavy truck was negotiating the highway; one moment the sound came very clearly, and the next it had been completely cut off. An effect of curves and hills, maybe, or some trick of foggy atmosphere. The truck made Simon think of all the lucky people over there, including most of the population of the world, who'd never heard of Vivian.

He wanted to simply walk away from her, and keep on walking. He would, as soon as he'd found Marge. Something told him that would not be easy, but he'd do it, and then the two of them would walk away. At the moment he felt capable of rebelling against Vivian's orders—of course he hadn't really tried as yet. It couldn't possibly be as easy as it felt right now. She wouldn't let him go. His special powers—and he could no longer doubt he had them—made him far too valuable for that.

A small bird flew close to him, in a half circle. There was something odd about its wing movements; could it have been a bat? Now it was gone again.

Leaning against a tree, Simon reached out with his free hand in the motion of a man trying to catch some fog. This was the world, the existence of psychic powers demonstrated, such stuff as dreams are made on. How did that whole passage go, in Shakespeare? Something about the fabric of a dream. But it would be too much, if the whole world-dream turned out to be a nightmare.

The bluff here was really not that steep, he thought. If the slope had been just a little more moderate, someone would probably have made a pasture out of it. Simon's knees were trembling. He gave a grunt of near-exhaustion, as if Vivian had really made him reenact that whole day of fifteen years ago, and sat down on the darkened stump where someone had long ago cut down a tree.

And almost jumped up again, when he thought he heard a broken cry, in a child's voice, or a woman's. It told of terror, but it was gone again in a moment, leaving no sense of the direction or distance that it had come from. And now, for just a moment as he peered through the fog, Simon thought he caught a glimpse of a ruined tower, broken and jumbled masonry, set a little back from the edge of the bluff not far ahead of him. Simultaneously he was aware of silent horror and pain, human anguish preserved as if by some arcane method of recording. Could the building have something to do with the old artists' colony? It had seemed too large for that. In the next moment Simon was unsure that the tower had been there physically at all. The sense of recorded suffering persisted, though.

Now for the first time he saw the rays of the morning sun, only momentarily visible through clouds. And when they were gone the figure of a lean man dressed in black was moving slowly toward him along the edge of the bluff, through wreaths of morning mist.

Simon stood up. But he could sense nothing about the approaching figure that demanded flight or a defensive confrontation. There was potential danger, but it was not overriding. There was potential benefit as well; and there was strangeness.

The man, as he approached, looked at least equally puzzled as to what he should make of Simon. He offered a deep-voiced greeting in French. Simon was surprised but managed to reply in the same language. The man gave a little shake of his head and switched to modern English. "I think you are a sojourner here, even as I am."

"Here?" Simon didn't know at first how to interpret that. "On the south bank of the Sauk, you mean?"

The man's dark eyes gazed at him with interest. "Is that where you think you are?"

"I've been—wandering."

"Indeed." The other smiled faintly; he had an engaging way about him. "I also. I have been touring castles. My name is Talisman, by the way. And I think you must be Simon Hill, professional conjurer. Sent here by the woman you know as Vivian Littlewood."

"Are you working for her? What name do you know her by?"

"I certainly am not. Another name for her, a much older one, is Nimue."

Simon had the impression of hearing that name before somewhere. Now, somewhere in the fogbound middle distance, a man's voice had started singing. The language again was French, to Simon's ears oddly accented. The melody had to be nothing other than some simple old folk song; but Simon felt a chill.

He asked: "If I'm not on the Sauk, where am I?"

Talisman was watching him closely. "At the moment, on the border of Brittany."

Many places, many times. "And . . . that river down there?" The more the mist cleared and the light grew, the stranger the world looked. For example, there was a structure in the distance—farther than the broken tower he'd glimpsed earlier—that looked very much like an old factory chimney.

"The river is the Sèvre," said Talisman, in the tones of one cautiously giving guidance. He turned his head and nodded in the other direction, away from the edge of the bluff. "And if we were to walk a few paces that way, we will find ourselves standing on the bank of a moat."

"A moat."

"I told you that I have been touring castles. Not of my own volition, unfortunately. I have even revisited, briefly, my own former residence." Talisman sighed. "And, before that, the house of evil that is now reconstructed on the Sauk. I saw it in its original location, where the earliest stones were set in place by men named Comorr and Falerin—ah, you have heard of those names, at least. From Nimue, I take it."

"I've heard of them." Simon moistened his lips. "I don't want anything to do with them, or Nimue either. What now?"

Talisman gestured in the direction of the ruined tower, now once more partially visible through mists. "Now this. This was once part of a great domain—the Château Tiffauges. Does that name convey anything to you?"

"The name? No." But ancient horror, preserved in time, still drifted with the mist.

"It should, perhaps." Behind Talisman, as the morning fog dissipated further, the broken tower was once more to be seen. It was immense, like the stump of some bombed office building. "But we are obviously too late to see this establishment at the peak of its fame—if fame is the proper word. I deduce, from various considerations, that we are now standing sometime in the middle of the nineteenth century."

Simon didn't doubt it. *Many place, many times.* Looking away from the river now, he could see the regular depression in the land that Talisman had called a moat; it was deeper and wider than Simon had imagined moats to be. Great trees growing on the bottom of it had their crowns at his eye level. Beyond it he could just make out the vague shape of the keep, more than half ruined, not quite deserted. In one exposed interior corner a thatched hut had been built, and the voice of the singing peasant seemed to come from there.

A picture of something silvery, utterly beautiful, came and went in Simon's mind. Almost he managed to grasp where it was. But before he could quite do that it was gone again. He turned toward the ruined chateau, stretching out one hand and letting it fall. "The Sword," he murmured.

Talisman came a step closer to him. "Yes, that is what we are both seeking, are we not? We have both been sent here for that purpose, even if the one who sent me did not do so consciously. At first I was surprised by the idea that the Sword might be here—of all places."

The last three words contained an emphasis that made Simon look more closely at the speaker. "I don't understand. What is this place?"

"If Joan the Maid," said Talisman, "once truly had the Sword in her hand—as I have come to believe she did—then what more natural than for her to leave it to one of her trusted lieutenants, a powerful man who could be expected to survive the English wars? On the other hand, it might have been stolen from her by such a man, who really saw in it no more than magic to be turned to his own advantage. And once it was in his hands, by gift or theft, he might well have brought it here, to the seat of his power, his personal dominion." Falcon paused. "He was a Marshal of France, and his name was Gilles de Rais."

TWENTY-FIVE

During the long hike Marge had formed a more or less definite mental picture of the Strong Fort. In her mind she saw it as something like a miniature castle. The reality was quite different: a broad and gentle hilltop, fortified by two concentric earth-and-timber walls, each higher than a man. Lush grass covered the lower portion of the hill, and still grew in patches between the broad paths and roads and barren spots that had been worn over most of the upper portion by feet and hooves and wagon wheels. The area surrounded by the inner wall was several acres in extent and contained two deep wells, plus enough simple buildings to qualify the place as a small town.

When Artos and his party arrived, escorting Marge and the Ladies, tents were already going up between and beside the permanent buildings, to help shelter the burgeoning population. The place was badly crowded, but Marge gathered that no one expected that to last for more than a few days. A big, decisive battle was expected soon, one in which Artos would of course thrash the invaders, among them his own traitorous bastard son Medraut. There was also low-voiced gossip about Artos' wife, whom Marge had not yet seen. Her infidelity was an open secret.

Marge had not yet finished helping the Ladies get settled in their temporary House—the usual occupants had been moved into tents for the duration—when a man came with word that Artos wanted to see her at once. She found the leader dismounted, surrounded by people wanting to make reports and/or ask favors. But his business with Marge had evidently a high priority in his own mind. As soon as he saw her he raised his voice, putting off the others, and came to take her by the arm. His first words were: "I've not seen him yet, have you?"

She had no doubt of who Artos meant. "No, I've no idea where he is."

"I've managed to find out that much, at least."

Artos led her to the main street of the miniature town, a rutted road going straight out through the main gate of the inner wall; after that they walked a quarter-circle between walls, then out through the main gate of the outer defense. Despite his relatively short legs, Artos set a pace that was hard to match. He paused twice on the way to shout orders to workmen about defenses. He and Marge dodged incoming wagons laden with what Marge supposed must be food to sustain a seige, or military supplies of some sort. When they had got outside the outer wall, the scene still bustled with activity. More tents had been put up out here, as Marge had noted on her way in; she realized now that these must be temporary storage facilities for non-essentials, and housing of a sort for various hangers-on.

On the outer rim of this suburb, a number of men were gathered around a small lean-to tent, one side of it supported by a wagon; from the sour smells wafting from the direction of the tent, Marge realized that it must be the establishment of an itinerant wineseller. When some of the men saw Artos approaching, the little crowd dispersed like morning mist.

But for once the leader showed no interest in what his troops might be doing. There was an aged and mellowed dungheap not far from the wineseller's tent, and a crumpled figure in clothing once fine, now badly stained, was taking advantage of its softness. Artos marched straight to the figure and turned it over. To Marge the face of the old man, dozing and drooling, looked definitely familiar; though he was younger now than the last time she'd seen him, his hair and beard not so far gone in moldy whiteness, indeed still containing broad streaks of black. It was borne in on her that once even this man had been truly young; and somehow that was one of the most eerie thoughts of all.

"Wake up," said Artos, gently cuffing the old man's face.

Ambrosius woke up. He looked at Artos, whether with comprehension or not would have been hard to say.

Artos said: "People tell me that you have some plan of going to Londinium."

The old man grunted. He hardly glanced at Marge. His red-rimmed eyes were still the color of storm-cleared skies, but not yet deeply hooded by age-carved lids.

Artos told him: "The roads are far from safe. And I can spare no escort for you. You understand that?"

"Understand that, of course I understand that." Marge could recognize the voice at once. "But I do you no good by staying here. Not any more. And no one's going to bother me on the road."

"How do you . . ." Artos let it trail off. There

was a little silence. Then he gripped the old man
again, and raised him a little, helping him settle
into a more comfortable sitting position. The old
manure he sat on was as soft and dry as dust.

Artos remained squatting by the elder's side.
"Father," he said quietly, and Marge understood
that the word used did not denote true parentage.
"Father, I want you to speak seriously with me
for a little now. Then do whatever you must do."

Ambrosius either didn't understand, or didn't
want to understand. "Go 'way. I gotta get some
rest, then it'll be time for me to leave."

"No, hear me first. I won't try any more to keep
you confined. I won't try to take away your drink.
I see now that those efforts did no good."

"Speakin' of drink . . ."

"First, tell me something about this young
woman you see before you."

Those remarkable eyes turned to regard Marge.
She felt a nervous shudder, that ceased as
abruptly as it had come. It was followed by the
strangest sensation, as if some gentle bird the size
of a small aircraft, as silent as it was invisible,
had just flown over her head, almost brushing her
hair with its unseen wingtips.

"Pretty thing," said Ambrosius, regarding
Marge tenderly. He spoke now in some tongue far
older than the one in common use here, but she
still understood him perfectly.

"What's that?" said Artos, who hadn't understood. "I wish you wouldn't do that."

The elder ignored him for the moment. "Little
one, do I know you? Lately I've been forgetting
things."

Marge would have bristled at being called
"little one" by any man of her own world that she
had ever met. But when the appellation came
from Ambrosius, and in the particular ancient
tongue that he had chosen—well, she would have
felt guilty of bad manners, if not worse, if she'd

objected. She replied only with a gesture, one she knew would signify agreement to any speaker of that ancient tongue.

Ambrosius was momentarily intrigued. "How is it you can understand me, one of your tender years? No, forget I asked that. It's often wiser not to know . . . tell me one thing only, are you from Nimue?"

Artos sighed; probably he had caught the name at the end. Marge said: "No, grandfather." The honorific title came quite naturally.

Grandfather belched, a brutal sound. Gross manners—but no, here a belch probably had nothing to do with manners at all. On the tip of her tongue Marge had marveling questions for the old man, interrogations about how he'd managed to make it through the centuries to where she'd met him first. If he could do it maybe she could make it back as well. But maybe she shouldn't mention their other meeting. *Often wiser not to know:* he might have said that as a warning to her.

Artos stood up, with another sigh. The old man's attention, Marge saw, had abruptly gone away from both of them, was somehow turned inward. But she and Artos both had things to settle with the old man, and time was a pressure on them if not on him. She knelt down, put out a hand, and gently touched Ambrosius on the arm. Shifting back to the tongue that Artos could understand, she said to Ambrosius: "On the march here, people were saying that you were dead."

That got his attention back, if only briefly. "Ah, little one. Now you've seen what I am, do you think I'm still alive?"

No words spoken in bright daylight, thought Marge, ought to chill the way those did. She could find no answer. Meanwhile the old man's gaze had once more shifted inward, to the contemplation of some private grief or problem.

Turning to Artos, Marge said: "He obviously

hasn't been like this all his life. I mean, he can't have been this way for very long. What happened to him?"

Artos frowned at her for a moment. "I'll allow the possibility that you truly do not know," he said at last. "All right. What happened to him was that he was enchanted by a young woman, a sorceress of surpassing skill. Besotted, by one he doted on—he could never say no about anything to a pretty young girl. That was his weakness, and they found it out. He taught Nimue the secrets of his craft, and he taught too well, by far. She was for a time one of the sacred Ladies, you know—the very one whose place you may be allowed to fill."

"I've heard her name spoken since I've been here in your land. That she is one of your enemies. Beyond that I knew nothing of her until now."

The military leader was growing angry. "For the last few months, Ambrosius, when he is not too drunk to do anything at all, does nothing but sit and mope after her, yearning to see her, wondering why she left him for Falerin, begging all the gods to let him hold her once more in his arms." Artos's wrathful gaze shifted back to the old man. "There's nothing strange about the fact that people call him dead. Nimue's spells have forced him to destroy himself."

"Can't anything be done?"

"I've tried about everything that I can think of. And I have more other work to do than ten men could accomplish."

As if his curtain of withdrawal had somehow been penetrated by the viciousness of Artos' quiet anger, Ambrosius stirred himself, came back to them. Now he too appeared silently angry, at Artos for disturbing his morbid contemplation. But the old man's feeble rage was hollow and could not last long; presently it was gone. Now he looked once more at Marge, but as if he had already forgotten who she was.

Artos looked at her too, and when he spoke it was still to her—or to himself. "And yet," the leader mused, "he has somehow managed to touch you. He brought you here, for some purpose, from—wherever are you really from?"

"From a far land, lord. I don't know if I can explain."

"His magical games. I've always taken them on trust. Try explaining to me later. But the fact that he brought you here raises hope in me that all's not lost. Even though I don't know why he did it."

Artos was interrupted by a burst of oaths from the old man, who was getting unsteadily to his feet. "Where's Nimue?" Ambrosius demanded of them both. "What've you done with her?" He glared at Artos. "Tell me, or I blast you inside out!"

Artos spoke gently and sadly. "Do you think I fear you, father?"

"Where is she?" But even as Ambrosius spoke, his rage was faltering back into fear.

"She's with Falerin, as you know." That much was said brutally. Then Artos seemed unable to keep his voice from softening. "Do you think I'm going to tell you how to reach her?"

"I cannot even use my powers to look for her. She has forbidden me that." Ambrosius groped around him in the air with trembling hands, as if trying to seize something that could not be seen. His fingers, large, muscular, and powerless, bore great jeweled and useless rings. Never before had Marge seen an alcoholic derelict who still wore expensive-looking jewelry; but she could understand why no one had yet stolen these.

Ambrosius rambled on: "Where's that wineskin? I had it right here . . ." Then he stopped, staring hopelessly at the young man. "I tell you, Artos, a great stone crushes me. I do nothing but think of her."

"And drink." Artos' voice almost broke, then with a leader's power regained steadiness. "You damned old fool. But I cannot spend my whole life trying to save yours. Not when kings depend on me to lead their armies, not when . . . you see, there's a way the common folk have, of *looking* at me when I ride by. I can't just leave them all to be part of Falerin's dominion. You know what kind of a fate that would be."

There was a wagon coming out of the fort's main gate toward them now, noisily empty as it jounced over ruts. It was drawn slowly by some kind of sturdy-looking cattle that Marge could not have named. Ambrosius watched it approaching for a moment, then turned back to Artos. "I've arranged for a ride. I'm going to Londinium. No, it's all settled. If I'm not here you won't be worried about me, wasting your time trying to do something for me. I'll be no worse off in Londinium than anywhere else." It was as if Ambrosius, by some trick, or great effort of the will, was managing to hold himself momentarily sober.

Artos could find nothing to say.

The wagon pulled up at the roadside nearby, stopping with a final jolt into an old rut. The lone driver, in poor garments, looked very tired, Marge thought, and worried as well. Probably about having to drive all the way to Londinium, wherever that was, without an escort.

But the old man was not quite ready. He put out a tentative, unexpected hand and took his leader by the arm. "Before I go, will you show me the Sword?"

"Sword?" It took Artos a moment to understand. Then slowly he pulled the weapon from the sheath at his side and held it up, hilt down, point to the morning sky. It was a little fancier then the other handmade weapons Marge had seen during the last few days. Otherwise she could see nothing remarkable about it.

Ambrosius raised a gnarled finger, touching the half-polished steel. "Do you remember how it must be hidden? When the time comes?"

This time Artos paused a little longer. Then in a hardened voice he answered: "I remember."

"Good; *she* doesn't know about the Sword—not yet. If I were to see her again—she might find out. But I'm not going to see her again. She probably wouldn't let me if I tried, and—"

The old man's voice collapsed, and with it his sobriety. He clung to the young man for support, and Marge could see the tears squeeze from his eyes. He repeated: "A great s-stone, Artos . . . she's put me under it for good. There's no way out. No way."

Artos abruptly turned fierce. "Don't say that! In time, with all your powers, there surely must be something . . . tell me, what will it take? What materials will the counterspells require? I'll get them. I'll find other wizards who can help. It's madness for us to give up like this. I'll mortgage this land if need be, I'll strip the kings who pay me of their wealth. I'll tell them I cannot win without your help."

Ambrosius groaned. In a voice of solemn doom, fallen almost to inaudibility, he said: "It may not be."

"I'll bring the new priests, with their nailed-up god, to pray for you."

"No . . . it may not be." Ambrosius paused, as if trying to recover himself again. He held one forefinger upraised, as if what he was about to say next would be of great importance. But then he said only: "There's a street I know of in Londinium . . . it reaches all the way around the world. I think this is one alley to it, here."

He lurched away from Artos to the side of the waiting wagon, then abruptly altered his course and made it, in a few staggering steps, to the wineseller's counter. Marge saw a bright coin appear between gnarled fingers, in a hand she knew, with professional certainty, had been empty a moment earlier. The villainous-looking proprietor glanced nervously at Artos; the commander's sword was sheathed again, and what the wineseller saw must have reassured him, for he took the coin and handed over a full wineskin. Ambrosius reeled under its modest wobbling weight back to the wagon. He hung on the side of the vehicle, staring into its flat bed, which was empty but for a few inconsequential bundles that doubtless held only the driver's personal effects.

Then Ambrosius began to sing, loudly and drunkenly in a cracked voice: "Lon-din-i-um, Lon-din-i-um, I'm going to Lon-din-i-ummm." Suddenly his countenance collapsed into a mask of grief. One word croaked from his lips.

The face of Artos had hardened into a mask of duty. He grabbed the old man around the waist, and, as if he were a bundle of freight, hoisted him with easy strength up over the wagon's side and in. Then with a wave, as if throwing something from him that he did not want, he sent the wagon rumbling on its way.

TWENTY-SIX

"Gilles de Rais," Simon echoed aloud the last words that Talisman had spoken. "Bluebeard. The one who murdered hundreds of children . . ." His voice trailed off. The echoes of old horror that hung in the air here were explained.

Talisman nodded. "He also performed many experiments in alchemy and magic, trying to recoup his squandered fortunes. If he had the Sword here, it would have been an irresistible temptation to profane it by trying its power in some such attempt. After that it was somehow hidden again. Perhaps here, perhaps elsewhere."

"Not here," said Simon, conscious of a sudden inward revelation.

Talisman stared at him, then startled Simon by spinning and moving two steps with utterly inhuman speed. The effort stopped there, as abruptly as it had started; whatever Talisman had had in mind, it was too late. Now Simon could see the ring of half-wraiths, demihuman shapes, surrounding the two of them at the distance of a pebble's toss.

There might have been thirty or forty of them in all, and they were the color of the dissipating fog where they were not as thin as glass, and their faces were the faces of beings who had been for a long time in hell. Among their number were things like beasts, and other things more like men or women. Some crouched, some stood, and some held weapons. Some were clothed, some not, and the naked among them were not always those who looked the most like beasts.

The ring they formed was not quite closed, and the open side of it was along the rim of the bluff. Talisman turned to face in that direction, and in a moment Simon saw why. Directly below them, three figures were climbing the steep hillside. They were ascending straight toward Simon at a steady trudging pace. The central figure was a woman's, and he saw as they came into clearer light that it was Nimue—the woman he had known as Vivian. She was still dressed in her red party gown. A couple of paces behind her, at her right, climbed Gregory, while Arnaud limped along in a similar position on her left.

Simon blinked, taking a closer look at Arnaud. The man had recently been hurt again, had suffered what seemed to be a minor bullet-wound in one leg. But Simon now could perceive a much more fundamental wrongness in him. One symbol of it was the brownish fur-stubble that had begun to sprout across his cheeks; it superficially resembled an ordinary beard, even as Arnaud had a surface resemblance to a human being. Under the surface there was a different kind of nature to be seen. Repelled and frightened, Simon looked away.

His eye fell on Gregory, who he saw was truly human. But his human nature had been altered drastically. And he had incorporated in his very

self things that Simon could not name, but that
stunned him with the feeling of evil that they pro-
jected. The base of true humanity only made the
horror the greater.

With some half-formed idea of appealing for
help or understanding, Simon turned to Talisman.
He was surprised to observe in the man at his
side something akin to Gregory's altered nature,
though with deep differences.

Simon had only an instant for each of these dis-
coveries. The woman he had known as Vivian had
almost finished her climb, and she was still climbing straight toward him. The long red dress
molded to her thighs, as with perfect balance she
stepped across a fallen log. When Simon looked
deeply at her now, he saw . . . no, there was more
than he could dare to see. He held his vision on
the surface. Nimue's expression was grave, and
once her eyes had caught his they held them in a
commanding stare.

She stopped a pace in front of Simon, on the
very lip of the bluff. "Find it for me," she ordered
urgently, without preamble.

This woman was someone he'd never known before. He said: "It isn't here."

Nimue glared at Simon as if he'd dared to
threaten her with a blow. She declared: "You saw
it here. I can tell, now, what you see and what you
don't. You can't imagine what it's cost me to come
here myself. Find it!" Her voice vibrated, almost
growling, and she gestured imperiously toward
the nearby ruins.

"I can't," said Simon, and expected to be struck
down on the spot. "I thought for a moment that it
was here, yes. But it's not." Under Nimue's gaze
he could not lie, could not even try to hold back
knowledge. "It's not. I was fooled, by the way it's
been concealed." Simon shook his head a little,
awed. "The magic."

"Where is it, then?"

"In our own time. My own time. That's where we can reach it. It's somewhere, as you thought, in—or near—the castle."

"Then we will go to where it is. At once—"

At that moment Talisman struck. He lunged straight at the woman, from his position eight feet to Simon's left. But Gregory and Arnaud had alertly positioned themselves close to her as bodyguards. They intercepted Talisman's rush, caught him between them. Fast and powerful as he was, he could not break through. Wraith-figures closed in from the circle.

The sound of the struggle was unearthly. At the moment of greatest violence and noise, Nimue's eyes let Simon go, and he was able to turn and run. But he had not gone half a dozen steps before another of the figures from the circle was in his path, confronting him. Then it vanished, but at once he felt its hands clamping his elbows from the rear, pulling his arms behind him, bringing him to a stop. The thing laughed with a high shrieking sound, and Simon saw other figures of the circle close before him, jeering at him. The pressure of the grip on his elbows increased until he screamed with pain. If his arms were pulled a centimeter closer together, the bones around his spine would certainly crack.

"Gently," said Nimue's controlled voice, somewhere behind him. "Simon is still my friend. We still must treat him gently."

The pressure did not vanish, but it eased out of the region of pain, and Simon could see clearly again. When the grip on his arms turned him back toward Nimue, he beheld Talisman now stretched out unconscious on the ground, his two chief opponents standing over him. One of them, Gregory, kicked the fallen man savagely. The jarred body on the ground looked less human than before, more like a puppet or a statue; for a moment Simon thought that Talisman was dead, but inward vision showed otherwise.

Gregory had put on his foolish-looking hat now and was squinting into the east. "Shall we just leave this one here, mistress, for the morning sun to find?"

There was a little silence while Nimue considered; the peasant's cheerful singing had stopped some time ago. "No," she decreed at last. "Too uncertain, for one of his power. But daylight has him frozen in man-form. Finish him now, with wood."

Arnaud growled in his throat. It was a low, regular sound, of which he appeared to be no more conscious than of his breathing. He looked round him, then seized a green tree-limb, thick as a man's arm. In a moment he had plucked it, like a flower. As Gregory stepped out of the way, Arnaud raised this weapon in both hands and brought it down like a spear at Talisman, splintery end first.

The stroke dug deep into leaves and earth, the end of the branch going two feet deep in solid ground. Talisman's body had disappeared.

TWENTY-SEVEN

Kate had brought along a new shirt and an un-damaged jacket to the hospital on Sunday morning, along with a lot of other stuff. The doctors were ready to let Joe go, and early Sunday afternoon Charley Snider was there helping him get the fresh upper-body clothing on. Kate had gone up to her folks' place on the North Shore to give them the facts, or some version of the facts, about the shooting incident in which the news media reported their son-in-law had been involved.

As he dressed, Joe reflected that Kate was probably mad at him for going right back to work from the hospital, without even coming home to her for a rest. But some of Carados' friends, as much murderers as he had been, were known to be still on the loose. And Kate was religiously strict about not trying to interfere with any of the vital aspects of Joe's job.

The bandage on his right arm wasn't all that hard to work into a sleeve, with Charley's gentle

help. Trouble was, the hand was still just about
useless. A nurse brought him a plain sling of dark
cloth; Joe wasn't sure if the sling was going to be
a help or a hindrance, but he meekly enough let
his arm be guided into the thing after his coat was
on. Maybe at least the sling would be a reminder
to other people not to bump him.

"You up to this, ain't you?" Charley asked him
when at last Joe was fully dressed.

"Now's a good time to ask that. Yeah, I'm up to
it. I'm lucky, the bullet missed the bones and the
big blood vessels. And we'll just be riding around
for a few hours in a car, right? No harder than sitting around in a chair somewhere." Still he
wished he could be home.

Charley grunted, and picked up Joe's bag.
"Well, it's important, so they say. They wanna do
it today, on Sunday, I guess they figure they'll
find more people home. We got an FBI honcho
comin' along, a state police captain, some big shot
from the attorney general's office. Maybe they figure they could never all get together during the
week."

Now it was necessary to concentrate for a few
minutes on the details of getting Joe officially
checked out of the hospital. As soon as they were
effectively alone again, with Charley carrying
Joe's bag for him across the lobby—it had taken
Joe some arguing to keep from being forced to
ride down in a wheelchair—Charley said: "Another reason, as I get it, is that there's actually a
couple—three big old houses out in that direction
that could actually be described as castles.
Owned naturally by some pretty big people, so we
don't want to bother 'em unnecessarily. And our
star witness is a little vague on his geogra-
phy—he's gonna ride in the car with you and me,
by the way, once we get our caravan organized.
Seems he requested it that way."

In front of the hospital Charley's unmarked police car waited, under the usual cloudy Chicago sky. When they were in the car and moving, and Charley had reported in on the radio, he asked: "What you think it is, anyway, with all these different names our star witness likes to use?"

"Who is he now? And did you find out how he got out of that cell at headquarters?"

"He just keeps sayin' the door was open. We don't want to push him on that until we find out if he can help us with Carados' friends. And he's still Falcon, as far's I know. We still don't have any better make on 'im than that. No fingerprints, nothing."

Joe turned the subject over in his mind, not for the first time. Feathers, Hawk, Falcon. There was certainly an association there, even a progression of sorts. "A falcon's a kind of hawk," he said. "Isn't it?"

"Yeah. Well, with or without a real name he ain't much as a star witness. But maybe he can put us onto something if he can recognize this castle where he claims he was. Some of Carados' people from New Orleans are still runnin' loose somewhere, that much we do know. Including the one you shot at and hit down the alley. There was a good blood trail there and I thought we had 'im. But then the trail just cut off. How come your gun was loaded with silver bullets?"

"What?" said Joe, weakly. Then understanding, of a sort, came, a few seconds after shock.

"You heard me, man. Silver. The bullets that you fired. The ones we could find, anyway. You emptied your piece and we found three, two in Carados and one ricochet all flattened out of shape, on the alley pavement." Charley didn't sound really perturbed. More as if silver bullets were something you were likely to run into maybe once a year.

There was one man Joe would have liked to be able to consult before he had to discuss this subject any more, but that man didn't happen to be available. Somewhat to Joe's surprise, he found himself wishing that there'd been a vampire in the hospital last night, to give him a nocturnal briefing.

But he was going to have to answer on his own. "Suppose," he said carefully, "I say I don't know what in hell you're talking about?"

"Then," said Charley, "we would have to hypothesize." He brought the word out in carefully polished tones, but nonchalantly, as if he thought that coming from him it might have a certain surprise value. "And what we hypothesize is something like this: some unknown friend of yours was in that alley too, and carrying a piece, and his just happened to be loaded in that silvery and unorthodox style. And after your friend had departed, taking with him all his spent cartridge cases, we found some of his bullets but none of yours. This theory, however, however attractive it may *be*, fails when we hear from the lab that the silver bullets were all fired from your gun, don't bullshit me, man."

And all the time Charley, unperturbed, drove on quietly and safely through spattering rain. Not looking at Joe, he waited for an answer.

For years now Joe had been expecting the arrival of some moment like this one, when he would have to try to make such things as vampires and magic a part of some official record. He'd even had bad dreams about it a few times. He wasn't ready to face the moment yet, if there was any way at all in which it could be avoided.

He said: "No regulation that I know of against loading silver."

"And your old lady can afford it, if you can't. Oh shit, man, don't come on to me now with regulations." At last Charley was irritated. "Off the record, now. Nobody in the Department really gives a damn if you fired diamonds or money-market certificates at that cat, long as you wasted him. I don't think any reporters gonna get their hands on any of that silver. But—well, I didn't figure you for going to fortune tellers, any of that jazz."

"No," Joe sighed. So far the reporters had been put off effectively, but sooner or later they'd have to talk to the hero who'd shot Carados. That would be another thing to face. "I didn't figure myself that way either. Can we talk about all this later?"

"Sure. But you're gonna have to talk about it pretty soon, with some people a lot higher up in the Department than me."

"Thanks for the warning."

Their arranged rendezvous with the other lawmen was at a state police station in a western suburb. They reached the place a little after three o'clock, and Joe was introduced to FBI, State's Attorney, State Police; they all gave him looks of large respect, somewhat tinged with envy. He was the wounded waster of Carados.

And they had Falcon with them, and were of course watching the old man continuously if casually. It was the first glimpse Joe had had of the old man since they'd both been carried out of the alley the night before. The old guy was unhurt, dressed now in a fresh issue of jail clothes, though not officially under arrest, and appeared to be much wrapped up in his own thoughts. When the large all-male party had been reshuffled and dealt out into four cars for the long drive, Joe found himself in the back seat of a CPD vehicle. Falcon sat at his left side, with Charley on the other side of Falcon. Christoffel, another Homicide detective, was doing the driving, with a man from Intelligence, whose name Joe hadn't really caught, beside him.

When they had got under way, Joe asked conversationally: "How's it going, Mr. Falcon?"

The old man hardly turned his head, and didn't really answer. With a worried expression he appeared to be contemplating his own right thumbnail, which stuck up from his hand clasped in his lap. The car was heading now for an entrance to the westbound/northwestbound interstate, the three other cars of the convoy with it, two ahead and one behind.

Joe's wounded arm hurt. He eased it out of the sling, and tried to arrange support for it by crossing his legs. "Or have you decided to change your name again?" It wasn't a a jeer, but a respectful request for information.

"Wish I could, sometimes." The old man's voice was surprisingly clear, reasonable, thoughtful. If they could put him on the stand like this they'd have a good chance in court, provided of course that they could catch someone for him to be a witness against. Wherever his voice was coming from now, it was a great distance from Skid Row. The old gray-blue eyes looked at Joe from behind their hoods, took note of him, and gazed on through.

"We're going to look at some buildings, big houses, ask you to look at them. I guess they've told you about that."

"Yeah." A sigh. "I'll look at 'em. I'll tell you what I can."

"That's good."

The old man went back to his thumbnail. Joe stared out the window at passing suburbia. For some reason he found himself wondering what his life would have been like if he'd been born on a farm.

Time passed silently in the car. The old man had already been questioned on every subject where it was thought he might know something. There were other topics the men might have talked about but didn't want to bring up in front of him. They were probably all tired, wishing they could be spending their Sunday on something else. The caravan kept moving at a good clip along the highway, keeping up with all but the fastest traffic. A half hour had gone by with no conversation of consequence, and suburbia was being replaced by farmlands, when suddenly the old man sighed. There was that in the sound which got attention.

"I'm gonna have to take a hand," he announced. His hands were still clasped together, but he was staring straight ahead, no longer at his thumbnails.

The Intelligence man had hitched himself around in his seat, and was looking back at the potential witness with a psychologist's estimating eye. "Take a hand in what matter, sir?" he inquired.

"Once a man realizes who his real enemies are, then he's got to do something about it."

Joe felt a chill.

"Like his kidnappers," said the Intelligence man.

The old man stared at him blankly for a while. Then at last he said "Right," as if his thoughts had been racing a long way ahead and had had to come back to answer belatedly.

Satisfied, the Intelligence man nodded, smiled, turned to face front again, letting well enough alone. Joe still felt a chill.

"And a man has to help his friends," murmured the old man, very low. "His allies; even if he doesn't like 'em." He fell back into a near-trance, staring at his hands.

Charley Snider had seen a lot of psychos in his day, and probably thought he knew the harmless ones. He glanced at the old man once now, then out at cornfields. Then, as if something the glance had shown him had caught belatedly at his instincts, he looked back again. "Mr. Falcon?"

"Don't bug me now," said the old man in a voice

of fierce concentration. "Gimme ten minutes to—think." And something in the way he said it made Intelligence turn his head again, open his mouth, and then decide not to interfere. Christoffel looked back in the mirror, and then just kept on driving.

Five minutes later the driver commented: "Looks like some heavy weather up ahead. Damn. Some of those back roads'll be . . ." He let it go. No one bothered to take it up.

A good seven minutes more passed, before the old man relaxed, with a sigh that seemed to come out of some vault of the dark past. He let himself sink back in the seat, suddenly looking worn and almost frail. "That's it," he breathed. "Talisman's out, just in time."

Joe looked round sharply. Charley asked: "Who's that?"

"Just thinking out loud," said Falcon weakly. Before anyone could ask him anything else, he added: "I think we're gonna meet some people up there, this place we're going to."

"Someone named Talisman?" asked Charley. "Who's that?"

"We'll see," said the old man, letting his eyes close. "I can identify the place for you. I'm sure of that now."

It was the first time he'd ever made such a confident assertion, and the others exchanged hopeful looks.

"How about the people?" Charley asked him. "The ones who kidnapped you. If they're there."

Another great sigh. "Yeah, them too."

After that, nobody wanted to push any more questions at him right away. Five minutes more of silence and it began to rain; as the driver had foreseen, heavy stuff. The wipers monotonously flogged the windshield.

"Helicopters won't do us a damn bit of good in this, if we should need 'em," someone in the front seat complained.

"They're still standing by."

The car radio signalled, and the Intelligence man talked for a time on its handset phone. Joe couldn't hear much of what the conversation was about. He wasn't trying very hard. He had other things to think about.

The first "castle" they were to take a look at was near Sycamore. Pale stone and pointed windows, behind a towering hedge. Joe might have described the place as a castle himself, but the old man dismissed it with an absently contemptuous wave of his hand.

"You sure? Take a good look."

"I'm sure. Let's get the hell on with it. This is not the place."

"You said you didn't get much of a look at the outside of the place where they were holding you."

"I got a quick look. This ain't it. Let's go."

They stopped at a drive in for hamburgers and coffee. An hour after that, they discovered that the road by which they had intended to approach the Littlewood castle was flooded, the river here up with the rain, over the floodplain that lay along its southwestern bank.

"Okay. Back through Blackhawk then, and we'll go around, come in from the other direction." Men were looking at their watches and swearing to themselves.

"Do these people know we're coming?"

"Couldn't reach anybody there by phone; they say the phones are connected, though."

"I gotta take a leak," the old man said. "How about stopping somewhere?"

A gas station near the outskirts of Blackhawk was honored for the occasion. While the cars' tanks were being filled again the men for the most part stood around beside the cars, talking about the rain and watching it pour down just beyond the edge of the high canopy sheltering the pumps.

Joe and a state trooper were both keeping an eye on the door of the men's room while the old man was inside. There was no window, they'd made sure, no other possible way out of the closet-sized chamber. Still Joe was almost surprised when Mr. Falcon reappeared in perfectly normal fashion.

The state trooper now took a turn in the closet himself, leaving Joe for a moment effectively alone with the old man. Joe didn't waste any time.

"Mr. Falcon, thanks."

"Oh?" Falcon gave him a shrewd look, and didn't ask him thanks for what.

"But they picked up some of those bullets I fired. Turned out they're silver. They weren't when I loaded 'em, but . . . I'm in for some kind of an investigation."

The old man chewed this over for a few seconds, as Joe stood before him more supplicant than guard. At last Falcon offered: "Deal?"

Joe nodded eagerly, then hesitated. "What've you got in mind?"

"Tell me how you know about the Sword. I can fix it about those bullets."

Joe considered, mentally crossed his fingers, and said a prayer. He'd noticed in the past few years that he was getting into the habit of doing that. He decided. "A man named Talisman told me."

"You know 'im, huh?" The old man gave a wise, slow nod, as if impressed; and in the next moment burly policemen were milling aound both of them, talking about the roads and the weather.

As they were driving along the highway on the north bank of the Sauk, some miles west of Blackhawk, the old man began urging them to stop. Presently the whole caravan had pulled over. The sun was setting and they'd all just put their headlights on. They were right at some wide place in the road called Frenchman's Bend. The few houses and shacks were all dark and silent, looking totally uninhabited. The rain had stopped, for the time being anyway, and the swollen river looked ominous and dirty.

The old man got out of the car on the side toward the river, and then just stood for a moment peering across, as if he could really see something on the far side. Joe could see the dark, humped smudges of the wooded bluffs over there and an enormous full moon struggling to get airborne above some of those trees and between the clouds.

"That's the place," the old man said. "Right over there." He sounded eager, but not in any particular hurry.

"Might be," someone muttered. "It oughta be about there."

Someone even raised the idea of trying to get a boat, but no one else had any enthusiasm for that idea.

Once they crossed the river again, at the next bridge thirty miles below Blackhawk, they started having some more trouble with roads. With a little luck and daring they got through, but it was full night by the time the caravan reached what had to be the castle. The main building was invisible, but headlight beams fell on a massive stone wall, and after they had driven a little way along the road that followed the wall they came to where a private drive went in through an old chained gate.

The full moon was now well above the trees in the east; it evoked bizarre shapes and shadows among the trees inside the grounds.

"We're not going to bother the owners tonight, correct?"

"It's not that late, we could give them a try."

Men got out of their cars, looking for a doorbell or something similar. They milled around, some of them with pocket flashlights in hand.

"Where's Falcon?"

"Where's Falcon?"

"He was right here, sonovabitch. Sonovabitch, come on, guys, where *is* he?"

"He was right—"

But he wasn't anymore.

When the screams started from the direction of the house it gave them an even better reason for breaking in.

TWENTY-EIGHT

Hildy Littlewood was running for her life, fleeing from her husband, from the man with whom she'd once sworn love, undying love. On flying feet she sped through darkened stone passageways, past midnight vaults. The lights in the castle were few, and seemed to be going out one by one. Once she stopped running in a place where she was sure there was a light switch, and ran her hands over the wall for what seemed like hours, whimpering all the while, until she found it. She flicked the switch up and down a score of times but nothing happened. Somehow the electricity must have been turned off. Maybe the lightning . . .

Now she could hear Saul's pacing feet, not running after her, pursuing patiently instead. His voice, a room away, called: "Hil?"

She fled again, gasping with the effort, knowing this was all a dream, taking comfort in the fact that before much longer she would simply have to wake up. To find herself where, and doing what? Hildy came to a door that she knew had to lead to the outside. She threw herself at it, wrenching and pushing at the latch and knob. They would not turn or move, they would not even rattle. As if the whole door and wall had been carved in one piece from wood, or built in one piece of reinforced concrete. Hildy almost collapsed, sobbing.

Here came Saul's patient feet again, pacing and pausing, once more a room away. Saul probably feared that if he came into the same room with her she'd had another hysterical screaming fit.

His voice was still patient too. "Hil, in a little while they'll all be back, Vivian and all her helpers. Then there won't be even this pretense of hiding, of getting away. So you'd better stop pretending now. You'd better be sensible. If Vivian finds out that you've been trying to cut and run . . ." There was a faint quaver in the unfinished sentence. Hildy knew Saul well enough to realize that he was now really, badly, frightened. It made her own terror all the worse.

Hildy ran once more. She couldn't have stopped running if she'd tried. This time her sprint brought her to a door she'd never opened, as far as she could remember; she was in one of the parts of the castle that she had never had the time to explore fully. The door opened for her, and she went through in a burst of desperate hope. To stop almost at once. She was on a balcony, halfway up the wall of a circular room, very high, maybe thirty feet across. Below her on a stone table, dark puddles were half-congealed in the light of a ring of torches. The bodies of the Wallises lay there, naked, broken, stabbed with a hundred wounds and drained of blood. Blade still in hand, wearing the face of Grandfather Littlewood, the executioner looked up at Hildy and smiled. She screamed and screamed and screamed and then someone or something had seized her from behind.

The moment Talisman's body vanished, Simon tried to take advantage of the confusion that suddenly appeared among his enemies. He turned, and leaped past Vivian, over the edge of the bluff, ready to die in a rolling, bouncing fall rather than stay where he was. No one, nothing stopped him, and it seemed for a long moment that he had got away. His leap turned into a fall into mist and darkness, and the fall went on and on, long past the moment when he should have struck some portion of the hillside. He felt no fear, only relief that he was going to be killed, and would not have to exist any longer as a pawn in Vivian's service. And just then he landed with a thump, arms and legs collapsing under him so that his face was pressed into sodden leaves. Their wetness had a faint, familiar smell, and Simon knew that he was once more somewhere near the castle on the Sauk.

He got to his hands and knees and looked around. Again it was near sunset on a cloudy, warm day; it seemed to him that it was always near sunset in this place. The sky was ominous, but only a little rain was falling at the moment. Only another leap away was the edge of the bluff, and below that would be the river, the way out to sanity. Simon sprang erect, ready to leap again.

A shadowy figure, almost invisible, moved at the corner of his eye. As if it had been waiting for him here, it seized his elbows from behind, and marched him back toward the castle. He did not try to turn his head to see what it looked like.

In the grotto, a ring of torches was flaring in the twilight, supported in ancient-looking wrought-iron stands that Simon had never seen before. The familiar statues looked on uncaring. There were other figures about besides the statues, creatures in and of the twilight, that Simon could not fully see. He made no effort to see them better. A hand unlocked the barred cave-door and Simon was thrust inside, and the door closed and chained tightly again after him.

Looking out across the grotto, he could now see no one, no presence, nothing moving but the wavering torchflames that ringed the waiting, empty stone. Drops of rain hissed sullenly in the torches. Was this to be yet another test? He could see without turning that the secret tunnel was no way out this time. It was forbidden, pre-empted, occupied by something, some process, so hideous—

There was the tiniest sound behind Simon, and he spun round. In a small natural alcove, on the opposite side of the cave from the mouth of the descending tunnel, the twins from the antique shop, still dressed as medieval servants, sat huddled together like small children in a corner.

Simon stared at them. They returned the stare, but he could not tell if it was with hope or fear.

"What are you doing here?" he asked at last.

They looked at each other. Neither wanted to answer him.

"You've got to tell me what you know about this. If there's going to be anything we can do, we have to—"

"Sacrifices," said the boy at last. It was a small child's voice. "She's going to kill us. You too. You're in here."

"He's started coming through the tunnel now, to our world," said the girl. "The Master is. I did what Vivian wanted, I did, but it won't be needed now."

"What? What won't be needed?"

"The baby. The Master is coming now. Vivian won't need any more help."

"What baby?"

"Mine." The girl looked steadily up at Simon. "Yours."

Hints and fragments of explanation, each more dreadfully suggestive than the last, struggled to take form in Simon's brain. "You mean you're pregnant—from me. That time I thought that you and I—I wasn't dreaming—you were in bed with me—"

The girl was nodding. She sat there clasping her knees, looking ugly. "It's how we all live here. It's how we do things. Vivian breeds people. People with powers, the powers she needs to help bring the Master. But now he's coming at last. Now she needs the sacrifices more, that's what she said. Needs us to be killed. Needs our blood. Help me!" The girl seized Simon by one leg, clung to his knee with a burst of weeping. Suddenly she looked up at him again and said in a clear voice: "You're my father."

"Mine too," the boy said next to her.

For a moment Simon truly did not understand.

"And Lissa and I bred a baby once for Vivian," the boy added, looking at his sister. "It didn't turn out good. Vivian already used it up. Now she's going to use us up."

Simon backed away from them, one step. It was as far as he could move. Father. Daughter. Baby. To himself he mumbled words that he was unable to understand.

His body pressed against steel, and he turned. Outside the jailbars of the cave, in the light of the ringed torches hissing in the rain, a guardian power stalked, a jailor with a crooked walk. Simon could recognize old Grandfather Littlewood, from the portrait—no, it was only something in old Littlewood's shape. At close range he could see how the thing was wearing old Littlewood's human likeness like a mask. He could see everything, and it did him no good at all. On its shoulder the creature bore what appeared to be a giant cleaver, stained with blood.

"Prepare," ordered a disembodied voice, Vivian's voice, out of the nearby air. And the Littlewood-figure came to the jail door and somehow pulled it open. It seized Simon by one arm when he tried to run, and held him paralyzed.

Somewhere in the distance, down inside the secret tunnel, an awesome procession was approaching. There were sounds, a muttering of many voices that were not all human. There was reflected light, beginning to be faintly visible to the physical eye. The colors of it were sickly. Falerin the Master was approaching. Evil wafted ahead of him, like the stench of his wagonloads of corpses.

And now, along the path that led through woods to the grotto, came Vivian and her supporting crew. There came Gregory, right after her, and there was Arnaud. Around them, a score or more of wraith-figures slouched or capered. Two at least dragged captives with them. Simon didn't want to look.

Abruptly there was a sound of purely human movement inside the secret passage. Saul climbed up out of it, carrying his wife Hildy in his arms. She was alive, and her eyes were open, but they no longer saw, or perhaps no longer wished to see. Behind them the inhuman muttering grew a little louder, became distinguishable as some kind of a chant.

"Quickly!" ordered Vivian, stopping her own advance near the altar.

Hildy was borne there by her husband, and put down, as he might have carried her and given her to a doctor for an X-ray examination. Relieved of the weight, Saul stood back and rubbed his eyes. Somehow, Simon realized irrelevantly, he tended to think of Saul as wearing glasses.

Thoughts about Saul vanished. Vivian was looking straight at Simon himself. "Find the Sword for me," she commanded him.

"I won't." Whether it was a benefit of actual physical imprisonment, or something else, Simon found himself at least momentarily free of fear. He could at least try to defy her now.

Vivian nodded to the executioner.

"Slow bleeding, Lady?" the thing that wore old Littlewood's shape inquired of her from over the sightless staring Hildy.

"Quick death. We have no time tonight for squeezing the fine essences, or playing tricks with what's left afterwards."

Simon beheld the cleaver rise; he heard but did not watch it fall.

Now Vivian was looking at Saul. "Now *you* are not needed any longer. But we require your blood and death."

Saul looked about him, in his usual abstracted, business-like way. "I thought it might have worked out differently," he said to no one in particular. He rubbed his eyes, and again Simon had the impression of an accountant's or bookkeeper's eyeglasses being handled. "I thought—"

One of the wraith-figures pushed Saul violently from behind. He went face down on the stone altar. The cleaver swung, and this time Simon was not quick enough looking away. He saw the flying blood.

With each violent death, the presence of Falerin came closer through the tunnel, his music a notch louder, even the sickening smell became a little harder to deny.

Suddenly Simon noticed Marge, in the background behind Vivian, being brought closer to the altar by the figure that held her. Her eyes were on Simon, but not as if she expected anything from him or even saw him. Beside Marge, another creature was holding Sylvia, who appeared to be in no better shape.

At the mouth of the cave, the boy-twin was being pried from his sister's almost catatonic grip. He was dragged helplessly out and thrown upon the altar.

"Flesh of your flesh, Simon." Vivian's voice bored at him relentlessly. "Now will you find the Sword for me? Then we'll need no more sacrifices. Or, a few more deaths, a bit more blood, and my powers will be strong enough to force the passage despite the Sword. Which way is it to be?"

Simon saw that the hope Vivian offered him was a lie, as was her confidence of being able to overcome the hidden Sword. And he saw much more than that.

He spoke his discovery aloud. "I see now where it is . . . no, where it was for a long time. It's not there any longer." Before Vivian could interrupt, he raised an arm, pointing uphill to where the towering keep was shrouded in night and mist. "In the great hall. There's an oak beam right above the fireplace. Open it."

There was a swirl of rapid movement among Vivian's inhuman followers. Only seconds later, muffled crashing noises sounded from inside the castle. And very quickly after that, two of the powers were back, bearing ten feet of torn-out beam between them.

At once Vivian commanded: "Break it!"

In the grip of those hands it crumbled as if it were termite-eaten. Amid a cloud of dust there came to light a carven, sword-shaped nest. One creature pulled from the debris a brittle relic, powdered with ancient wood, that might once have been an ornate scabbard. Of a blade there was no sign.

Vivian snarled, and signalled; the boy died on the stone, the ominous presence in the tunnel once more advanced. "Bring the girl here!" she cried. Then she looked at Simon. "Where is it now?"

"I'll not say." As the cleaver fell once more, Simon looked at Vivian, looked deeply and freely; now he had little to lose. He saw that she was his mother, and beyond that horror he could see nothing at all, and never would.

Marge, from her position as sacrifice-to-be, watched Simon go into shock, his body contracting on the ground into a fetal curl. Beside her, Sylvia had lost consciousness, and Marge envied her.

Gregory prodded Simon's inert body with a foot, then bent and with his hand tried some other brisk revival method. The he looked at Vivian. "What shall we do, mistress, to bring him back?"

"Never mind, we do not need him now." Vivian's anger was spent, vanished, as if evaporated in the glow of a coming triumph. She paused, smiling. "Here's one who'll tell us all we need to know."

Gregory hoisted Simon's body and threw it onto the altar. The cleaver fell, and Marge saw Simon's head roll free. She was unable to look away, but in her terror of being next, even Simon's death meant little in itself.

Now what? What was everyone waiting for? Gradually she realized that all action was suspended. Everyone was waiting for something. Slowly Marge turned her head toward the woodland path, following the common gaze.

The figure shuffling along the path toward the paved court looked ordinary enough, what she could see of it in the moonlight and the light of torches. It was only the figure of a man. A gray old man, not very big, his dress modern, drab blue and humble, almost a slave's or servant's uniform. Two huge powers guarding the start of the path looked down on him like contemptuous sphinxes as he passed between them. But they let him pass. The impression of meek humility was damaged when the old man stumbled briefly at the very edge of the paving, and told the world about it in foul language, as boldly as if there had been no one else within a mile.

But he understood perfectly that a sizable assembly was waiting for him, and he must have understood its nature pretty well. For he showed no surprise when he stopped to look them all over. Nodding to himself, he calmly took in the gory and fantastic scene. Nimue's bodyguards sidled a little closer to her.

When the old man spoke, his words struck Marge, even in her present state, as a ridiculous anticlimax. He said only: "The police are out there, at your gate."

Nimue made a sound of astonishment, a faint purring whine, and shook her head as if she marveled at him. "But they won't be able to come in, my dear old man. Lucky for them."

"I think they may. They represent the law." He said this very soberly and seriously, but at the same time he spoke as if he were announcing something new, or something that his hearers perhaps had never heard before. "There's laws for all of us. Even you. Even that . . . foulness that you serve."

"Where is the Sword, old fool? I have brought you here to tell me of the Sword."

"Fool?" The old man sounded surprised and angered by that, and there was a pause. He actually scratched his head. Then at last he had to agree. "Yeah . . . yeah, I was. Enchanted too, of course. But enchantment comes half from the inside. Yeah, I was a fool from the very start. Fool all the way." He paused again, and went on in a gentler voice. "You were very young then, really young, and beautiful. There's . . . something about beauty. Beauty and wine beat me, a long time ago. Power and gold could never do it."

He looked contemptuously past Nimue, to the cave and the tunnel mouth, where a pale glow was growing brighter, throbbing faintly with the chant of whatever creatures and powers might be advancing through the tunnel. "He's not gonna make it here, you know. He'll have to stay in his own land, his own time, with his own limited power there, and let his own people eventually burn him at the stake the way they do. As the book says, it is written. Maybe you meant to bring me here this time to help you, but this time I came willingly. Not even your enchantments last forever."

Nimue made a gesture, as of producing something hidden, small, and vitally important. "I have kept one command, one order that I may yet bind you to. That is what is really written."

The old man bowed, an almost courtly motion. "So you have, I see. I must submit to it. Much good may it do you."

"The command is this: Tell me where the Sword is now." Behind her the glow in the cave mouth had brightened again, and in the very heart of it, the doorway where the barred door stood open, a dark slender column of something had begun to waver in the air.

The old man answered: "Gladly. For a long time it was where none could see it. I've moved it, though. The Prince of Wallachia, standing there behind you, has it in his hand."

Nimue turned, to see the man Marge had known as Talisman, standing tall in the mouth of the opened passage, gravely salute the old man with his blade. To Marge the Sword looked much like common iron; nothing out of the ordinary at all. If there had been a jewel or two in its hilt when Artos wore it, they had been dulled or stolen by now. But Talisman held it like one very well used to swords. When the executioner lunged at him with cleaver raised, the Sword flicked once only, with invisible speed. The cleaver clanged on the pavement, the mask of old Littlewood beside it, the creature who had borne them obliterated. There followed a mighty roaring from down the hidden passageway, and Talisman turned to look in that direction over his raised point.

Nimue screamed and screamed again, echoing the hoarse offstage voice of her Master. From their places at her side, Gregory and Arnaud both leaped at Talisman; he twisted round, thrust once, thrust once again. Nimue screamed; and the old man, a long wooden staff come from nowhere into his hands, strode toward her. "Your last command is spent," he said.

The moonlight was clear, but Marge thought that lightning had shattered roof and sky together, to bring the castle down around her head.

It was one thing for men to yell at each other with determination that now they were going to break in. It was quite something else, Joe had been able to observe, when you got down to the nitty-gritty of dealing with inch-thick steel bars in a gate as high as the twelve-foot stone wall it pierced. Bold decision promptly degenerated into something like slow farce. With only one good arm Joe couldn't be of much direct help. At last Charley Snider managed to climb over the gate, from a start on two bowed and burly backs. In the effort Charley burst seams in his coat, and one in his pants, but nobody was laughing. Once he was over and down, sure enough, there was a way for him to unbolt the great gate from inside. Cars started rolling in.

The screams had been terrible, but they had stopped while Charley was atop the gate. Now pocket lights were being flashed at the many doors of the closed garage, and around the darkened lawn and courtyard of the immense and silent main building. No light showed in any window.

"Watch out, swimming pool. Don't step in that."

Joe saw the bottom in a flashlight beam: weed-grown, cracked, dry for what had probably been decades. On the other side of the pool, French doors led into the ground floor of the main building. The doors were closed, and, as it soon proved, locked.

"Go ahead."

Glass tinkled, a single small pane. The doors were readily enough opened.

The voices of the men first to go in reported nothing but more emptiness, and long disuse.

Joe was still out in the courtyard when his eye was caught by a slight movement in a dark moon-shadow some yards away. He looked again, carefully, making sure.

"I'll stand by out here," he volunteered then. "Man the radios. My arm's starting to give me hell."

No one argued with this. They were all busy being active cops, getting into the building, searching aggressively for the screaming victim, or victims—there had seemed to be more than one voice in agony.

Joe, left alone, walked warily past the cars with their radios buzzing alertly. He moved close to the shadowed corner. Talisman was standing there, carrying some kind of bundle in his arms. When Joe got close enough he saw it was the limp body of a young woman.

"The searchers will not find much, Joseph. I wanted to reassure you that things have turned out—much better than they might have. The world is as safe as can be expected." There was no hint of mockery in Talisman's voice.

"If you say so. What about her?"

"She goes with me, for tonight. You have my word she will be safe. But I must strengthen the merciful forgetting she has been blessed with by one more powerful than I. One whose art makes a semblance of neglect and abandonment around us now. I have seen marvels tonight, Joseph—yet I myself have some little skill in helping people toward forgetfulness."

He glanced down at the young woman, who stirred, looked up at him. Then like a child she closed her eyes again.

"Who is she?"

"Marge Hilbert. But you will probably never hear her name again. I have told you, Joe, she will be safe."

"Where's Falcon? I mean the man who—"

"I know who you mean, Joseph. You will not find him. He will soon sleep again, in some retreat of his own devising. Which I myself would not try to find, even if I thought I could succeed. He will sleep, I think, until the founts of magic are recharged. A new day of the earth had dawned. The Sword is with him."

"Wait . . ."

But Talisman and the woman were gone.

THE END